18

JEWISH STORIES TRANSLATED
FROM 18 LANGUAGES

Cherry
Orchard
Books

18

JEWISH STORIES TRANSLATED FROM 18 LANGUAGES

Edited by
Nora Gold

Foreword by
Josh Lambert

BOSTON
2023

Library of Congress Cataloging-in-Publication Data

Names: Gold, Nora, editor.
Title: 18: Jewish stories translated from 18 languages / edited by Nora Gold.
Other titles: Eighteen
Description: Boston : Cherry Orchard Books, 2023.
Identifiers: LCCN 2023019159 (print) | LCCN 2023019160 (ebook) | ISBN 9798887192062 (paperback) | ISBN 9798887192079 (adobe pdf) | ISBN 9798887192086 (epub)
Subjects: LCSH: Short stories, Jewish—Translations into English. | LCGFT: Short stories.
Classification: LCC PN6120.95.J6 A14 2023 (print) | LCC PN6120.95.J6 (ebook) | DDC 808.83/1088924—dc23/eng/20230522
LC record available at https://lccn.loc.gov/2023019159
LC ebook record available at https://lccn.loc.gov/2023019160

Book design by Tatiana Vernikov
Cover design by Joseph Weissgold, with Ivan Grave

Published by Cherry Orchard Books, an imprint of Academic Studies Press
1577 Beacon Street
Brookline, MA 02446, USA
press@academicstudiespress.com
www.academicstudiespress.com

Copyright credits

The translation has been made with the support of the Hellenic Ministry of Culture and Sports / Hellenic Foundation for Culture (HFC) within the framework of the GreekLit Sample Translation Grant Programme. This excerpt is from the novel *The Researcher*, originally published in Greek by Patakis Publishers in November 2020 and awarded the prize for best novel by the highly respected literary magazine *O Anagnostis* (The Reader).

Contents

Foreword

By Dr. Josh Lambert

You could easily read the story of the Tower of Babel as telling us that multilingualism is a bad thing: after all, the linguistically unified people who challenge God in that story are punished by having their speech "confounded," mixed-up. But I prefer to think about this a little differently, focusing not on the punishment but on why this story gets told, and the pride of place it receives, in the eleventh chapter of *Bereshit* (Genesis). Why would whoever put the Torah together consider it necessary to explain multilingualism, right up there with the account that book gives of the origins of the sky and the sea, of animals and people?

The answer, I suspect, is that the authors of the Torah knew that multilingualism was as much a part of their world as light and dark, heavens and earth. They believed that every reader of the Torah, in their time and after, would live in a multilingual situation, and just as kids would inevitably ask where the sky comes from, they would also wonder about the linguistic profusion around them. The authors of the Torah turned out to be prescient on that topic: multilingualism has been a major facet of Jews' experiences throughout history. Even more so, it has been fundamental to the development of Jewish literature.

That's why I'm grateful for Nora Gold's *18: Jewish Stories Translated from 18 Languages*. This anthology presents fascinating modern and contemporary Jewish literature translated from Russian, Ladino, Portuguese, Turkish, Danish, Yiddish, Hebrew, Greek, Romanian, French, Spanish, Hungarian, Italian, Croatian, Czech, German, Albanian, and Polish. In a few cases, the authors are already well-known in English—including the Nobel Prize laureates S. Y. Agnon and Elie Wiesel, and the incomparable Russian story writer, Isaac Babel—but many of the authors gathered here came as news to me. In a few cases they were the first Jewish writers writing in a particular language I had *ever* read, despite decades of reading Jewish literature voraciously. In fact, I'd venture to say that rarely in Jewish literary history has such a linguistically wide net been cast. The resulting anthology matters both because of the literature it introduces and because of the editorial model it offers.

The creation of such an anthology was no small feat. It's difficult enough to read through magazines and journals and pick out excellent writing in a language in which one is fluent, but to do so in languages one doesn't read or speak is very challenging. Gold has succeeded by planting a flag with her journal *Jewish Fiction .net*, where all the stories in this book were originally published. For over a decade, it has been one of the only places on the internet one can go to reliably encounter contemporary Jewish literature in translation. People around the world, discovering *Jewish Fiction .net* and its mission, seek Gold out, while she also searches actively for works translated from languages she's never published before.

The 18 stories in this book reflect a wide range of styles and themes, as one would expect, given the diversity of places and time periods in which they were written, as well as the idiosyncrasies of individual authors. That variety is entirely the point here. As Gold rightly says in her introduction, the stories in this anthology cannot be understood as representative of languages or communities. To get a real feeling for modern and contemporary Hungarian-Jewish or Croatian-Jewish literature, you would need to read quite a bit more than one translated story in one collection.

For that reason, the most urgent reaction that I had, reading through these stories, was to feel how crucial it is that Gold and her colleagues acquire the support they need, and the enthusiastic readership, to go on and continue their work. There's always more translation to be done from the languages covered here, and surely there are also modern or contemporary Jewish short stories we haven't read yet in Arabic, Persian, Mandarin, Swedish, and Hindi, let alone in other Jewish languages like Juhuri and Judeo-Arabic. Before too long, we can hope, we'll see stories from those languages in *Jewish Fiction .net*, and in another book like this one.

In the meantime, I hope you will enjoy the treasures prepared and gathered for you in this collection. You will, without a doubt, encounter Jewish voices you've never heard before, and expand your vision of what Jewish literature can be and where it can come from.

Josh Lambert *is the Sophia Moses Robison Associate Professor of Jewish Studies and English, and director of Jewish Studies, at Wellesley College.*

Introduction

By Dr. Nora Gold

This book owes its existence in part to an arrogant, ignorant, American Jewish man, a writer, who told a group of Jewish authors from around the world (all writing in languages other than English) that at that time there was no Jewish fiction of any significance being written anywhere other than in the United States (and perhaps in Israel, where there were one or two writers worth reading). This happened twelve years ago in Jerusalem, during a coffee break at an international conference of Jewish writers, and the listeners to this comment were some of the most illustrious writers of Jewish fiction in their own languages and countries. By this point, I had begun *Jewish Fiction .net*, the online literary journal, which was then, and still is, the only English-language journal, either print or online, devoted exclusively to Jewish fiction. Envisioned from the outset as an international, multilingual journal, *Jewish Fiction .net* was soon to publish the work of some of the writers present at this incident: stories or novel excerpts translated into English that had never before been published in English. These eminent writers listened politely while they were insulted by their colleague. I was appalled by his obliviousness and rudeness.

Unfortunately, however, this man was, and is, not alone in his lack of awareness of the amazing Jewish fiction being written around the world. Generally speaking, when native English-speakers hear the phrase "Jewish fiction," they think only of American Jewish fiction. Not of other English-language Jewish fiction, such as Canadian, British, Australian, or South African, and certainly not of fiction written in other languages. Some people may have read literature translated into English from Hebrew, Yiddish, or Judeo-Spanish (or Ladino, as it is usually called), but are unaware of most of what exists in Jewish fiction. This is especially regrettable since one of the unique features of Jewish fiction is its multilingualism. Because Jews have lived for two thousand years scattered among other nations, Jewish literature has been written in the languages of virtually every country where Jews have dwelled. Unlike other peoples that typically write in their own language (for instance, Italians in Italian, the French in French, etc.), Jews have written their stories in dozens of languages. There are currently some specifically Jewish languages, for example Hebrew,[1] Yiddish, and Ladino, but the fiction written in these languages constitutes just part of the Jewish writing that exists globally.

One reason that so few people are aware of the extent of multilingual Jewish fiction is that only a small percentage of this treasure trove has been translated into English.[2] Furthermore, much of what has been translated is not easily accessible. Even with Google, it can be challenging for anyone other than scholars in this field to learn about, and locate, these works. Whether you, reading this now, are among those who have wondered about Jewish fiction written in other languages but did not know how to track it down, or never even knew that it existed, now it is available to you. In this anthology you'll find eighteen (*chai!*) brilliant works of Jewish fiction translated from Albanian, Croatian, Czech, Danish, French, German, Greek, Hebrew, Hungarian, Italian, Ladino, Polish, Portuguese, Romanian, Russian, Spanish, Turkish, and Yiddish. Here you'll discover stories and authors you've never heard of before and will want to meet again.

This anthology is the first of its kind in twenty-five years. Two anthologies of multilingual Jewish fiction came out in 1998,[3] and since then no others. This book, created to fill this lacuna, differs from the previous ones in three ways: it features significantly more languages, it contains only translations (no works originally written in English), and it is the first one to be conceptualized and structured by language.

This book is a natural outgrowth of the thirteen years—the bar mitzvah, if you will—of *Jewish Fiction .net*, the online literary journal that I founded in 2010 and have edited ever since. *Jewish Fiction .net*, which has readers in 140 countries, publishes first-rate Jewish fiction from around the world that was either written in English or translated into English, but never before

---

1 The transliterated words in this anthology follow the Encyclopedia Judaica system for Hebrew and the YIVO one for Yiddish, with the exception of words currently included in the English lexicon.

2 One laudable initiative to rectify this situation was the Contemporary Jewish Writing series: nine books published by University of Nebraska Press between 1998 and 2010.

3 Marsha Lee Berkman and Elaine Marcus Starkman, eds. *Here I Am: Contemporary Jewish Stories From Around the World* (Philadelphia: Jewish Publication Society, 1998); Ilan Stavans, ed., *The Oxford Book of Jewish Stories* (New York: Oxford University Press, 1998).

published in English. All the works included in this anthology appeared for the first time in English in *Jewish Fiction .net*.[4] I started this journal because the publishing crisis triggered by the advent of digital publishing resulted in many fine writers, including Jewish ones, suddenly being unable to find places to publish their work. *Jewish Fiction .net*, a donor-supported journal that is free of charge, was founded to create a publishing space for this first-rate Jewish fiction that couldn't find a home.[5] Alongside these works by emerging writers, *Jewish Fiction .net* has published stories or novel excerpts by some of the most eminent Jewish authors, including Elie Wiesel, Chava Rosenfarb, Aharon Appelfeld, Nava Semel, A. B. Yehoshua, and Steve Stern, to name just a few. *Jewish Fiction .net* publishes not only new stories and novel excerpts, but also classic works that have never before been published in English and new translations of classic works, for example stories by Shmuel Yosef Agnon, Isaac Babel, Dvora Baron, Eliya Karmona, Mendele Mokher Seforim, and Lili Berger.

Among the jewels in the crown of *Jewish Fiction .net* are its translations. Out of the 575 works published so far in *Jewish Fiction .net*, nearly 30 percent have been translations from other languages. Discovering these translations from around the world[6] and connecting with the fascinating, evolving field of translation[7] has been one of the joys of publishing this journal—indeed, of

---

4 Boris Dralyuk's translated excerpt from "Red Cavalry" was published for the first time in English in *Jewish Fiction .net*. Prior to this, other translators had translated "Red Cavalry" into English, but Dralyuk's was a new, original translation.

5 I chose the name "Jewish Fiction .net" not only because this journal owned that web address (it also owned, and still owns, jewishfiction.com), but because the image of a net resonated with me and matched the goals I had for this journal. To act as a safety net positioned under high-wire writer-acrobats. And a net, like one that catches fish, so all these great stories wouldn't get lost.

6 Discovering these translations usually occurs in one of two ways: either through a story arriving over the transom at *Jewish Fiction .net* or by an active search on my part for a translation in a specific language. In both cases, the relationship that has developed over the years between *Jewish Fiction .net* and an international network of translators, authors, and publishers often plays a part.

7 As an example of the evolution of this field, translations were once perceived as "copies" of "original" creative works, but now they are recognized by many as creative works unto themselves, as new works of art (Yaakov Herskovitz, "The Origins of National Culture: Self Translation, Originals, and Split Authors," Webinar hosted by YIVO Institute for Jewish Research, October 25, 2022, Video, 10:32–11:34. https://www.youtube.com/watch?v=ZQINdqSYcVY). Consistent with this, some translators are now demanding to have their names on the front covers of the books they translate ("Translators' Names

the four decades I've spent in the field of Jewish fiction as a writer, editor, and publisher. So it is a great pleasure to share the marvelous works in this anthology. The main purpose of this book is to showcase the rich multilingualism of Jewish fiction, and thus change the way people think about Jewish fiction and its parameters. By presenting in one volume a sampling of eighteen magnificent works, each originally written in a different language, this anthology offers readers the opportunity to experience the diversity that exists within Jewish fiction, as well as its common elements. It is also a useful resource for introducing non-Jewish readers to Jewish fiction, thereby facilitating the inclusion of Jewish fiction in conversations in the international literary community about translation and world literature.

~

Crouching at the heart of this book is a question: What is Jewish fiction? To some people, this question is merely a theoretical one; for me, running a literary journal devoted to publishing Jewish fiction, it is essential to our decision-making process. The question, What is Jewish fiction?, has been much written about,[8] struggled with, reflected on, debated, and, in some cases, skirted.

Must Be on the Cover," Interview in the Frankfurt Buchmesser newsletter, Issue 1, January 2023. https://www.buchmesse.de/en/news/translators-names-must-be-cover?utm_source=newsletter&utm_medium=email&utm_campaign=january).

8 For example: Victoria Aarons, Mark Shechner, Avinoam J. Patt, eds., *The New Diaspora: The Changing Landscape of American Jewish Fiction* (Detroit: Wayne State University Press, 2015); Marsha Lee Berkman and Elaine Marcus Starkman, eds. *Here I Am: Contemporary Jewish Stories From Around the World* (Philadelphia: Jewish Publication Society, 1998); Melvin Jules Bukiet and David G. Roskies, ed., *Scribblers on the Roof: Contemporary American Jewish Fiction* (New York: Persea Books, 2006); Justin Cammy, Dara Horn, Alyssa Quint, and Rachel Rubinstein, eds., *Arguing the Modern Jewish Canon* (Cambridge, MA: Harvard University Press, 2008); Leah Garrett, "The Kvetcher in the Rye: J. D. Saligner and Challenges to the Modern Jewish Canon," in *Arguing the Modern Jewish Canon*, ed. Justin Cammy et al. (Cambridge, MA: Harvard University Press, 2008), 645–660; Ruth Gilbert, *Writing Jewish: Contemporary British-Jewish Literature* (Houndmills, Basingstoke, Hampshire: Palgrave Macmillan/Arts & Humanities Research Council, 2013); Dara Horn, "The Eicha Problem," in *Arguing the Modern Jewish Canon*, ed. Justin Cammy et al. (Cambridge, MA: Harvard University Press, 2008), 687–700; Sheila E. Jelen, Michael P. Kramer, and L. Scott Lerner, eds., "Intersections and Boundaries in Modern Jewish Literary Study," in *Modern Jewish Literatures: Intersections and Boundaries*, ed. Sheila E. Jelen et al. (Philadelphia: University of Pennsylvania Press, 2011), 1–23; Ray Keenoy, Mark Axelrod, and Saskia Brown, *The Babel Guide To Jewish Fiction* (London: Boulevard, in association with the European Jewish Publications Society, 1998); Adam Kirsch, *Who*

Out of all the definitions of Jewish fiction I have encountered over the years, the one I consider most comprehensive and persuasive is that of Ruth Wisse, presented in her book *The Modern Jewish Canon.*[9] Wisse's definition, like any definition, inevitably has its limitations, some of which she herself acknowledges, such as her including in her proposed canon only works by Ashkenazi authors. Additional limitations of her perspective have been articulated by other scholars, as well, including contributors to the book *Arguing The Modern Jewish Canon* which was dedicated to Wisse herself.[10] Still, I agree with her definition that Jewish literature is literature that is "centrally Jewish," a phrase

---

Wants To Be A Jewish Writer? (New Haven: Yale University Press, 2019); Josh Lambert, *American Jewish Fiction* (Philadelphia: Jewish Publication Society, 2009); Josh Lambert, *The Literary Mafia: Jews, Publishing, and Postwar American Literature* (New Haven and London: Yale University Press, 2022); Julian Levinson, "Is There a Jewish Text in This Class?: Jewish Modernism in the Multicultural Academy," *Michigan Quarterly Review* 42, no. 1, https://quod.lib.umich.edu/cgi/t/text/text-idx?cc=mqr;c=mqr;c=mqrarchive;idno=act2080.0042.122;view=text;rgn=main;xc=1;g=mqrg#end-of-header; Vivian Liska and Thomas Nolden, *Contemporary Jewish Writing in Europe: A Guide* (Bloomington and Indianapolis: Indiana University Press, 2008); Alan Mintz, "Knocking on Heaven's Gate: Hebrew Literature and Wisse's Canon," in *Arguing the Modern Jewish Canon,* ed. Justin Cammy et al. (Cambridge, MA: Harvard University Press, 2008), 23–34; Dan Miron, *From Continuity To Contiguity: Toward A New Jewish Literary Thinking* (Stanford: Stanford University Press, 2010); Cynthia Ozick, "America: Toward Yavneh," *Judaism* (Summer 1970), 264–282; Cynthia Ozick, *Art and Ardor* (New York: Alfred A. Knopf, 1983); Antony Polonsky and Monika Adamczyk–Garbowska, eds., *Contemporary Jewish Writing in Poland: An Anthology* (Lincoln: University of Nebraska Press, 2001); David G. Roskies, "Gimpel the Simple and on Reading from Right to Left," in *Arguing the Modern Jewish Canon,* ed. Justin Cammy et al. (Cambridge, MA: Harvard University Press, 2008), 319–340; Derek Rubin, ed., *On Being (and Not Being) a Jewish American Writer* (New York: Schocken, 2005); Maxim Shrayer (ed.), *Voices of Jewish-Russian Literature: An anthology* (Brighton, MA: Academic Studies Press, 2018); Ted Solotaroff and Nessa Rapoport, eds., *The Schocken Book of Contemporary Jewish Fiction* (New York: Schocken, 1996), previously published as Ted Solotaroff and Nessa Rapoport, eds., *Writing Our Way Home: Contemporary Stories by American Jewish Writers,* New York: Schocken, 1992; Ilan Stavans, *Jewish Literature: A Very Short Introduction* (New York: Oxford University Press, 2021); Ilan Stavans, ed., *The Oxford Book of Jewish Stories* (New York: Oxford University Press, 1998); David Stern, *The Anthology in Jewish Literature* (New York: Oxford University Press, 2004); Hana Wirth-Nesher, ed., *What Is Jewish Literature?* (Philadelphia: Jewish Publication Society, 1994); Ruth Wisse, *The Modern Jewish Canon* (New York: The Free Press, 2000).

9 Wisse, *The Modern Jewish Canon.*

10 Cammy et al., *Arguing The Modern Jewish Canon.*

originally coined by Cynthia Ozick that Wisse borrows.[11] To Wisse, "centrally Jewish" means reflective in some way of Jewish experience, Jewish consciousness, or the Jewish condition. She offers as an example of Jewish experience a novel by Isaac Bashevis Singer describing a seventeenth-century Polish town in the grip of messianic fever that "plunges us into the Jewish condition."[12] Her examples of "fiction [that] yokes us to a Jewish consciousness"[13] are Isaac Babel's *Red Cavalry* (an excerpt of which, in an original translation, is included in this anthology), and the writing of Shmuel Yosef Agnon (also represented in this anthology), where "all the layers of Jewish civilization and learning surface through quotations, allusions, and stylistic imitation in the richly intertextual Hebrew."[14] To Wisse, in a work of Jewish fiction, "the authors or characters know, and let the reader know, that they are Jews,"[15] and the characters not only have Jewish ancestry or affiliation, but share in the fate of the Jewish people.

Of course, what it means for a work of fiction to reflect Jewish experience, Jewish consciousness, or the Jewish condition can be complex to define. From my perspective, a story[16] that is Jewish expresses Jewish identity on either a religious or cultural dimension, and it relates in a fundamental way to Jewish experience, whether in the past, present, or future. Sometimes at *Jewish Fiction .net* we receive a story that is very good, but when we consider it in terms of the above criteria, we are unable, try as we might, to find anything Jewish about it,[17] so that is not a story we publish.

---

11 Wisse, *The Modern Jewish Canon*, 11; Cynthia Ozick, "Toward A New Yiddish," in *Art and Ardor* (New York: Alfred A. Knopf, 1983), 168–169. Previously published as Cynthia Ozick, "America: Toward Yavneh," *Judaism* (Summer 1970): 264–282.

12 Wisse, *The Modern Jewish Canon*, 14.

13 Ibid.

14 Ibid., 14–15.

15 Ibid., 15.

16 For simplicity's sake, in the title of this book and sometimes in this introduction, I use the word "story" to refer to both stories and novel excerpts, given that the novel excerpts in this anthology all stand on their own like self-contained stories.

17 Someone else might react differently to this story, of course—inevitably there is subjectivity in this process. But at *Jewish Fiction .net*, we always have at least two, and often three, readers evaluate each submission we receive, and we engage deeply, seriously, and open-mindedly with every one of them. So all the submissions that come to us get a very fair reading.

The stories and novel excerpts in this anthology touch on many themes, including the Jewish family; antisemitism; morality; outsider identity; relationships (both positive and negative) with non-Jews; the Holocaust; pride in, and love of, Jewish tradition; and critique of this tradition and of the Jewish community (for example, because of its sexism). Among these stories there are various commonalities, as well as great diversity. Each of these works is a world unto itself, and there is no implication here that any of them are representative of the literature or the language in which they were originally written, thematically, stylistically, or otherwise. For instance, the story translated from Czech should not be viewed as "typical," or representative, of Czech, or Czech Jewish, or Jewish, fiction in general. Furthermore, the writers of the stories in this book—like other writers of Jewish fiction—are diverse not only linguistically and culturally, but in multiple other ways: in political outlook, sexual orientation, birth religion, skin color, and more. So it is worthwhile, when reading these works, to remain cognizant that Jewish fiction and its authors are far from monolithic.

~

So far, in using the phrase "Jewish fiction," I have been focusing on the first word in it: "Jewish." But now let's pause on the second word. Since this is an anthology of fiction, a few comments about fiction as a genre are in order. In my view, fiction has a special kind of power. This is because when we read a story or a novel, our defenses drop, our boundaries relax, and we enter the inner life of the main character. Once we decide to keep reading a book, even if the protagonist is a serial killer, we enter this person's reality and see the world through his or her eyes. Through fiction we are introduced to different kinds of people than we usually meet, as well as to places, cultures, and experiences distant from our own. So fiction brings us into intimate emotional contact with differentness and otherness—and this changes us. There is actually psychological research showing that reading literary fiction increases our capacity for empathy, and consequently our behavior, in real life.[18] Fiction-reading is a transformative experience, one that can alter us for the better.

---

18 Raymond A. Mar, Keith Oatley, and Jordan Peterson, "Exploring the Link Between Reading Fiction and Empathy: Ruling Out Individual Differences and Examining Outcomes," *Communications (Sankt Augustin)* 34, no. 4 (2009): 407–428; Raymond A. Mar, Keith Oatley, Jacob Hirsh, Jennifer dela Paz, and Jordan Peterson, "Bookworms Versus Nerds:

This, of course, is not the only reason, or even the main reason, for reading, or writing, fiction. But it is why fiction in general, and Jewish fiction in particular, gives me hope. We are living now in a fearsome time—a period, under the shadow of a pandemic, of enormous global upheaval and uncertainty, politically, socially, economically, and environmentally. For Jews, this is also a time of skyrocketing antisemitism and a worldwide Jewish community that is extremely divided and polarized. Many people, I among them, are concerned about the growing chasm between different groups of Jews—between left/right, Orthodox/non-Orthodox, Ashkenazi/Mizrahi, Israel/Diaspora, and more. In this challenging context, I envision Jewish fiction as a place of meeting. A bridge, arching over the many fissures below, where, sharing in the beauty of our literature, Jews can discover some empathy and mutual understanding. It has happened many times that, after publishing a new issue of *Jewish Fiction .net*, I received emails from readers saying that, until then, they'd never read a story by (for example) a Turkish Jew, or an Argentinian Jew, or a Croatian Jew, and had never thought about these Jews' particular perspective or experience of life. Yet reading these stories changed their feeling about people from these places, made them think more deeply about what it means to be Jewish, and broadened the parameters of the Jewish world as they knew it.

This gives me hope. Since fiction has the ability to alter how people think, feel, and act, perhaps this anthology can help bring Jews closer together and make us more knowledgeable about, and accepting of, each other. Like a water hole where many diverse, colorful species of wildlife assemble to refresh themselves, I see this book as a gathering place where, despite our differences, we can all drink from the nearly inexhaustible richness and strength of our people's stories. There is also room, of course, at this water hole for non-Jewish friends and readers. So they can sip from our waters and share with us theirs.

Now, onto these wonderful stories! They will speak for themselves. *L'chaim*—Drink deeply and enjoy!

Exposure to Fiction Versus Non-fiction, Divergent Associations with Social Ability, and the Simulation of Fictional Social Worlds," *Journal of Research in Personality*, 40, no. 5 (2006): 694–712; Megan Schmidt, "How Reading Fiction Increases Empathy and Encourages Understanding," *Discover*, August 28, 2020, https://www.discovermagazine.com/mind/how-reading-fiction-increases-empathy-and-encourages-understanding.

18
Jewish Stories

Hostage

By Elie Wiesel

Excerpt from a Novel

Translated from French *by Catherine Temerson*

So from one day to the next, Shaltiel Feigenberg and his family became famous. Their names and faces appeared on the front pages of newspapers. *The Mysterious Disappearance of a Jewish Storyteller* was one headline. They were discussed on television. President Gerald Ford, when brought up to speed, made his concern publicly known. His secretary of state, Henry Kissinger, followed developments closely. The prospective presidential, senatorial, and congressional candidates published statements condemning "all forms of terrorism and proclaiming their solidarity with the Jewish people." Blanca and her nieces reluctantly submitted to the journalists' questions to assuage them.

Time magazine quoted Malka saying that the investigations should focus on antisemitic groups: "It's simple. They're everywhere. They won't forgive us for having survived and for having children." (The magazine pointed out that the hostage had no children.)

The *New York Times* published excerpts of a short story that Blanca had found in the jumble of her husband's desk drawers. A literary agent contacted her and asked whether she wouldn't consider publishing his short stories in a book that could be produced in a matter of weeks.

An Israeli evening daily printed Shaltiel's Israeli short story in its entirety. It was hardly characteristic of his oeuvre, if oeuvre is the right word. It lacked the intellectual, let alone mystical, preoccupations of his other writings. This one was an action narrative.

Brooklyn was in turmoil. Some young Hasidim created a small self-defense group and offered to protect the Feigenberg family. Their elders announced a day of fasting and invited the entire community to join them in reciting the appropriate psalms: Heaven will help the Jews when men prove to be powerless or indifferent. A great mystic spent the entire night in silence, in strict reverent meditation, trying to locate and protect Shaltiel.

~

In Israel, for understandable reasons, official circles and the public were following the Feigenberg episode with ever-greater interest. Are people more interested in the fate of a writer, no matter how modest, than in the fate of an anonymous person? Possibly.

The special adviser to Prime Minister Yitzhak Rabin, General Peleg Har-Even, summoned Dan Ramati. Tall, elegant, taut with an angular face, looking perpetually curious and vigilant, he was feared, dreaded, and admired.

Ramati, who had been nicknamed "the great," had had a legendary life. In his youth, before the creation of the Jewish state, in the years 1942 to 1948, he had been a member of the famous Berger Group, whose members were called terrorists by their opponents and resistance fighters by their supporters. The number two man on the English security services' most-wanted list, he was reputed for carrying out bomb attacks. In the official structure of the state of Israel, as the director of the Mossad, he had exceptional authority, both professional and moral. His opinions were sought after and respected.

"What do you think of the Feigenberg case?" asked the prime minister.

"I don't know yet. I've sent two of our best people to New York. We have excellent relations with the FBI and the CIA, so that shouldn't be a problem."

"I want you to make this affair a priority. And to take charge of it personally."

"Why? Is there something here I'm unaware of?"

"No. But there *is* something that seems important to me, an intimate connection that has to exist between the Jewish state and the Jewish people—I mean, the Jewish Diaspora. This may be taking place in America, but I think we have a role to play in it. In my mind, wherever a Jew is threatened or persecuted just because he's Jewish, we're responsible for his fate. Keep me posted."

Dan Ramati nodded his head approvingly.

~

They are in a dilapidated, foul-smelling basement with a few odd chairs and overturned benches. A small window near the ceiling is full of dust and produces a cloudy beam of light. A smell of acrid smoke causes occasional sneezing. Huge cobwebs hang from the ceiling and fill the corners.

There are two men and their hostage. An Arab, Ahmed, is impatient and speaks with a guttural, nervous voice. An Italian, Luigi, seems more easygoing. His voice can be gentle, almost warm at times.

"What do you want from me?" Shaltiel asks. "What have I done to you? Why did you bring me here? Who are you? What am I to you?"

"We can be whatever you want us to be, your salvation or your death," says Ahmed. "Don't have any illusions: You can yell until hell freezes over; no one will hear you. And even if they do, no one will care about your fate. They'll write about you in the newspapers for a few days, then they'll forget all about you. We have three days left. If our demands aren't met, too bad for you."

Shaltiel can vaguely make them out through his ill-adjusted black blindfold. They're looking hard at him, as if they expect to see him change in some way. He can see their silhouettes. Odd, it's not like in the crime films where the prisoner can't see a thing. Is he dealing with amateurs or professionals?

He can distinguish half their faces, like masks. He sees huge eyes. I'm speaking to eyes, not human beings, Shaltiel thinks.

Somewhere in his subconscious, a voice keeps whispering: This must be a case of mistaken identity, a monumental, stupid mistake. These things happen. They must somehow think I'm a dangerous person. But I'm not a danger to anyone. He had been on his way to Srulik Silber's, an old collector friend, whose house, near the ocean, was crammed with books and esoteric manuscripts. It was an unplanned visit. Shaltiel was going home and suddenly felt like seeing Srulik, especially since he had to return an eighteenth-century Sabbatean pamphlet that he had borrowed the week before. He liked Srulik. Last month, Shaltiel was telling him that his erstwhile dreams had evaporated a long time ago. The Messiah would not be coming. The world, cursed through its own fault, would not be saved; the Messiah would arrive too late, or, as Kafka said, on the day after. Srulik smiled when Shaltiel said that. "Do you really think I don't know?" he asked.

He never got to meet Srulik again because Satan meddled. Footsteps came up behind him, someone was suddenly rushing, shadows were approaching. Shaltiel walked on, heedless. He was struck on the back of his neck and collapsed, his head on fire. As he regained consciousness, everything was swirling around. The stars were falling with a thunderous noise.

And what about the book he was going to return to Srulik, full of calculations sketched out in concentric circles? It was meant for the initiated and was particularly interesting. Why was everything being sabotaged by some curse plunging him into this makeshift prison?

There is an unpleasant half-light. He is *clinging*. At first, to pass the time, he plays mental chess against an imaginary opponent. If he wins, he thinks, God will smile down on him; he'll get his freedom back. But it's difficult. The white bishop makes a marvelous opening. The king is too old, too slow. The queen is too nimble, too quick, too eager to win. The knight is a prisoner. The game is interrupted by his torturers.

Timidly, a pale beam of sunshine infiltrates through the basement window, protected by two wooden bars. Is it daybreak or dusk?

"You're Jewish," says an Arab voice. "Your name is Shaltiel Feigen-something. Feigenberg, that's it. It's in your papers. Married. You're a peddler. What do you sell?"

"Words," says Shaltiel.

"You making fun of me?"

"No, it's the truth. I sell words."

"I don't believe you. No one buys words."

"They pay for my living."

How do they know these things about me? Shaltiel wonders. Oh yes, my documents. It's all listed. But then they surely know that I've done no harm to anyone and that I have no money. My wristwatch is worth all of twelve dollars. I don't get mixed up in things that are none of my business. I'm happy to have a few friends, who, like me, are in love with words and the silence between them. My life is of no consequence, except for my family. I don't understand what's happening to me.

"You want my poverty? You can have it."

"And he thinks he's funny," the Arab says as he laughs.

"Not so clever," the other one adds. "Do you think we don't know?"

"Well then . . ."

"Well then what? We know you're not rich. But we'll get something out of you, something that's not money. We're fighters in the Palestinian Revolutionary Action Group, and you're our prisoner."

"Why me? I'm not important. No one will satisfy your demands for my sake, you can be sure."

Then, in a neutral tone, with no sign of hatred, Luigi explains, as if to a student: They're not looking for money; they couldn't care less about money. That, they could get more easily and with less risk. Others give them money. They are interested in playing their part in the life and history of Islam. His organization decided to try to do on the American continent what his comrades are doing in other places, all over the Middle East. It's the first time. Yes, it's the first operation on American soil, which is supposed to be safe, secure, impregnable, according to the boasts of its leaders. Hostage-taking is more profitable than ordinary attacks in Tel Aviv, Paris, or London. It doesn't cost them anything in human lives and brings them worldwide publicity, as well as the liberation of their comrades-in-arms. So this is a new strategy of the radical Palestinians, faithful to their military, national, and religious objectives. They are gambling on Jewish solidarity and taking advantage of its influence on Western governments.

~

At first, it all seemed unreal to Shaltiel, a crazy scheme staged by men obsessed with pointless, criminal violence.

The first night dragged by, populated with predatory, threatening shadows. It's a tale, Shaltiel said to himself, a frightening tale, senseless and improbable, in which I'm both the witness and victim. It's a tale in which someone like me is tormented. It's not me who is aching, who is thirsty. I'm somewhere else. I live in another city, in another world. In another body, another story, another mystery, another person. Soon I'll wake up, find I'm intact and serene, impatient to string together words that make people dream.

All Ahmed knows is how to insult, swear, and curse. He is playing the familiar part of the wicked inquisitor alongside the nice one. Drunk with frustration, he takes it out on his powerless victim. His favorite words are "done for." "You're done for, you're all done for, the Jews are done for," he says. In the first few hours, that's as far as he goes. Mental torture is enough for him. Everything about him spreads anger and hatred: hatred toward the Jewish state, the Jewish people, the Jewish past, the Jewish religion, Jewish money, Jewish power. These are his obsessions, his phobias, complete and all-enveloping. At least, this is the impression he wants to give. Every word coming out of his mouth is a gratuitous insult, an obscene swearword, a poisoned arrow, or a call to suffering, humiliation, denial, murder.

In his view, the Jewish infidels will survive only so they can be punished by Allah and oppressed by his devoted servants. They are the cause of all evil weighing on the world. They are the incarnation of transgression, impurity personified, the vermin of the earth, society's cancer, the enemies of peace, the negation of happiness. Realizing that Shaltiel was guilty only of belonging to the accursed people, Ahmed quickly saw how he could take advantage of the situation: He had to coerce his hostage into signing a "voluntary" declaration condemning the Jewish state for "all the crimes committed against the unfortunate Palestinians." He also wanted to get him to request that men of goodwill, on every side of the political spectrum, save his life by obtaining the liberation of the three Palestinian "prisoners of war."

Between the obscenities punctuating the Arab's orders, Shaltiel finds himself regretting two things: that he never acquired the mystical powers that would make him invisible and that he never studied the Koran. Does the Muslim holy book, held to be sacred by countless believers, really preach bloodthirsty violence? His mind, molded by the study of Jewish sources, refuses to accept this. If the Koran represents contemporary Islam, as practiced by his abductors, he feels it is a religion much to be pitied.

Ahmed believes that he is the Prophet's personal servant. It is He who commands him to do what he does. Hence his conviction that he can do as he pleases. Shaltiel is his enemy and the enemy of his brothers in the desert; he must be denied pity. He must be crushed, his will shattered, his faith ridiculed, his honor sullied, his reason denounced, his dignity destroyed; he must be smashed, trampled on, his soul emptied of its powers and treasures. Ahmed's immediate goal is specific: compelling the masters in Tel Aviv and Washington to accept his political demands. In front of his implacable, inflexible determination, they will show themselves to be weak and cowardly. The key to his victory is here before him: this pathetic Yid, Shaltiel Feigen-whatever.

Little by little, Ahmed convinces himself that, in addition to the liberation of the Muslim prisoners, it will be essential for him to force the hostage to disown his people—those manipulators, renegades, criminal gangsters, children of the devil and death.

"Whether you admit it or not, from the fact of being Jewish, you've got Muslim blood on your hands," he says to his prisoner. "What the Jews are doing at home, they're doing in your name, too."

"No, no, no!" protests Shaltiel, who hasn't yet understood the meaning of this accusation. "I'm Jewish, but I've never humiliated anyone. I've never committed a crime! You've made a mistake about me. I'm not the person you're looking for. I'm not your enemy! I'm against all humiliation, all persecution; I'm opposed to violence in every form, for violence includes violation. The Jew that I am, the storyteller I am, repudiates it with all my heart and soul."

Ahmed isn't listening to him. There is no discussing theology, sociology, and politics when someone is under the spell of a self-enclosed totalitarian ideology. Intentionally or out of ignorance, Ahmed, who is empirical in all matters, detests pointless and laborious philosophical imaginings, never-ending discussions, or clashes of ideas that might be respectful of nonbeliever opponents and sinners deserving only of complete contempt. His argument boils down to two words: yes and no. His vocabulary is meager, limited to threats and swearwords. His role is not to listen but to be listened to. As he sees it, every infidel is a potential hostage. He is the all-powerful, omniscient master; the slave owes him not just absolute obedience, but also his existence and survival.

Even torture that is only verbal reinforces the power of the torturer: the prisoner's imagination leads him to dread the next round of interrogations. And when it happens, the feeling of inferiority becomes more acute; it bores into the brain, and the cultural and psychological defenses that surround the brain disintegrate and vanish. The ego is dissolved. Could Ecclesiastes be right? Is a living dog worth more than a dead lion? Chased from his throne by Ashmedai, the master of demons, good King Solomon, the wisest of men, experienced mental torments, too. Physical pain comes later. For the tortured, all the knowledge acquired from childhood in the course of a lifetime won't protect you. The moans seem to issue from another body. In the end, the victim doesn't have anything or anyone to cling to. It's the feeling of falling into a bottomless well. Suddenly emptiness or the idea of emptiness appeals to him. Oh, to have an empty head, an empty heart, an empty future; to think of nothing, to feel nothing: This would be paradise in the middle of hell.

But Shaltiel knows this is impossible. His breath is not the only thing binding him to life. He has his parents, his wife, his close friends; they must be dying of anguish. What do they know? What are they doing? Who are they calling? What are the police doing? What is the press saying? In his imagination—and it fits with reality—he imagines Brooklyn in turmoil: the intense speculation in the study and prayer houses; the Hasidim consulting their Teacher, who advises them to recite particular psalms. In her powerlessness, Blanca must be agonizing. If there is anyone who is moving heaven and earth, it is she. Nothing stops her; nothing holds her back. Dynamic and full of ideas, she must be running from one office to the next, from one of the dozens of Jewish organizations to another. He can hear her motivating them, encouraging them, urging them to act: Surely someone can get to a congressman, a government official.

"So, you little bastard Yid," Ahmed yells. "Are you going to open your filthy mouth finally? If you don't talk, I'll make you drink your own blood! Are you going to ask for the liberation of my heroic comrades? Are you going to sign a confession and publicize your disgust for the Jewish army and the

Jewish politicians? They will be done for in time, I can guarantee that! And you first and foremost!"

Meeting with flat refusals, the Arab moved away and seemed to take his companion to task, as though he were testing his loyalty to their cause.

"We've got to get him to show his weakness and cowardliness publicly. Thanks to him, we'll force the liberation of my brother and the others, and also gain the respect of revolutionaries throughout the world. That's our mission!"

So there are only two of them, thinks Shaltiel. Two men, two terrorists, bound by hatred. Yet, listening to them, they're so different. One will never change because he won't entertain doubts, but is the other one capable of doubting? In the end, which of the two will kill me? Actually, what's the difference? Inevitably, they'll go through with it.

He says to himself that, like Dostoyevsky, he'll be a witness to the preparations of his own execution.

He hears a door opening and closing. One of the terrorists has gone out. It's the Italian. Ahmed begins to manhandle his prisoner, hoping he'll reach a breaking point.

Shaltiel takes refuge in his memories and in words, as usual. He calls them, but they don't obey. Ideas and images overlap, become distorted, diverted, disassociated. Finally, a wave of panic turns to tenderness.

Suddenly, a weird thought pops into his head: Why not make a "confession" and sign their preposterous statements, to which no intelligent person will attach any importance, and put an end to this stupid, horrendous spectacle? Other men, ever so much more influential than he, have done this, in another day and age: Nikolay Bukharin, Lev Kamenev, Zinoviev—great statesmen, illustrious generals, admired revolutionaries, former companions of Lenin—when their suffering became unbearable. He can't do it, though he could perhaps advise the Americans and the Israelis to liberate the three Palestinians, but he could not accuse Israel of war crimes or crimes against humanity: His own memory and that of his parents won't allow it. Yet it would be so simple: Saying yes under threat is not a disgrace. If he gave in, surely Jews would understand. Didn't he write articles supporting Jerusalem in an obscure Jewish monthly put out by the Department of Literary Studies at a Jewish college in Ohio? He used a Hebrew name, Shaltiel ben Haskel.

He suddenly finds himself trembling. Is it possible these Palestinian terrorists have read his articles and discovered the real name of their author? Perhaps his abduction was calculated. But why would they read a publication whose readership was so limited that it had to close down for lack of a subsidy? Yet in his feverish pain, he says to himself, Now that electronic communications are becoming global, anything is possible. How is he to know? Should he ask Ahmed if he is familiar with the articles? Bad idea. He might torture him even more cruelly.

Clenching his teeth, he decides not to say or do anything for the time being. He'll wait for the Italian.

~

In the course of the following night Shaltiel succeeded in persuading the Italian to remove his blindfold.

"In any case, it's of no use to you," he said. "I've studied esoteric subjects that have taught me how to 'see' voices. So I can describe you and your friend, your faces, your bodies, your behavior. Do you want me to prove it?"

The Italian nodded his head silently. He was surprised when his prisoner began to describe facial characteristics of both men—one bearded, the other just badly shaved; the first having well-defined eyebrows, the other bushy ones.

Luigi is thrown by what Shaltiel has to say, failing to account for the blindfold having been askew. He removes it. Shaltiel has won. He squints, adjusting his eyes to the meager light.

Am I dreaming? Is it the dream that makes my body tremble? wonders Shaltiel. He is so afraid of torture, so afraid of fear. His brain is muddled, disoriented, especially when he must wear the blindfold. He keeps repeating prayers, but they are beginning to seem less holy. His thoughts are bizarre; he's not even sure he's *thinking*. Does he cry for help? The cry may well be silent. But he hears it and he's not sure it's him. He suddenly sees himself surrounded by a group of masked children who are threatening him. They're reproaching him for not having children. They demand a story, any story, as long as it's beautiful. He suggests a poem; they refuse. He insists. They put their hands over their ears. He gets angry. A little girl makes a face at him. He finds it unbearable. Finally, he submits:

This is the story of a young, sad tiger who, from afar, tells a beautiful story to an exhausted old lion. Listen, children, grandchildren, listen and don't cry. And you, old people, listen and don't laugh.

Don't look for your father, says the tiger; he is gone. Don't call for your mother; she is hiding.

What do you say, children, when you're saying nothing? And you, old people, what are you doing against the forest with its bruised arms?

And you, jailer, who is the real prisoner, you who erects great walls, or me, your victim who dreams of freedom?

Let's listen, children, nice children, let's listen to the beggar who keeps silent and the blind man who sings of dusk and the tramp who sings of his thirst.

The Guest

By Varda Fiszbein

Story

Translated from Spanish *by Andrea G. Labinger*

Intuition or luck? The opportunity was in his hands and he knew how to seize it.

The fact is that he guessed someone like my grandfather could only react as he did.

In a God-fearing man, one respectful of Mosaic Law, the sense of tradition prevails even above feelings.

He may not have been rich, but every year when the Pesach festivities rolled around, he would conduct his Seder surrounded by his family like a king.

Elegant in his dark suit, with a gold chain draped across his chest, he sits in an armchair at the head of the table as if it were a throne, his head resting on a cushion designed especially for that day, a cushion on which the Star of David, delicately embroidered, stands out against a blue velvet background.

At the other end of the table, wearing an expression that betrays the fatigue resulting from the turmoil of several days' preparation, sits his wife, wearing a soft, black silk dress. She has chosen the correct place, opposite her husband and close to the door, because throughout the course of the evening she will make many visits to the kitchen, hurriedly transporting bowls and trays laden with steaming mounds of delicacies. Comings and goings that will leave damp little tracks on the skin of her décolleté and accentuate the tense furrows beneath the rice powder with which her daughter has tried to conceal the intense redness of her mother's cheeks. The three older sons will occupy their customary seats, accompanied by their wives and offspring. They will look happy and well-groomed.

Perhaps at some point in the evening one of the little ones will lift the hem of the embroidered linen tablecloth, squeaky with starch, confirming that this year, once again, nearly all the women have called a truce with their feet by slipping off their new shoes.

Raquelita, the youngest, will sit to the right of the head of the table, as befits the princess of the house. Light of their eyes, balm of her father's old age, flower of her mother's yearnings. An unexpected, only daughter on whom she has bestowed the name of the Patriarch Jacob's wife.

Many are the expectations her progenitors hold for her. Intimate, unconfessed illusions: that her lovely dark eyes, her slender fingers, trained through long hours at the piano, her wispy, almost adolescent figure might succeed in attracting a young man from a wealthier family than her own; though, should the situation arise, a somewhat older, but wise, gentleman, well-connected in worldly, cultured circles, would not be frowned upon either.

The unmarried son will sit beside his mother. On this occasion it will be his honor to fulfill the duties of hospitality, which are regarded so favorably in the eyes of the Almighty. With his sister's joyous complicity, he will be responsible for choosing a guest. Someone who—poor soul—does not have the good fortune to share the Pesach meal with his own people. The son will count on his family's approval because the guest will have already visited their home and shared moments of leisure with the youngest sons and exchanged polite greetings with the parents.

Forty light bulbs on the enormous chandelier suspended from the middle of the ceiling illuminate its carved crystal arms, projecting line and color, hitherto unremarked, on the silverware, an effect achieved thanks to the diligence of the daughters-in-law, who came over the night before to help with cleaning.

The delicate aroma of gefilte fish and stewed meat blend together and waft toward all corners of the house, caressing the diners' senses along the way.

In his role as king, my grandfather presides over the rites with great precision, ensuring that in the middle of the table, equidistant from all the place settings, meticulously arranged on porcelain dishes, are the bitter herbs that must be eaten as a reminder and a lesson for the youngest ones of the hardships suffered by the Hebrew people when they were forced to live the bitterness of exile and slavery at Pharaoh's court.

The glorious saga will be read from the Haggadah, which tells of how the Magnanimous One sent Moses to liberate his brethren, for which we must be eternally grateful, since otherwise we would not yet be free.

The celebration proceeds uninterrupted with the reading of the Haggadah, followed by everything from soup to nuts and topped off by exquisite desserts, gladdening flesh and spirit.

Four times the glasses will be raised in unison, the last time to welcome the Prophet Elijah, encouraging his spirit to visit such a pious home.

Just as tradition demands, after dining my grandfather will give the order to search for the *afikoman* that he had hidden earlier that evening. A rectangular piece of unleavened bread, the whitest and crunchiest, the most delicious part of the matzah, evoking the kind of bread the Hebrews were obliged to take with them when they hurriedly fled Egypt, as they did not have the time necessary for the bread to rise. In order to get it back, he must pay the price demanded by the finder.

Although everyone present will participate, the adults will only pretend to search so as to give a greater chance to the little ones, who will return it in exchange for a sweet, or possibly a few coins.

After the *afikoman* is redeemed, he will break it into enough pieces to distribute all around. He will act in a generous and just manner, just as He Who redeemed us from our long, sorrowful captivity is generous and just.

And so the first night of the Pesach celebration will come to an end.

At that dinner in the year 1940, I, like everyone else, thought that the invariable ritual would be repeated. However, neither I nor anyone else had anticipated that the guest would take it upon himself to make a change.

I was only thirteen and felt slightly out of place. I was the oldest of the grandchildren, no longer of an age to participate in the commotion produced by the younger cousins as they stampeded through the house in search of the piece of matzah, but not yet old enough to join the adults who took advantage of the occasion to chat about this and that while pretending to look for it.

I remained in my chair, feeling uncomfortable, until, at the opposite end of the table, my grandfather, who hadn't moved from his seat either, beckoned me with his hand, and understanding my state of confusion, hurried to my rescue, pointing out the circle formed by my two youngest uncles and their friend.

Prepared to accept his suggestion, I started to stand up in order to join them, but at that moment the group dispersed.

I didn't know then, as I still don't know today, what my uncles did or where they went. From that moment on, and until the end of the evening, all my attention was focused on our guest's actions.

He folded his napkin before depositing it next to his unfinished glass of wine, and, noticing a loose thread on the cuff of his shirt, yanked it off brusquely. Once on his feet, he deliberately walked toward the head of the table.

He had a kind of languid gait that called attention to his misshapen jacket pockets. A careful look revealed that the jacket had originally been the same color as the pants he wore.

He asked permission to take the pillow on which my grandfather's head had been resting all night long. He unzipped the cover.

Intuition or luck? Inside, wrapped in tissue paper, was the object to be redeemed.

The opportunity was in his hands and he knew how to seize it.

He returned to his seat at the table, indifferent to the disappointed ruckus of the children.

On the adults' faces, the abundant dinner, drawn-out evening, and many toasts, both ritual and spontaneous, were now beginning to leave their first traces.

My grandfather tapped the edge of his glass with a spoon to call for silence before turning to the young man, who awaited his words with apparent nonchalance, and simply said:

"As tradition demands, now we must fulfill the obligation of sharing the afikoman. To reclaim it, I will give you something in exchange . . ."

The addressee was as familiar with the tradition as was the speaker, my grandfather. In our family, redemption of the white piece of matzah was governed by strict rules: no price limit, refusal, or bargaining was possible.

For whatever reason, something in the atmosphere changed. The distracted silence in which we awaited the game/ceremony that was carried out in almost identical form year after year and which concluded the Pesach dinner, suddenly turned attentive, expectant, perhaps more profound, as if silence could grow in cadence or degree.

There was not a trace of insolence or challenge in his face or in the tone he assumed: "I want to marry your daughter," we heard him reply in a quiet, but clear, voice, as he gently slid the product of his search across the table toward my grandfather, and we broke out in goose bumps at the sound of the tissue paper softly scraping against the tablecloth.

For the first time I noticed the many broken, overlapping lines that time had etched on my grandfather's face. I saw that the silver on his chin had long since won the battle against the original dark brown of his carefully trimmed beard.

His clear-eyed gaze bared none of the emotion that his soul must have harbored at that moment.

No gesture violated the purity of his aquiline profile as he turned his head, while at the same time his hand reached for the cane he used to stand up and walk out of the room with at his usual, measured pace.

That night a rift opened up in the tradition. It was the guest, not my grandfather, who distributed the pieces of the *afikoman* among us, standing beside the woman who was already his betrothed.

Three months later he married Aunt Raquel.

And the Crooked Shall Be Made Straight

By Shmuel Yosef Agnon

Excerpt from a Novella

Translated from Hebrew *by Michael P. Kramer*

Not so many years ago, in the town of Buczacz (may His city be rebuilt, amen), there lived a fine, upright Jew by the name of Menashe Chaim Hakohen, a native of the holy community of Yazlivitz. While he could hardly have been counted among the world's rich and mighty, nor have found his place among the nation's notables, still the income he earned from his general store was ample rather than meager. He lived with his wife Kreyndl Tsharne, with whom God had graced him in his youth, and together with his wife ate his fill of bread and pursued righteousness and mercy all his days. He truly embodied the maxim of the sages of blessed memory, "Who does righteousness at all times? He who supports his wife and children." At least partially embodied—for the man was childless. As they had no children, she, his helpmeet, put all her efforts into running their business, presiding over everything that had to do with the shop, as was customary among the scattered communities of Israel in those days.

Ordinarily, such a man expects to dwell with his wife in peace and tranquility, to spend his days pleasurably enjoying the good of the earth, and, when his appointed time comes, after a hundred and twenty years, to behold the splendor of the Lord. Alas, when it pleases God to subvert a man's ways, good fortune swiftly takes wing, and the Omnipresent has many emissaries to fling a man down upon the dunghill of need. While they sat safe and sound in their home, fearing no evil, offering praise and thanks to the blessed Lord for their shop and its serenity, fortune's fury sprang upon them. Their shop caught the eye of one of the town's prominent shop owners and he coveted it, seeing how good their portion was. Having close ties to the authorities, he went to the court of the town's lord and offered him significantly more rent than Menashe Chaim and his wife were then paying, and the shop nearly fell into his hands.

For in those days, the government of His Majesty, Emperor Franz Josef, had limited the authority of the rabbinic courts. High-handed Jews could flout their people's covenant and challenge the established claims of others with impunity. Who could prevent them? Had Menashe Chaim's wife Kreyndl Tsharne not added to the rent several guldens, who knows if they would even have finished out the year there. From then on, it seems as if the Evil Eye (may the Merciful One spare us) oversaw everything they did, and their business declined dramatically. Neither did their competitor stand by idly, hands in his pockets. He devised various schemes to ruin their business and deprive them of their livelihood. He lowered the price of his goods. He maligned their shop. When Menashe Chaim attempted to alleviate their plight by bringing in a new machine to grind cinnamon, peppercorns, and coffee beans, rumors spread through the town that a demon from Hell turned the grindstone, that devils danced upon it, and other such calumnies that are best not committed to writing. In short, on the day the shop's rent was due, they had not a penny to pay the lord of the town, let alone the extra guldens they had already added, as explained above. Then there were the bribes to the deputies and lackeys and to the court go-betweens and to anyone who could advocate on their behalf. Taxes and duties consumed the rest of their efforts. As the government levied taxes on shopkeepers based upon the rent they paid, now that the shop cost them more, the taxes for the government's coffers, for municipal upkeep, and for paving roads naturally increased as well. Their stock dwindled markedly. More and more of their shelves stood bare until, as the Talmud says, the breach in the wall was greater than what remained standing. But the Lord's steadfast love does not cease, and His compassion does not fail. Divine Providence (may He be blessed) always dilutes the bitterness of the bad by mixing it with some good, so even in this time of trouble Menashe Chaim and his wife despaired not of His mercy. Their faith remained strong. Soon He would rescue them from the grip of misfortune.

Indeed, as we are told in Kehal Hasidim, nothing stands in the way of faith. Once the Baal Shem Tov (may his merit shield us all) received a heavenly call to journey to a certain village to learn the true character of faith, so that he might in turn teach the people an invaluable and much needed lesson. When the Baal Shem Tov and his disciples arrived at the village, they lodged with the local tavern-keeper, a dignified old man who welcomed them warmly, prepared a great feast for them, and rejoiced at such distinguished guests.

At daybreak, when the Baal Shem Tov and his disciples rose for prayers, a Cossack, an officer of the nobleman who ruled the village, entered with a corded whip in his hand. He struck the table with the whip three times, then left. None of the tavern staff said a word. The guests were baffled, having no idea what these cracks of the whip might mean. They turned to the host. He was as cheerful as before, had not reacted at all. As they completed their prayers, the Cossack returned. Again, he struck the table with his whip three times. Again, not one of the tavern staff said a word to him. The disciples looked at each other in bewilderment. The Baal Shem Tov finally asked their host why the Gentile had thus struck the table. The host answered, "It's a warning. Today I must pay the lord of the village the rent for the tavern." He warns them three times, and if the bundle of money is not ready after the third time, the nobleman will take the tavern-keeper and his entire family and throw them in the dungeon. "From the look on your face, it appears that you have the money," said the Baal Shem Tov. "Hurry then, take the money, go to the nobleman now, before our meal. We'll wait till you return safely to us." "As of now I haven't even one penny," the host responded, "but the blessed Lord will surely provide for me. Let's eat and drink. We needn't hurry. We have three hours before the time arrives. The blessed Lord will surely provide for me." They all sat down to dine, they took their time, and the host's face showed not a hint of worry about the money. The guests looked at one another in amazement. It was truly wondrous to see. When they finished eating, the Cossack came a third time and struck the table thrice with his whip. The host neither stood nor stirred in his seat. After they ate and recited a proper, unhurried, even-paced grace, the host dressed in his fine Sabbath clothes, girded himself with his wide sash, and announced, "Now I'll go to the court and bring the rent to the nobleman. I'll not tarry. Stay here. I'll quickly return." The Baal Shem Tov asked him again, "Do you have the money you need?" He answered, "As yet I haven't even one penny, but the blessed Lord will soon send His aid." And he left.

The Baal Shem Tov stood in the doorway with his disciples and watched him go. As the tavern-keeper walked briskly toward the court, a wagon veered from its path to meet him. He stood beside the wagon, spoke with the passenger, and left empty-handed. The wagon continued toward the tavern. But before it arrived there, it slowed and stopped. The tavern-keeper was called back to the wagon and handed some money. When the wagon arrived at the tavern, the disciples inquired of the new guest, "What happened between you and the tavern-keeper? Why did you call him back and hand him money?" He explained, "I ordered liquor from him to be delivered next winter, may it be well for us, and at first we could find no common ground and agree on a price. But when I saw that he insisted on his price and wouldn't haggle with me, and because I know him to be an honest man, I gave him the amount he wanted. We didn't speak much more than that, as he said he was on his way to the nobleman with the rent for the tavern."

"Today you have seen the extraordinary power of faith," said the Baal Shem Tov to his disciples. "No need to worry. The blessed Lord will help us in our hour of need, if only we truly trust in Him, may He be blessed."

Dear reader, please do not be angry with me for going off to tell of the tavern-keeper's triumph and abandoning Menashe Chaim and his wife to their sighs. As God is my witness, my sole purpose is to illustrate the principle of *ma'aseh avot siman le-vanim*, that what happened to God's servants in earlier times may happen to His faithful in latter days. The rewards of faith are great, and happy are they who wait for Him. Even with a sharp sword at his throat, a man should not lose faith. But let us return to our tale.

As they wondered whence their help might come, Menashe Chaim and his wife lifted up their eyes and saw a large wagon hitched to three horses pulling up to the door of their shop. A villager climbed down from the wagon. Trembling, they went to greet him. They wanted to know what he was doing there, but he kept his mouth shut, did not utter a word, as though he were dumb. He rummaged through a pile of straw, probing its depths as God probes a man's dark secrets. He took out a trough and filled it with feed for his horses. He turned his attention to the wheels. Then he opened his broad belt, clutched his whip, spit this way and that, entered their shop, and asked whether he might be able to obtain various sorts of goods there. Kreyndl Tsharne and her husband received him cheerfully. "Where would you be able to get such goods if not here?" they answered in unison. In a blink the two of them sprang up—he here, she there—showing him all sorts of things, whether he asked for them or not, quoting him their prices. Even though the prices were fair and the measures just, the customer complained and haggled over the transaction for several hours. He was paying cash and could obtain all the merchandise from the supplier at cost, he argued, so why should he waste his money? He seemed to mean what he said. What would they do if the churl went elsewhere? Are there no other shopkeepers in Buczacz; is there no other merchant there? They needed his money as sorely as the dead crave the dew of resurrection. What had they to lose if they sold their merchandise for no profit, just this once for no profit, if as a result they earned enough to keep the shop for another year? Still, as merchants will, they put him off at first, trying to cajole and entice him in various ways, pleading that they could not possibly sell their merchandise below cost. The uncircumcised fellow remained unmoved by their pleas. He switched his whip from left hand to right, turned his back on them, and marched out. They rushed to usher him back in, took his hand and patted it, partly as a show of affection, partly as an act of supplication, appealing to him in the name of God to add a bit to his offer. But in the end they closed the deal on his terms.

The Gentile opened his money pouch, bought all the goods he wanted, and went contentedly on his way. Kreyndl Tsharne and her husband recounted the money and were overjoyed to see that they had almost enough to pay the shop's rent for another year. They deliberated how to obtain the amount they still lacked, whether from the free loan society or by borrowing on interest, no matter the consequences, which is what they did. That very day, between the afternoon and evening prayers, Kreyndl Tsharne dressed in her best clothes, wrapped her head in her silk Sabbath kerchief, put on her jewelry, went up to the court of the lord, and presented him with the payment. Glad, though faint-hearted, she renewed the contract for the coming year on the past year's terms. Breathing a sigh of relief, she returned to her shop where her husband Menashe Chaim sat beside a table, drowsing over a book. He awoke when Kreyndl Tsharne entered and announced that it was time to close the shop, that footsteps no longer fell in the marketplace and no customers might be expected. As usual, Menashe Chaim went out to see whether his competitor had closed up, lest it come to pass that a customer happen by and turn into his rival's shop, God forbid. Kreyndl Tsharne, exhausted by the day's trials, sank into a chair to rest.

For a short while, she didn't budge. She was simply unable to stand on her feet. But when she got her wind back, she looked around the shop and let out a loud and bitter cry. The cupboards were bare, the boxes and crates emptied. Nothing remained. Tearing at the fringes of her garment, she rained curses upon the head of Menashe Chaim, her careless, good-for-nothing husband who, dozing while she was out paying their debt, let some thief clean them out. Menashe Chaim swore that he had not taken his eyes off the shop, not even for one minute, but to no avail. Once the tongue begins to swear, it cannot stop. Kreyndl Tsharne heaped curse upon curse. "Did I go out dancing tonight?" she cried bitterly. "Did I paint my face for some fancy party? I went for you,

you idler, for you, so your livelihood wouldn't collapse! And you couldn't even sit like a golem and guard the fruit of my labor! Mercy! Why did God give you eyes? Only to see me toil away? Only to see the food that I serve you, the food that I earn by the sweat of my brow, with my blood and my fat?" Menashe Chaim was dumbstruck. His face turned as dark as a blackened kettle. The Mishnah states that a woman's earnings belong to her husband, but at that moment this fact escaped him. And when he failed to respond, she berated him even more. Finally, she grew too weak to curse him any longer—such is the strength of a woman—and the wrath of Kreyndl Tsharne subsided.

Menashe Chaim took the bundle of keys, followed his wife out, and locked the shop. Kreyndl Tsharne began to sob again, pouring out her bitterness. "This is what they mean when they say, 'locking the barn door after the horse is stolen.' You lazy, good-for-nothing idler! Why are you locking an empty shop?" Still, she bolted upright, rolled up her frayed sleeves, checked that each and every lock had been secured, and left for home. The black cast-iron lock, dangling down upon the dingy, yellowed, frost-flecked door, looked like a snake's tooth whose venom had already dripped out.

The First Christmas

By Gábor T. Szántó

Story

Translated from Hungarian
by Walter Burgess and *Marietta Morry*

He was shuffling among the Christmas tree vendors in the Lehel Square Market. He had never before bought a Christmas tree but in this winter of 1969 he felt he could no longer hold out; his two children were complaining in an accusatory tone that everyone in their class would have a tree except them. His wife, Anikó, also looked at him with such despair as if the whole world would come to an end if the children had to do without a shitty tree.

Robi, his older son, sniveled when the father blamed him for not understanding: Christmas is not their holiday; neither is Easter even if they get some chocolate eggs every year.

"It's not fair that others have their holiday and we don't," the younger son Peti said sulkily. Then he went on blinking and watching with trepidation. His brother did not argue. He felt that his rebelliousness would cause pain to his parents. He also feared the consequences and so preferred to close himself off and suffer quietly.

"The reason we don't celebrate Jewish holidays either," the father explained, "is that for modern enlightened people religious things are outmoded. Family holidays, birthdays, wedding anniversaries are different, but not saints' days because they have nothing to do with us."

~

The children seemed to accept the explanation, but he was aware that they were suffering; when he walked with them to and from school holding their hands, they would glance sadly at the Santa Clauses in the shop windows. Once they even remarked resignedly: "Let's watch it here even if we won't have a Christmas at home."

This was a jolt to the stomach. He had no counterargument. His children were in distress.

"You decide! I don't want you to regret it later that you gave up your principles because of the children or because of me," Anikó whispered at bedtime when he told her that he was being ground down by indecision.

"Why me? You decide," he said. He felt that his wife would like their children to be happy but she wanted to shirk the responsibility because she was not capable of going alone against the taboos her parents had hammered into her.

~

He stood there in the whirlwind of the market, the characteristic scent of the pine trees filled his nose and as he examined the more suitable ones (their apartment, a modern condominium in the Újlipótváros district, was two meters, eighty centimeters high), even after twenty-five years he recalled vividly the Christmas of 1944 when their work camp was near a snow-covered forest.

He had not smelled pines since. He had not gone hiking. It was their elderly neighbor who would take the boys walking in the woods or to the top of János Hill, the same lady who babysat them from their early childhood; he, on the other hand, had no desire to go into Nature, thank you very much.

"I have walked enough for a lifetime," he grumbled to Anikó, who sighed: "You need fresh air." And she knocked on Tante Klári's door.

~

He stood there among the pine trees which were tied up in twine and remembered how the stove in the wooden barracks flickered. They did not know whether they should be glad that they had not been driven farther west in the snow or if this unexpected calm should be taken as an ominous sign. Under the circumstances it was impossible to want to push forward even if they suspected that the relaxed attitude was not a good augur. Food was getting scarce, they could not count on a new supply in the middle of the forest. The nearest village was two days' walk away in snow which reached up to their knees.

In the morning, another group showed up, they also set up camp there. Those who were aware of the date knew that they were spending Christmas Eve with the remainder of another forced labor battalion and its guards. A few ornaments hastily made from newspapers were fastened to one of the trees, along with a couple of candles.

To celebrate their meeting and the holiday, the soldiers boozed up on apricot brandy and ordered the laborers out of the barracks. They had to line up and be harangued by the senior officer, Captain Ferenczy.

"It's Christmas, you Jews! Don't you know that it's a holiday of brotherly love? That is when Jesus was born, the one you crucified. But to prove that we are not like you, we will give you a chance. We will organize a race and only those who fall behind will have to croak. The rest will be let off the hook. This is your Christmas present." He turned to the soldiers. "Teams of five will compete with each other from the two battalions. You can only shoot at those who fall behind and belong to the other battalion. Is that clear? You've got to have rules both in games and in life."

There were loud guffaws from the guards on both sides.

"All right, let's get ready. If it gets dark you'll shoot wildly and you might get some of those who are strong enough to carry on."

The laborers pulled off their coats, jackets, and sweaters in silence. A few even removed their trousers and stood there freezing in long johns or just their underwear to be sure that nothing would slow them down.

They had to run sixty meters in the snow from the starting line to reach a cliff in an abandoned quarry. Both groups took off when the starting gun was fired. Those whose turn would be later were completely numbed. All they could hear in the surrounding silence was the crunching of the snow, their panting, and the whistle of the bullets. They sank up to their knees in the virgin snow as they lifted their legs with panicky movements. The bullets that missed them ricocheted from the rock with an ear-piercing sound.

"Does blood stink?" asked Váradi from the textile trade, as the two of them hit the wall side by side.

It was not clear whether his companion was just trying to catch his breath or was hit.

"I have no idea, why?" he said, panting. He did not realize that he was still alive.

"Because if it doesn't then I shit myself."

At that moment whimpering sounds came out of him, neither he nor his companion could tell whether he was laughing or sobbing, and he just collapsed in the snow.

~

He wanted to get the boys presents which would make their first Christmas memorable. In the import company where he worked, his colleagues could, with special permission, get duty free items. As there were two weeks left until Christmas he could make sure that the surprise gift he had looked up in the catalogue would arrive from Czechoslovakia in time. On the other hand, he was not willing to buy Christmas ornaments, lights, sparklers, and special candies that would be hung on the tree.

"You go and buy these lousy trinkets," he said to Anikó, who nodded in silence, and she thought: Once they had made up their minds to go ahead, why did he have to spoil everything by his attitude? Why did they have to feel bad when they could actually enjoy themselves?

~

Their agreement was that he would carve the trunk and set up the tree in the living room by the window and she would decorate it. He did not even enter the room until it got dark and his wife told him, embarrassed but with childish excitement, that he should get the present from its hiding place because the boys were getting impatient. They lit the sparklers and called the children to come in. The boys stood in awe with flushed faces in front of the tree. The younger one watched the zig-zagging sparks and the blinking colored lights with his mouth agape. They took in the smells of the phosphorus and pine which filled the room; Robi, for his part, glanced first at the tree and then at his parents, as if expecting them to indicate what he was supposed to do.

His wife pressed his hand behind his back. He let the woman touch him but did not react. When the sparklers had burnt out, the only illumination came from the colored lights. Anikó turned on the dim lamp beside the sofa but he switched on the chandelier in defiance.

"What is this?" Robi asked, fingering the joint present with excitement. Peti was already tearing off the golden wrapping paper from the long package. When they had removed the wrapping, the present was still not visible: it was covered in a brown cotton bag.

"Could it be a fishing rod?" Robi looked at his father, wondering.

"But we never go fishing!" Peti, crestfallen, let go of the wrapping paper.

Their father's poker face and enigmatic smile gave them no hint. The boys undid the narrow opening of the bag but they needed his help to remove the quite heavy Slavia 6-20 air rifle with its black steel barrel, still protected by nylon, from its case.

"Wow, this is really cool!" the boys exclaimed in appreciation. They kept touching the weapon and, each in turn, put his arm through the sling and hoisted it across his back, and marched around the room. They aimed it to find out how heavy it was. Their mother watched them in alarm. Up to that point the boys had not had even toy guns.

"Make sure you don't aim it at each other or at anyone else!" and she whispered in her husband's ear, "Isn't this going to cause trouble?"

He embraced her and pressed her to his side. Anikó's alarmed face did not relax. In the meantime, the boys managed to bend down the barrel with a joint effort to fill the container with air and with their father's approving nod fired the empty weapon.

"Well boys, do you want to try it out?"

"Yes, yes!" Robi and Peti shouted.

"Just watch! I will show you how to load it," and took it out of their hands.

"But how can we try it out?" Robi asked. "We don't have a bull's eye."

"Just wait," the father said, still smiling like someone who had thought this through in advance.

The Christmas tree stood in front of the window. He pulled aside the curtain and opened the window. Across from their five-story apartment building there was a pitch black space that used to be a lumberyard, where now empty lots were awaiting redevelopment. He went back in the middle of the room to join the boys.

"We won't shoot the candy, only the ornaments!" he said as he put the tiny lead pellets into the rifle and handed it to his elder son.

Robi took a step back in shock. His eyes were searching his mother's face, she was clenching her younger son with tears in her eyes.

Purimspiel

By Jasminka Domaš

Story

Translated from Croatian *by Iskra Pavlović*

Every day Tamar passed the pastry shop with a little terrace where the people in the district where she lived ate different cakes with chestnut, chocolate, or fruit of the season.

On the way to her flat she noticed many people hurriedly and happily carrying hot doughnuts or plates, or taking them wrapped in white paper, like pillows. And it seemed to Tamar that the doughnuts were breathing with the soft, fragrant, and sweet flavor of soft sugar. In this way she could determine that the carnival was in full swing, when such cakes are sold.

And she stated: "Once this mass of dough, crazy and swelling in a strange heaving carnival procession is gone, and when doughnuts are gone from the pastry shop and window, Purim will come. And in the four corners of the world, in Purim plays Queen Esther will appear, multiplied in her numerous characters, as if she was reflecting herself in the infinite holographic cosmic mirror of the Purim story."

And this woman, like many others after her, in Persia and outside Persia, will learn that when she is losing, she is losing double, irrelevant of who Mordecai is, and who Ahasuerus is, or Haman. And while she was thinking about it, she was not consoled by the fact that Purim is the only Jewish feast to be included in the World to Come. And, again, she was absorbed by the destiny of Esther, the woman who prayed not only for herself but for all her people, who was at the same time frail and strong, tender and still ready to sacrifice herself, opening windows in the future world in her singular way.

For she who believes in this cannot lose even when she is losing. From this musing and deep pondering within herself, Tamar was startled by the sound of her mobile phone, and she answered.

"Listen, Tamar, are we going to make the Purim party at my place? This might be the best thing because my flat is the biggest, and you know I like cooking, and it won't be difficult to bake a heap of *hamantashen*," chirped Rina happily, always ready and prepared to undertake the organization of a celebration, or a friendly evening with informal company.

Tamar immediately agreed to Rina's wish, and in a split second she thought: What mask shall I put on this year? What will I find when I turn the world upside down, what will I find at the bottom of myself after the second or the third glass of liqueur? And can this world be any more weird and crazy than it already is?

And while time is speeding up, and everything is destroyed and disappears in earthquakes and tsunamis—villages and towns, together with people who until a moment ago were living with their simple human worries—the only solution she can see is to slow down her pace of life. She does not have to be present at the opening of every exhibition, and every film, theatre, or concert première, she does not have to come to every gathering where someone wants her to come. And she is convinced that being in her flat with a wonderful view of the park is the best rest and the best use of time. The time of silence, serenity, and relaxation, regardless of the disaster-predicting stories and the prophecies that the world will soon perish and—as it says in *The Zohar*—birds will peck flesh from the mountain of human bones.

When she forgets all this, she relaxedly writes her poems, stories, novels . . . And she smiles, because every time a book comes out people ask her: "Were you writing about yourself? This is you, the main character, but you are also in the minor characters!" And she is sick and tired of such questions. The only thing she wants is freedom and peace, although this sounds like a manifesto by Marx and Engels!

Sometimes, when someone rings her up and asks what she is doing, she quibbles, because sometimes she does nothing at all, knowing that leisure breeds new ideas, and sometimes out of this Nothing she suddenly sits on her bed, takes a pencil and writes a poem. Later she herself wonders how it is possible that she has written such a long one in such a short time, and then she shrugs her shoulders, reconciling herself to the fact that she was just writing down what the One Above dictated, sending her words by his light channels, just as he sent to Planck his ideas about the speed of light, or to Tesla his inventions.

Tamar never gets too conceited, and this keeps her healthy in every respect.

Suddenly she remembers that two years ago she brought back from India a sari and little colored stickers to be put between the eyes as a sign. She unwillingly touches the point of her Spiritual eye, as though wanting to check if it is still functioning or if it has become completely stunted. Then she lightly shakes her head as if she could see whether *Keter* (the ultimate level of spiritual achievement according to Kabbalah) is swinging above her and whether it is getting enough light.

So the moment she unlocked the door to the flat, she moved to the wardrobe, where, at the bottom, in a bag, lay the folded sari, the skirt, and the matching golden flip-flops. And she looked at all this for a long time because she was suddenly struck by the smell of India, sometimes pleasant, sometimes unpleasant—the smell of memories.

On the day of the Purim party, she first soaked for a long time in the bath full of fragrant salts with flowers floating about her, and this reminded her of her short stay on Cyprus at the time when the oranges blossomed, after which she left for Israel and learned sentences in Hebrew on the plane. And when she took the taxi in Tel Aviv and told the driver where to go, he smiled, and when she looked at him questioningly, he said, "You've explained everything very well, only you keep using the masculine gender!"

When she pulled herself out of the bath, Tamar rubbed herself with a soft towel and applied jasmine-scented body milk, and her skin shone with the softness of feminine nature. It always seemed funny to her that many of her friends and acquaintances, no matter how hard they tried, were never able to find a husband, and lived alone for years, while men clung to her. And she would say to her companions: "If only I had wanted to, I could have got married twice every year . . ."

And then that thought disappeared from her head like a cloudlet which has drifted off from the bathroom.

Tamar first put on her underskirt and fastened it tightly around her waist, because a part of the sari has to be tucked into it. Then she started wrapping it around herself. This took some time because she hadn't had the chance to wear a sari in a long while. Finally, she threw a part of the sari over her shoulder. The sari was a strong orange-golden color, and this is why she chose an emerald green, oblong sign to put between her eyes. Then, tingling, she pulled on ten gold bangles which continued humming sweetly while she was brushing her hair.

At that moment she remembered a young woman in the outlands of India, poor and cheerless, and how, having washed her hair, she rubbed sesame oil in it, and like this came out on the dusty road which was winding between little cottages covered with palm leaves, and that heavy black hair which was glittering and shining was the only wealth and splendor of her youth.

Tamar looked at herself in the mirror again, and again she was not alone: she was in a small passage in the house of a Jewish merchant, originally from Iran, who had invited her to a Shabbat celebration in Kochin, India. Then this picture, too, paled, and she applied some more makeup to her eyes before calling a taxi.

Before leaving the car, she looked at the clock on the driver's dashboard and saw it was exactly 19:17. Then she stepped onto the street and entered the doorway of the building where Rina lived on the third floor.

Three weeks later, there was a small notice in the papers, at the bottom of a page: *Tamar Sonnenschein has mysteriously disappeared on her way to a Purim party. The police have not found her yet, and if anybody has news about her, they are requested to contact the nearest police station.*

At the same time, on the other end of the world, local papers in the Malayalam language reported that, in Ame ashram, a mysterious white woman in a sari had appeared, speaking a strange language and trying to explain something, but nobody understood her. The police asked that, if anyone knew anything about her, to please contact the nearest police station. They even printed Tamar's picture, slightly pale and blurred, but still there could be no mistake because there is only one Tamar like this in the whole world.

After some time, she said her name was Soumia. They asked if she knew how to do anything and she made her way straight to the kitchen, and by that evening she had baked ten trays of cakes, and told everyone, offering them in the ashram, to help themselves to the *hamantashen*. Everyone was too polite to ask her what *hamantashen* were, but with their mouths full, eating the sweet poppy-filled pastry, everyone said they were delicious. And she smiled, and explained what no one had asked her to, saying, "Purim, Puru, Purim, Purimspiel."

But this is not the end of the story. Somewhere Up There, in the eighth heaven, Adonai loudly scolded the archangel Michael, asking him why on earth, on the feast of Purim in 2011, he had turned the wheel of Tamar's destiny too strongly, and put her, instead of at the Purim party in Croatia, at the feast of Divali in India.

Michael was confused, but answered the Lord sincerely: "Didn't you say I could have an extra glass on Purim?" And then Adonai stopped scolding Michael and decided to return Tamar, two hundred and eighty-three years and four days later, to where she had started off on a long journey. And the angel Gabriel, who was watching all this, consoled Michael saying, "Well, if nothing else, at least she was properly dressed!"

Purchase of Goods of Dubious Origin

By Augusto Segre

Story

Translated from Italian *by Steve Siporin*

Concerning work, the holy texts and educated people have said very beautiful, important, and edifying things, even if the hard reality of life doesn't always coincide with their wise aphorisms. Thus, for example, there are the well-known words: "You shall eat your bread by the sweat of your brow." But it's not always so. Actually, as everyone knows quite well, there are those who drip sweat, and not only from the face, because of their hard, daily work—still they barely manage to earn a crust of bread. On the other hand, there are those who don't sweat, because they make others sweat, and yet they always have a sumptuously laid table.

One must, however, be careful and not allow oneself to be misled by hasty, superficial interpretations like these. Certain gnomic statements project themselves into a distant future, to Messianic times, and thus we have to wait with faithful expectation and, in the meantime, do things of value in order to draw this wondrous era nearer. And this has to be done with unshakable faith, even if it has happened more than once that the ideals and hopes of those who labored diligently for their entire lives, whatever their work may have been, have collapsed disastrously, and with them, as in our case, all the expectations of an energetic family uprightly engaged in labor for generations.

In the large courtyard "of the geese"—which was called that because of the intense and remunerative work with these fowl that took place on the ground floor—to the right, just past the front gate, there was a big storeroom of scrap metal. A vast room, where the most varied kinds of scrap metal were piled up: stoves, locks, keys, iron construction rods, beds, safes, all styles of trunks, plows and other agricultural implements. Elia Levi had run the business, which he inherited from his parents, for longer than anyone could remember. It wasn't necessarily a simple job because there was not only the matter of selling, but also of arranging for new acquisitions and thus maintaining a stock that could always meet the strangest requests. Elia was well known not only in the city, but even in the surrounding area, in the nearby countryside where he often went to track down something of interest to buy. This restocking would also take place right in the store itself when someone turned up who wanted to get rid of things that no longer served him or who had a pressing need to put together a few lire. Levi was well known in the Community too, particularly as the attendant to the Coén when he would bless the faithful with the traditional blessing.

The life of the Levi family was modest, like that of so many other families, but secure and dignified because it was perfectly balanced between faith, plainness, and honesty in business. Besides, Levi had come to understand the new times quite well. He certainly would not have changed his accustomed work, which he was very fond of—not for the world, not at his age. But his children, he was convinced, had to change their ways in order to take advantage of the new, better opportunities that the great freedom of the Emancipation offered them. Thus, they would make a life for themselves at a higher level, in the midst of that varied and attractive world in which they had been learning to live for several decades. He had three children, two girls and one boy. The two girls had married fellow Jews who were shopkeepers, and Elia thanked the Lord again and again for this gift, given the unhappy way things were these days with the ever more overwhelming wave of mixed marriages. The two sons-in-law had opened a splendid fabric shop, on Via Roma no less, and the joy of the old father was indescribable when he went to visit his daughters in the shop or in their homes, modern and pleasant, in a new quarter of the city. It was a significant step up, economically speaking, in quality and space, which consoled him fully for the many sacrifices he had made and continued to make, all for the benefit of his children. What's more, he had done it without ever having asked anything from anybody, habituated as he always was to standing on his own two feet.

Then there was his son, Giuseppe, who had been the special object of his dreams and plans. He was an intelligent, quick-witted boy. It had not been hard to get him to study, notwithstanding the onerous expenses that Elia had sustained, besides having to forego the help of the one who, according to the informal tradition, should have been his closest aide and heir in business. But the progress that his son regularly achieved in his studies, always shining, had driven the father to support him, to encourage him to go forward at all costs, even when the father realized that Giuseppe wanted to break off his studies, so as not to continue burdening the family's expenses.

When the gates of the university opened before him, the economic problems reached substantial proportions. Elia did not lose courage; at that point, a prestigious goal had appeared before not only the son, but also before the father himself, who in a little while would be able to pride himself on having a son with a degree. He redoubled and tripled his efforts at work; he enlarged his activities a great deal, and his business as much as possible, making new contacts in new milieus, always guided by his extreme prudence as a shrewd businessman. He felt confident in himself; he had the kind of experience—inherited for generations and consolidated by decades of work—that made him a true expert in dealing with ironmongery. This was demonstrated by the fact that he was often consulted by other shopkeepers to judge the quality of certain merchandise and the terms for selling or buying, which were no less important than the value of the merchandise itself.

When Giuseppe graduated in jurisprudence there was a celebration in the family and in the entire Community. At the reception, organized in grand style by Elia, *sur murenu*, the rabbi, and even the already multi-degreed president of the Community, spoke. The latter, to tell the truth, took part in the celebration mainly because he was driven by curiosity to see up close this strange type of graduate—the *homo novus*—who had sprouted miraculously amid the scrap metal of that store in the courtyard of the geese. *Sur murenu*, for his part, didn't miss the opportunity, after the formalities, to point out how even this splendid result was the fruit of the Emancipation, which had freely and generously given the most complete freedom to the Jews, and that it was their express duty to demonstrate—always, on every occasion—their gratitude toward the House of Savoy, increasing their commitment as upright citizens and as Italians devoted to their sacred homeland.

With his diploma in hand Giuseppe did not yet have a job, but there were plenty of possibilities; all he had to do was get on with it. Elia did not fail to contact all the authorities he knew. When his son, being free for the moment, dropped by the warehouse on his own, he wandered happily between those walls of his childhood and told his father that in the meantime he could lend him a hand. This elicited the sharpest protests from his father. Precisely now he wanted to ruin everything? Someone with a degree should not be in the middle of scrap metal, but in an office. Everyone in his place, doing his own work.

And Giuseppe found his place, in an office, and it was nothing less than the local law court. He was presented with the possibility of a career in the judiciary. It was a prestigious position of great responsibility, which would automatically rank him among the highest levels of local society. He would be able to become a judge, maybe even president of a law court, in one of those courtrooms that Elia Levi had sometimes visited out of curiosity when trials took place in which people he knew were involved.

A few years later, however, something happened that never should have happened, something that Elia Levi would never have been able to imagine could happen. One day, in fact, Elia Levi was to be found in one of those courtrooms not out of curiosity but as a defendant. Incredible!

In the warehouse in the courtyard of the geese, two persons had appeared whom Levi knew vaguely, having occasionally run into them at some market and, now he remembered, in the café that he frequented on Tuesdays and Fridays, the market days. They proposed to him the acquisition of rolled-iron sections, a very good deal, for both the quality and the price. The deal concerned a consignment of goods taken over because of a bankruptcy, and it seemed genuine. The only condition, somewhat burdensome, was the payment in cash upon the delivery of the merchandise. As was usual in all of his dealings, and in this case, too, more than a few doubts presented themselves to the mind of the old shopkeeper, who began asking questions endlessly. The answers, however, were always precise and thorough, and the official documents presented to him were exemplary. Still not completely convinced, however, Levi wanted to see the merchandise. He was accompanied by the two friends who led him to a warehouse at the edge of the city. What was there were rolled-iron sections of prime quality—of that there was no doubt—that had belonged to a firm that he did not know but whose name appeared clearly in the official papers that were produced and that had gone bankrupt a long time before. He reexamined these papers with the greatest care; they were authentic, according to him, in every detail. The deal was concluded, and the merchandise arrived at Levi's warehouse toward evening, when the first shadows had already spread over the old courtyard of the ex-ghetto. Payment for the delivered merchandise was made, according to the agreement, in cash.

A few weeks went by, and then the bomb exploded. One morning when the store had just opened, a fellow—wearing dark colors, with a southern accent—presented himself and handed Elia a subpoena to appear before the examining magistrate.

"But what's this about?" asked Elia in a trembling voice.

"This, my task it is not. To deliver I must the document, and you, sir, to sign here you sir must." And he handed Elia a notebook, after having written "delivered to the same" on the document. Raising two fingers to the brim of his hat signifying an official goodbye, the man left.

Levi felt faint. He seated himself in a chair and read and reread that strange document, which didn't seem at all clear to him. "Purchase of goods of dubious origin"—what did that mean, what did it refer to? And—this part he did understand—he was summoned to the examining magistrate "for information" in three days.

When Giuseppe returned home—in the meantime, after several competitive examinations (passed with flying colors) he had reached the position of clerk of the court—his father, who was still distraught, had him look at the summons. The son was also astonished, and he subjected his father to many questions about his recent business activities. Elia responded with his usual precision; he kept a register in which all the activity of the storeroom was scrupulously recorded. Giuseppe, with the technical eye of the profession, set himself to study all of the documentation with a great deal of care. All of a sudden his attention was arrested by the acquisition of the rolled-iron sections, which still lay in the storeroom. He examined the merchandise and was surprised to see the disparity between the quantity of the goods and the price paid for them.

He turned to his father: "Whatever possessed you to make such a purchase? I get the feeling that deep underneath this there's something that's not so clean. How is it possible?"

"Listen, don't talk nonsense. I'm not a novice," responded his father, all but offended. "I certainly didn't buy with my eyes closed. For me too, at first, the deal wasn't convincing, but then I saw the papers and looked them over—several times—and they were in perfect order, without any doubt. It was a clearance sale due to bankruptcy."

"But are you really sure?"

"How can you have any doubt? It's not the first time I've dealt with business like this. I've always bought goods from bankruptcies—a lot."

"But given the importance of the transaction, why didn't you have me look over these papers?"

"What need was there? They were very clear and understandable even for me, who has no degree. Maybe you've forgotten that your father isn't a simpleton and that he has long-standing experience? I'm not exactly the type who can be fooled so readily."

But this time, unfortunately for him, Elia Levi had been fooled and in the most banal way. The documents were false, the merchandise was the fruit of receiving stolen goods, and so he was indicted for the purchase of goods of dubious origin and sentenced to several months, with a suspended sentence (being treated as a first offender) and the confiscation of the relevant merchandise. From which we learn, yet again, that in court honorable people may also be seated among the accused.

This entire sad affair devastated not only the old shopkeeper, but especially, and it could be said more directly, his son, the clerk of the court. How would he be able to continue his work in that building where his father, his own father, had been convicted? He opened his heart to several colleagues, who took pains to tell him that for one thing he was blameless, and in the end so was his old father, a shopkeeper of flawless honesty, a fact openly acknowledged by everyone in the city, including even the president of the tribunal, who at the conclusion of the trial said to the convicted man:

"I am enormously displeased that you, sir, having reached your age after an irreproachable life, would have fallen into this trap. What does it mean? That when you work, you never stop learning, whatever your age, even when you are old. On the other hand, the law is the law, equal for everyone."

All fine words, mulled over in Giuseppe's mind, even at night when he couldn't sleep and tossed and turned from one side to the other. His career, he thought, was ruined forever. There was no doubt, especially considering his completely unique situation: Giuseppe was not just any magistrate's clerk; he was a Jew, the first to occupy such an important position in that small city. It might seem strange that there could be anyone who would want to link what had happened with a magistrate's clerk who was Jewish, but it's not that hard to imagine it, at least in certain circles. Something vague, barely whispered, had been reported about him, something said completely in confidence by someone who, in instances like this, was careful to declare himself a friend of the Jews ("and I always have been"):

"It's well known"—it was supposedly said—"that the Jews, inside or outside the ghetto, look after their own interests, just as they always have, and they're not too particular when it comes to making money. They haven't changed, and they never will . . . even if they get degrees."

One afternoon Giuseppe was at his worktable when an office boy came in and put some files on the table. He examined them one at a time, then stopped and stared at a folder opened before his eyes, thunderstruck. It dealt with the sentence pronounced against his father, which he would have to register. Was it simply a coincidence or was it instead the special gift of some colleague, for some personal reason of his own? Giuseppe's head swirled and he felt faint. He closed the file slowly and left the office to wander aimlessly here and there throughout the city. He walked along the bank of the Po, staring persistently at the flowing water and the dizzying whirlpools of the current. The river was in spate. But he quickly turned away from that view and tried to push away certain thoughts that had suddenly appeared in his mind. He returned home.

It wasn't the first time since this family disaster that Giuseppe had tried to comfort his old father through the compassionate devotion he felt for him, even though it cost him great effort because by then he considered himself a failure in life, facing the same dead end as his father. Entering the store, he saw his father seated behind his table. It was heartbreaking to see once again how much he had aged in such a short time. Deep wrinkles marked his face, and his eyes, staring sadly into space, signaled the measure of his despair. The father, who had finally become aware of Giuseppe's presence, made as if to get up. But the son, solicitous, was near him and affectionately put a hand on his shoulder and repeated words of comfort and resignation for the umpteenth time—as usual, without results.

"Listen, Papà," he said, looking at the gold watch his father had given him on the occasion of his graduation. "It's almost time for *'arvith*[1]; why don't you go to the *scola*?"[2]

"Yes, you're right," sighed Elia.

He got up with great effort, took off his *kipà*, picked up his black hat, gently waved goodbye to his son, and went out, walking slowly. Giuseppe's father, to whom Giuseppe had always been lovingly close, had grown even more tender to him now.

As soon as he was left alone, Giuseppe was overtaken by his tortured thoughts in a nearly obsessive way. Finding himself in that storeroom which, one could say, had made a magistrate's clerk of him, but had then also destroyed his career, gave him a sense of despair without end that brought him down, down to his heart, to the deepest part of his soul. He walked slowly in the midst of all that merchandise, and he noticed that toward the right side

---

1 Evening prayers.

2 Synagogue.

there was a big empty space, occupied up until a few weeks earlier by those cursed rolled-iron sections. He stopped at length in that corner, so empty and so full of appalling memories, and he felt something like a knot in his throat suffocating him. All that iron, in the midst of which he had spent so many carefree hours in childhood and adolescence, now seemed to him as if it had been transformed into so many bars in a prison in which he found himself enclosed, without probation. He wandered around, here and there until, guided almost by instinct, he stopped in front of a display case filled with iron that was not for sale. It contained weapons that were precisely catalogued and duly registered and that had been used in the various wars of the Risorgimento, in which so many Jews had distinguished themselves with heroic deeds, even giving their lives for the beloved homeland. Rifles, pistols, swords, bayonets, and bullets of different caliber were lined up perfectly and scrupulously maintained without a grain of dust; polished and well-oiled, they shone, as if they had to be ready for use. Authentic pieces, undoubtedly, awaiting lovers of antique weapons. Giuseppe studied those arms for a while, flooded by a hundred uncertainties, by ever more oppressive thoughts.

Almost reflexively he stretched out his hand and took a pistol. His movements, at first uncertain, now became sure. He looked for and found bullets of the right caliber. He loaded the pistol, closed the display case, and set off with uncertain steps toward the rear of the storeroom, which was slowly dissolving into the first shadows of the evening. Suddenly a shot was heard.

The glorious, alluring Emancipation had offered a new sacrifice on the altar of Liberty and of the Country of Laws.

The Rebbetzin's Sense of Justice

By Lily Berger

Story

Translated from Yiddish *by Ronnee Jaeger*

He was small, skinny, timid, eyes always downcast. She the opposite, big, full-bodied, a Jewish Cossack who tolerated no injustice. A big talker! These were my teachers, Reb Fishel and his wife Khaye.

Behind his back they called him "Fisheleh hunchback," although he was not a hunchback, merely bent over. And her they called Big Khaye. We, the seven-year-old pupils, called Big Khaye "Rebbetzin."

How two such opposites were brought together, only God in heaven knows. In our shtetl there was a story told that when Fisheleh saw his betrothed for the first time, under the bridal canopy, he almost fainted from fear. Opinion had it that this first scare pursued him all his life, not because Big Khaye was a miserable or wretched wife, quite the opposite. She had a good heart and could bear no injustice. She protected her husband like a mother hen protects her chicks, as if, without her, Fisheleh Hunchback would, God forbid, have drowned in the waves of life like a leaky ship in the ocean.

So what then? From their first moment together the contrast between the dreamy other-worldly Fisheleh and his down-to-earth Big Khaye terrified him.

It often happened that the absent-minded rebbe forgot where he put things, and most often this misfortune happened with his eyeglasses.

Here we sat, the whole gang of pupils, around the long scratched table, waiting for the signal to begin, while the rebbe wandered about, searching, sighing, and eyeing us with suspicion. Finally, he mutters "No one saw the glasses? My glasses? Which one of you . . . didn't see? How . . . ?" "We didn't see," the children answered in chorus. Helplessness and sadness were etched on the rebbe's face, but we pranksters didn't pay much attention. You couldn't say we disliked the rebbe and wanted revenge; we simply enjoyed these moments.

Whoever had anything in his pocket pulled it out, and away we went: a button for a string, a string for a glass, a peppermint for a macaroon. We settled all the old accounts: whoever was owed a pinch, a jab, a quick punch in the nose—this was an opportunity to repay our debts. The victim took the gift with a quiet groan, with resignation, or hit back immediately. So, without the captain's oversight, the gang around the table quietly waved their hands about, whispered, and would have continued happily who knows how long, were it not for the rebbetzin. In the kitchen, separated from the classroom by a folding screen, Big Khaye sensed that something was not right. Instantly she appeared before the unruly gang and with her thunderous voice shouted, "Quiet here immediately!" As though by a magic wand, all transactions, accounts, and tricks stopped. Three rows of urchins around the table were silenced, not so much out of fear, but because of the rebbetzin's authority. It didn't occur to any of us that we could disobey Big Khaye.

Then the rebbetzin went into the second act. She approached the table, where the rabbi's chair stood, sized us up with a severe searching glance, lifted one prayer book after another, and then, turning to face the rebbe, stuck her hand into the pocket of his robe and pulled out his eyeglasses. Once she had even pulled out a lost pointer from the rebbe's pants pocket. The rebbe, standing like a lost lamb, like a strapped school child, looked even smaller and thinner. The rebbetzin then faced him with these words: "Here are your glasses, clumsy, dummy. First have your glasses ready, and then seat the scamps at the table."

In addition to the women's work, of which the rebbetzin had more than enough, she also kept an eye on the whole classroom, and on each pupil. She knew who was a blockhead and who had a quick mind, who was capable of sitting a whole day like a block of wood, who was up to nasty tricks; who brought fine food for lunch, and who, unfortunately, chewed a dry piece of bread.

More than anything she sought justice and righteousness; most important for her was righteousness. Even in figuring out the school fees, not the rebbe, but the rebbetzin, decided. "You say that Reb Fishel let you down? What does he know?" she answered the haggling woman with a question and continued. "Why should you demand that Khane Dvoyre the widow pay the same school fee as you? You have a breadwinner, may he live to one hundred and twenty. Is it not fair that you should pay the entire school fee and Khane Dvoyre half? What do you think—has he become the decision maker? It is not his business for whom to lower fees and for whom not. His business is to teach the children!" And it remained not as the rebbe had agreed, but as the rebbetzin had judged.

In only one aspect of the school did Big Khaye not interfere: the pedagogical side, in the teaching method. Perhaps because Reb Fishel had a reputation in town as a God-fearing, honorable Jew, or perhaps because she respected him as a Torah scholar while she was a simple, unlearned woman, Big Khaye gave no suggestions regarding her husband's pedagogy and methodology. And Reb Fishel had a brilliant teaching method: he put the greatest emphasis on the individual child. The whole group was arranged sitting on the floor against the wall, and the rebbe called each one to the table, and kept each little prodigy until he was certain that he had knocked some learning into his head.

Only once a day, the rebbe seated all the children around the long table and taught them as a group, repeating the lesson in unison. This was indeed the rebbe's most difficult task. We, his pupils, knew the rebbe's weaknesses, his helplessness when he had to deal with us all together. "Why are you looking out the window?" "And you there, why are you staring like a clumsy fool?" "And you, why are you squirming like a worm?"

"Yankeleh always has a drippy nose."

"Rebbe, Shloimeleh pinched me."

"Dovidl made fun of me. Dov v id dle m-m-made fun of m me," stuttered Faivel Sepliak.

From words, the rebbe moved to action. He didn't have a strap at hand, the reason being that it was against his pedagogic philosophy. But he had two thin bony hands and, whether he wanted to or not, he had to use them at times. He slowly shuffled over to the guilty ones, to one he gave a tweak on the ear, to a second he gave a light slap, to a third a whack; then the rebbe returned to his place with a pained look, as though use of corporal punishment was a hard experience for him. Even Dovidl, the mischief-maker—a nickname the rebbetzin gave him—used to say that the rebbe's smack really didn't hurt.

I don't know, because his punishing hand never fell on me. I was the only girl among the entire group of boys. It is very possible that the rebbe, Reb Fishel, was a gentleman, or wouldn't want his hand to touch a female, because actually I deserved it. The rebbe used to say that I was worse than a boy. Oy, you will say, how does a girl get into a boys' classroom? About this I only know this answer: it was arranged between my mother—peace be with her—and Big Khaye; and when the rebbetzin agreed, the rebbe had to agree. For me it was generally good: I was a girl and never received my earned punishments.

But the rebbe's punishment would have been useless, were it not for the rebbetzin. She always knew, from behind the folding screen, that something was going on in the classroom. She appeared in full majesty to quickly make order.

"What? Again? You are as pale as a corpse." She looked at her foolish husband.

"They drive me out of my mind," the rebbe responded with a tearful voice.

"Well, woe to him who allows himself to be driven out of his mind. And from such unruly types. Is it worth raising a hand to them? You have to yell, such a look give them that they will feel it in their belly." After this lecture that she gave the rebbe, the rebbetzin turned to us, gave a look that actually cut through to the belly, and ordered: "Silence, do you hear?" Is there any question that we listened?

In addition to her inborn abilities to control people in times of upset, the rebbetzin had many more talents. She showed great womanly skills in baking macaroons and *fefferlakh*,[1] which the students purchased, some for one groshen, and some for two or three groshen. Faivel got them for free.

In the *kheyders* of our shtetl, there was a tradition for which a rebbe's wife was responsible: she baked macaroons and *fefferlakh* that melted in your mouth and looked like little yellow geese with red eyes. But none could compare to our rebbetzin's macaroon and *fefferlakh* that melted into all your limbs; Big Khaye outdid them all.

But mostly our rebbetzin had a reputation with us for her sense of justice. First, she didn't see it as fair that the littlest pupils should be stuck in school from early morning till evening. Every day at a certain hour she sent us outside for a bit and kept an eye on us through the little kitchen window. "Let's go! Be on your way, air yourselves out!" she ordered, opening the door wide. She didn't have to ask long. But the rebbe occasionally protested.

"You're already chasing them out? I haven't accomplished the day's work, I need more time."

"It's okay, tomorrow is also God's day."

"You are breaking up my classroom, you are destroying the, the . . . you don't let me . . ." whined the rebbe with his weak, crying voice.

"Destroyed? Destroyed? And where is your justice? To keep children locked in the whole day, in such a heat?"

---

1 Gingerbread cookies.

"We are still, heaven forbid, not Gentiles. Jewish children sit in school a whole day. Are you raging against heaven? And what in heaven has been . . ." The rebbe gathered his courage.

"When God almighty sends us such a beautiful day, with such a bright sun, He wants his children to enjoy it."

"You are a woman and . . ." the rebbe could not contain himself, yet he was not bold enough to speak his mind.

"And if a woman, so what? Just look at him, my big shot!" And the rebbetzin gave him such a look that the rebbe was immediately silenced.

On such a heavenly day, we used to stay outdoors longer than usual. When the rebbetzin considered that we had had our fill of air and sun, she again opened the door wide, and ordered "Into the classroom."

The object of the rebbetzin's greatest concern was Faivel Sepliak. Faivel was the young son of Khane Dvoyre the washerwoman, a widow. He was called "Sepliak" because he had been nursed a long time. Therefore, he started school late and was the eldest among us. It seems something was wrong in his head. When he spoke, his entire face moved, as did his hands. No one knew exactly what was wrong with him. We all had an affection for Faivel. Maybe the rebbetzin's concern affected us. Nevertheless, it was difficult to keep ourselves from laughing. Big Khaye forbade us from making fun of him, so sometimes we would choke with laughter, covering our mouths with both hands, and giggling. We had to be very careful not to call him by his nickname. If the rebbetzin caught someone calling Faivel "Sepliak," or mimicking his way of speaking, he got such a gift that he would be careful not to repeat it again. Faivel was given special privileges in the classroom. Like all the children, he brought lunch to school, but his lunch was dry dark bread.

Yoyne, the butcher's son, shared his warm lunch. Shakhne the butcher was more of a cattle dealer than a butcher. People used to say about him that he was a schemer, an "operator."

It seems that his youngest son Yoyne didn't take after the father. He was a round chubby boy with thick red cheeks and clumsy hands. He carried himself like a leaden bird.

"A blockhead, nothing goes in, go do something about it," the rebbe complained.

"A child shouldn't stuff so much into himself. He must have a hole in his stomach, or an endless intestine," the rebbetzin explained.

Yoyne used to bring a red linen bag of all the best foods for lunch. Big Khaye gathered the warm lunches together in the morning and put them on the high cupboard so that the children shouldn't "peck like hens at their lunches." At noon, each child received his lunch. Big Khaye was never mistaken; with closed eyes she knew what belonged to whom. Faivel Sepliak usually chewed a dry crust of bread, occasionally he had a piece of sugar which the rebbetzin had given him. Suddenly he was restored by a piece of stuffed chicken neck that came into his meager portion, or a roasted chicken liver. Faivel asked no questions—only his eyes shone and his mouth swallowed.

Everyone in the group of rascals knew from where Faivel's good luck came. We were happy that Faivel Sepliak also had some pleasure in life. Only one person, Yoyne, sat sulking, chewed, and looked at Faivel angrily.

Once at lunch, Faivel enjoyed a big yellow pear, chewing with obvious delight and relishing each juicy bite, maybe for the first time. His entire face ate. Every feature was at work. Often when he spoke, his eyes silently wept, but now they sparkled with glee. Yoyne also chewed a pear, chewed, looking angrily at Faivel. Suddenly he shoved his hand into the red bag and blurted out: "There were two pears, two, now there is one."

"One is not enough for you?" the rebbetzin spoke out from behind the folding screen. "That's why you are a blockhead, you stuff too much into yourself."

"One is not enough for you," the children repeated the rebbetzin's words, and took revenge on Yoyne, who was not liked by the pupils.

The next day Yoyne's mother appeared. A short woman, heavyset, her big belly preceding her. She rolled into the school, angry, and, without a "good morning," went straight behind the folding screen, where the rebbetzin, with a master hand, was preparing the macaroons and *fefferlakh*. The rebbe paled. Yoyne, learning at the table, turned his head away. Our unruly gang, seated against the wall, began stuffing into our pockets little buttons, pieces of string, small stones; we perked up our ears. We children knew that something would play itself out here, as soon as we heard this dialogue:

"Tell me, my dear Khaye, if it's true, what my Yoyne tells."

"What, for instance, does your Yoyne tell?"

"He says that you give half his lunch to Sepliak."

"Your Yoyne exaggerates. A half, no, but something yes."

"So tell me, my dear Khaye, is it right to take from my child's mouth and give it to another? Is it fair?"

"So tell me, my dear Bryne, is it fair that your Yoyne should eat so much, that it actually gives him a stuffed head? And a poor orphan should waste away?"

"Khaye, what are you thinking, Khaye? You think there are no rules in this world?"

"What I myself think? I think that there should be a little justice in the world. Meanwhile you stuff your Yoyne. Because of this, nothing goes into his head, and his stomach is always so stuffed that he moves like a leaden bird . . . and . . . and, don't take offence, he fouls the air. One shouldn't overstuff a child this way, and a poor orphan should . . ."

"What are you saying, Khaye? It is not yet a lawless world. We'll see about that, Khaye, we'll see . . ."

The butcher's wife was not finished. She was probably afraid that with big Khaye none of her arguments would do. Pushing her belly forward, she left the school in a burning rage, and repeated "We'll see yet! We'll see . . ."

The rebbe, pale, frightened, arose from his bench, took a few steps to the folding screen, and sighed. "You will . . . you will yet, God forbid, bring a tragedy with your mouth, with your ways, with . . . with . . . Horrors, such a tongue."

"You're already frightened? By whom? By Bryne, the butcher's wife? Just look how pale you have become."

"She is basically right."

"How is she right? Is this how you judge? Is this the way you have God in your heart? Where is your justice?'

"Justice, justice. Even in a rabbinical court she will . . . she will perhaps be found to be right."

"So let her take me to court! Am I afraid? Let her. I will prove to the rabbi that it is not according to law and not according to justice that one should eat to the bursting point and another should starve. Is it right that Bryndel's young son should stuff himself and an orphan shouldn't have enough to eat? There must still be a bit of justice!" the rebbetzin announced with such conviction and resolve that the rebbe went silently back to his place. It seems he understood that big Khaye was prepared to stand not only before the law, before the rabbis, but even before God Himself in order to demand that there should be some justice in the world.

New York

By Peter Sichrovsky

Story

Translated from German *by John Howard*

Park Slope, Brooklyn, 1995

Erich and Hanna have a small apartment on the second floor of a narrow brownstone. Each floor of this single family home was converted many years ago. Today, it's not so easy for the two of them to climb the steep stairs. A lawyer lives above them with his girlfriend. He often works late into the night. A family with two children occupies the apartment below them. The man is a policeman, the woman a nurse. They have the largest apartment and have use of the small garden in the back.

Erich and Hanna moved here from Vienna many years ago. They got married on the crossing from Lisbon to New York. Erich worked for many decades as an editor in a publishing house and was responsible for German-language literature. Hanna translated books from German into English. Literature and old books have always been their passion.

Now Erich tries to enjoy his retirement. He celebrated his seventy-eighth birthday this year. Hanna is five years younger.

They regularly receive invitations from the Austrian Embassy to events such as recitals, film screenings, exhibitions, and lectures. The Cultural Department of the Embassy seems particularly to care about topics that have to do with Judaism. Erich and Hanna like attending these so they can live a little in the past. But this time is different. They've received a card for a reception on the occasion of the fiftieth anniversary of the end of the war.

Erich has decided to wear his black suit and Hanna a long, dark blue dress. In the early evening they are both ready but still can't decide whether they should go.

Erich looks at the cuckoo clock above the kitchen table where they like to sit most of the time. "Hanna, it's getting late. We have to make up our minds!"

"What are my alternatives?"

"We can stay home or go. I can't think of a third possibility, unless we go to the movies and forget about this evening."

"If we stay home, they'll celebrate without us the fiftieth year of their resurrection. If we go, they'll celebrate anyway, and we'll have to watch."

Erich laughs. "But they lost the war. We can celebrate that."

"Lost? Do losers look like they do?"

"It wasn't always easy for them, especially in the years after the war."

"What, do you feel you must protect them? Do you think they need that?"

"No, they don't need my protection, not even my pity," says Erich. "But I'm old, and I've had enough of the memories."

"I'm no longer young either, but I'll never forgive them!"

Erich braces himself and leans forward. "I know. I've heard it a thousand times. Are we going? At least we could enjoy the buffet . . ."

"It's been fifty years. . . . But can't you still remember?" interrupts Hanna.

"How can you ask me that?"

"The way they brought us out of the basement. The light burned. Like when I was a child and got soap in my eyes. . . . The noise in the house, at first I thought it was the SS, and then it was the Russians."

"Two years living in a basement . . . who can even imagine that today?"

They are silent for a few seconds. Hanna fumbles for Erich's hand across the table.

"That last day, remember, that last day? Mrs. Werner, she always brought us food and water, she didn't come for two days. You wanted to go upstairs, but I was scared and persuaded you to wait. The water ran out, there was no more bread, we hadn't emptied the bucket for days, it stank so terribly down there. I was sure we were finished . . ."

Erich squeezes Hanna's fingers. "We were covered with old rags and always waiting. I was sure everything was lost, all those months spent in the dark," says Erich.

"And when I held you back, then you suddenly wanted to, in this situation. For weeks you didn't touch me, but then suddenly . . ."

Erich smiles. "I thought it would be the last time . . ."

"We were still so young. Every time was like a last time . . . In that basement there . . . We were the last ones, all the others dead . . . We were allowed to survive, enjoy that last day . . . And then the first one, the first one right after the last . . ." Hanna fights back tears. "Why us? Were we better people?" she says slowly.

"The Kleins dead, both starved, the Rosenberg girl dead, died from a simple diarrhea, Fried dead, hanged himself, the two brothers Grün dead, they ran out of their hiding place because they couldn't stand living in a dark hole anymore—"

"Stop it!" Hanna interrupts him and puts her hands over her ears. "And what did we survive for?"

"That you mustn't say!"

"We survived for our Thomas . . . And then . . . and then . . ."

"Stop it, Hanna, I don't want to talk about that!"

"How old would he be now?"

Erich waits for a moment as if he had to think about it. "Just about fifty."

Hanna nods.

"His life was probably created on the last day of the war, and ended a few decades later senselessly," says Erich quietly.

"He was not even killed by a German . . . Somewhere in a jungle . . . Oh, Erich, tell me, why have we survived?"

"How should I know?"

"If only we had remained in Europe after the war, everything would have been different. Today we would be playing with our grandchildren . . ." Hanna sobs softly. "Why couldn't we hold Thomas back?"

"He felt like he was an American, and remember, he was conscripted. There was a draft."

"Ha—American—what a crock! Such a stupid death, so pointless."

"I always wanted to go back," Erich says.

"I know. Can you remember the architect? He was at our home a few years after the war. He fled in '37, for political reasons. You asked him if he didn't feel homesick. 'Homesick? I'm not a Jew!'"

Erich laughs. "I know, I know, I remember it well. That's just how we are. Tell me, Hanna, did we actually win the war?"

"What do you mean?"

"Someone must have won."

"We were liberated, we survived, but not as great victors."

"So? Then, who won?" asks Eric.

"I don't know. Maybe the Americans, but Thomas was an American! And what did that get him? What did it get us?"

"Do you remember, back then, on that last day, when they pounded against the iron door? We thought about hanging ourselves."

"Yes, we came within a hair of it, and so close to the end. 'They'll never catch us alive!' You always said that." Hanna gets up and takes a glass out of the cabinet. "Would you also like a glass of water?" she asks Erich. "Above us, they slept in beds with white sheets and pillows. And for breakfast there was milk with honey." Hanna fills the glass with water and puts it on the table. "That's why I still hate them today. Unfortunately, because I would be glad to find some peace. I couldn't even sleep that first night we were free. So many were dead, kidnapped, disappeared: my parents, your mother, your two sisters, my uncles, two aunts, all gone . . . Just the two of us, we're still standing on this planet fifty years later."

"Should we really have stayed in Vienna? Would Thomas still be alive? Hanna, have we both lost the war?"

"I don't know. At least we are still alive!"

"When we came out of the cellar, Mr. Schneider stood there. Peter Schneider was his name. 'Thank God that you are still alive,' he said to us, and had no shame. Lived for years in the home of my parents, slept in our beds, ate with my fork from my plate. 'Thank God that you're still alive!' That bastard!"

"You never got the apartment back."

"I got nothing back! Instead, they invite me to Vienna now for a tour in a horse-drawn carriage. Fifty years later! With the same money they stole from me, I could buy the whole team of horses and the fiacre to boot!"

"And the poor woman, Mrs. Werner, who hid us, what good did it do her?" Hanna says.

"The contempt of the other tenants. She died in her apartment two years later, and for a week no one noticed."

"A shit people!"

"Hanna, you mustn't talk like that."

"All the same, a shit people, hypocrites with big mouths."

"If we go now, they will tell us how much they lack the Jewish intelligentsia, the Einsteins, the Mendelssohns, the Freuds, the Kafkas, etc. They have never regretted the fact that they murdered Jewish workers and artisans," said Erich. "The worst is when they start whining: The terrible past, how sorry they all are!"

"Calm down, Erich. It doesn't make any sense for you to get so upset."

Erich goes into the living room. A large mirror is on the door of an old cabinet. Erich stands in front of it and looks at his reflection. Hanna comes and stands beside him.

"How emaciated we were then! Down to the bone. Old rags full of lice. Eyes blood red. I looked like an old man. You like an old woman. We were ashamed that first day. There was no joy. We had been two young beautiful people everyone admired, the most beautiful couple on the street. What had they done to us?"

Hanna seeks Erich's hand again. "A year later, here in New York we were the most beautiful again."

"On the outside, maybe, but here in my stomach the rat from the basement is still gnawing!" Erich looks at his watch. "And we have missed the buffet!"

Golem

By Maciej Płaza

Excerpt from a Novel

Translated from Polish *by Antonia Lloyd-Jones*

They had been in haste, that was Shira's lasting memory of those times, those days. Two years had passed since her first blood, barely two years since the morning when her mother had noticed a stain on her night shirt, raised her eyes to whisper a short blessing, and said with affection: "Look out," then slapped her in the face before adding: "Now you are a woman, may you always be rosy-cheeked, like blood and milk." They had hastened, because now the blood was flowing within her in harmony with the moon, and this brought her into the sphere of both adult and sacred, mysterious matters. Her mother and father had hastened, because a daughter is indeed a gift from the Eternal, but also a burden; they had hastened, although, or maybe because, there was no lack of devout young Jews in the neighboring towns whose family merits, whether books of *responsa* and moral works written by fathers who were rabbis, or the healing powers and prophetic visions of fathers who were *tsaddikim,* or the *shtiblekh* and yeshivas funded by fathers who were merchants, and above all the fortunes they'd amassed, had secured them seats of honor by the eastern wall of the synagogue, and from almost the time of her first blood, as if they had heard about it from somewhere, as if they had learned about it from the rising and setting of the moon, they had been sending their offers to Nachman, the Liściska matchmaker, for after all, the daughter of the saintly Reb Gershon, who as a *tsaddik* lived modestly, but was famous for his wisdom and righteousness, was a splendid match. They had hurried, all those rabbis, *tsaddikim,* and merchants, the fathers of frail boys, who had only just relaxed following their bar mitzvahs and begun to put on *tefillin,* only just managed to sprout their first moustache, had not yet entirely forgotten the pain in their backs and rears from the lashes of the *melamed's* birch, and were already on the market for marriage.

Also in haste was the rival family that Nachman praised the most ardently, singing genuine paeans in its honor, as a matchmaker should, though in fact he was only doing it in keeping with time-honored tradition, because Reb Gershon was well acquainted with Reb Eliezer Golan ben Akiva, a wealthy *tsaddik* from Zasławie, the father of six children, and when his offer came, he did not hesitate to accept it. Fourteen-year-old David must have been hastening too, Reb Eliezer's second-to-youngest son, whom they had decided that Shira would marry. In fact, the haste did not concern the wedding, which could wait, so much as the engagement, which would be harder and worse to break off than the marriage, so another two years went by before they first set eyes on one another. During this time, all she could do was imagine him, and so she did, thus conquering the impassable distance separating her from her betrothed, only a three-day journey by britzka, but also several hundred years of tradition, which forbade them to meet. She listened out for rumors from Zasławie, with flushed cheeks she tried questioning her mother, sister, and brothers, and approached visitors who came from there to ask if perhaps any of them was familiar with David, if they had seen what he looked like, heard how he spoke, and knew if he was handsome, wise, and godly. She would glance bashfully for comparison at the young Hasidic boys milling around the yard. She wore the silver ring that David had sent her, and when one of his brothers arrived, she asked him to read her the letter that came with this prenuptial gift, which must have been dictated to the Zasławie scribe, for not even a *tsaddik's* son would be able to write easily in the sacred language at such a young age, and she asked again and again, until she had learned the entire letter by heart, though there wasn't a word in it about her or him, just solemn sayings, pledges, and quotations from *Shir Hashirim*. All this she did, until finally her husband elect began to take shape before her yearning yet fearful eyes. She imagined his skin the color and sleekness of olive oil, his tight, springy sidelocks, his round eyes staring from under his hat, and his narrow, boyish shoulders wrapped in the black of a festive *bekishe*. She imagined that once they were finally standing beneath the chuppah, he would gaze at her as at a lily among thorns, an apple tree among the trees of the forest, a dove in the clefts of the rock.

There was haste when her future father-in-law and his entourage arrived in Liściska to draw up the *tnoim*, which was to tie the two families together with a knot of marital and material affairs and set a date for the wedding. Reb Eliezer and Reb Gershon had hastened to drink a toast to the health of the young couple, Rebbetzin Hagit had hastened to shatter a pair of china plates against the floor to mark completing the agreements. David must have been in haste too; just as Shira had imagined him, in faraway Zasławie he had been imagining her figure, her eyes, her voice. There was haste, because all the signs and prophetic dreams, all the answers that both *tsaddikim* received from the Eternal to the questions in their prayers led them to believe that, like all the previous marriages in both families, the union of Shira and David was registered in heaven. Only the Liściska scribe Reb Symche was not in haste, as for many evenings he sat with his pens and multi-colored inks over a sheet of parchment and wrote out the *ketubah*, the marriage contract, which was to join the betrothed couple forever. This *ketubah* came out beautifully, adorned around the rows of black letters with images of the sacred sites, a picture of the Temple, drawings of flowers and trees, doves and foxes, as flowery and colorful as the papercut *mizrekh* that hung on the eastern wall in the main chamber of Reb Gershon's house. But when at last two years had passed and it came to her wedding day, Shira was too overwhelmed to hear much as the *ketubah* was solemnly read out, and she only admired Reb Symche's beautiful script and drawings once the din of the seven-day wedding party had gone quiet, the klezmer bands had stopped playing and left the town, and the tables set for the local poor had vanished from the streets. By then the noise of celebration was just buzzing in her head, though neither the cheers inflamed by honey, wine, and hooch, nor the frenzied wail of clarinets, concertinas, and fiddles, nor the clowning performed by the *badkhen,* nor the choral Hasidic wailing had deafened her remembrance of the moment when a decked-out britzka harnessed to six horses entered the manor gateway amid an escort of Zasławie Hasidim, whom Reb Eliezer, by special permission of the governor, had dressed up as Cossacks, singing a wedding niggun specially composed for the occasion, with no words at all, just a thunderous *yombi-yombi-yom* pulsating with joy, or of the very next moment, when David, awaited and imagined for two long years, stood there before her, no less fearful and delighted than she was, shining with the black of his shoes, his silk *bekishe,* the fur shtreimel on his head, and the white of his stockings and his wedding *kittel,* and for the very first time they looked each other in the eyes. The sense of elation was stronger than the shyness, so they could not tear their gaze from one another, as with trembling fingers he lowered the veil over her face and recited the wedding speech, as the guests solemnly intoned: "Our sister, may you become thousands, the mother of thousands, of ten thousands, and may your descendants possess the gates of those who hate them," as she circled him seven times in the ritual dance, while he impatiently turned his head to follow her, and as at last, beneath the chuppah that obscured the stars of a spring evening from their view, he placed the wedding ring on her finger. At one of these moments, joyful as the most fervent prayer, she was beset by the strange, unsettling observation that the face of her betrothed was indeed as she had expected, the color and sleekness of olive oil, but that this dusky, olive tone had an overlay of whiteness, semi-transparent, but clearly visible, as if his skin were sewn from the same material as his wedding *kittel* or a funeral shroud. Though hardly a word of the entire ceremony remained in her mind, not even the text of the nuptial blessings, her most enduring memory was of the flawless white of the wedding attire, hers as well as his, for she was dressed in a gown that shone like the wings of a dove, and the unsettling whiteness of his skin. She also remembered sips of wine the color and sweetness of blood, the crash of glasses shattering against the ground, the trembling of her legs and heart, the quivering of both their voices, drowned in a chorus of joyful cries of "Mazel tov!," and the look in his eyes, which said ever more clearly that he was in haste: to enter the *yichud* room, where for the first time they would be alone together, to reach the moment when they would break their day-long fast and sit down to golden chicken broth, when they would unwrap their wedding presents: a silver Chanukah menorah, a Seder table set, a *tallis* smelling of starch, the next morning, when he would wipe away her tears and comfort her as she sobbed for the loss of her hair, shorn for the first time in her life, and the day when the wedding would finally come to its end and they would live together, when they would tell each other things they did not understand, and start their communal life, adult, sacred, and mysterious.

At that point, like any girl or boy standing beneath the chuppah, she thought all this haste was not the result of human desires and decisions, or human impatience, but of more significant causes than those of individuals: the monthly pulsating of her blood, the cycles of the religious year and the even more powerful cycles of Jewish life, greater than the life of any Jew, let alone Jewess, and that since in David's eyes, apart from youthful shyness she perceived tremulous impatience, as if he feared that what he was being given might instantly be taken away, it only meant that David was already eager for that life, stretching before them without end, that he wanted it to be filled as soon as possible with offspring, wisdom, godliness, people's respect, maybe wealth too, all the various goods that God's blessing might send down to a Jew. So she was in haste too, they were both in haste. They hastened on the first Shabbat eve after the wedding celebration, and then for the next dozen, no, the next twenty or thirty nights, as in dense darkness she waited, clenching her teeth with fear, feeling the light touch of his trembling fingers, for him to be intimate with her, for the monthly cycle of her blood to couple with the cycle of a life mightier than she, for this powerful life, regulated in accordance with the sacred order, to take deeper hold of them, and they would both become its, Jewish life's, humble servants forever. But they hastened in vain, for some reasons David could not be intimate with her, although she waited patiently. He doesn't know how, she thought, maybe he's afraid, and surely that was true, he was afraid, but not as she had thought at first; he wasn't afraid of life, but of death, as she finally discovered. This was why he and his family had been in haste, as she discovered one night when he sank heavily onto the bed, then curled up beneath the quilt, racked by a fit of shivering, and in the darkness she could sense that it wasn't the same as on previous nights, the shiver of helpless weeping, but of fever. She put a hand to his brow and felt the heat of a burning oven, then David suddenly coughed hard, and in the thin streak of moonlight that came creeping through the blinds, she saw that the white bedclothes were stained by a splash from his mouth, which when she leaped up and lit a candle, glinted ominously with the red of blood.

Less than a year later there was haste to allow him to pass on, there was haste, despite the teachings of the Talmud that hastening someone's death is close to murder, there was haste, for although he was dying quickly, he was in torment, and it is said that the final agony is worse than the actual dying. As the Angel of Death insistently forced its way into their house, the old women recognized it in various forms—one day a vagabond with silver hair turned up with a begging bowl, another time, so they said, a black, winged shape flitted over the house at midnight, glittering with a thousand eyes—so nothing could help: none of the several doctors summoned, nor the requests, tinged with angry resentment, of both pious men to the Almighty, nor the communal fasts, nor the family prayers. Also to no avail was changing David's name to Yosl, to mislead the messenger. On the final day, his advent was heralded by Reb Gershon's prophetic dream, the nearby cawing of a raven, and the distant, but audible, howl of a dog in the goy district, and that night, too, the behavior of the domestic cat, who for no visible reason raised his hackles, leaped up from his place on the bench by the kitchen stove, and darted out of the window. When at last the Angel of Death burst into the house, although to all but the dying man it was invisible, they knew that it too was in haste, for before David Yosl had fully opened his eyes wide with terror, a drop of deadly bile had dripped from the blade of the angel's sword into his gaping mouth, which he choked on painfully, spouted blood one last time, and finally died, and all the gathered assembly had to do was to draw aside in reverent awe, for the black messenger to leave as fast as it had entered. Once it was all over there was more haste, as the Liściska funeral fraternity hastened to complete the posthumous ritual in a single day according to tradition: to wash the dead man, clothe him in a wedding *kittel*, whose whiteness this time was the white of mourning, wrap him in the *tallis* his father-in-law had given him as a wedding present, place shards on his eyes, and to the laments of the mourners that set the panes of glass shaking in the houses they passed, to escort him in a black crowd of Hasidim and townsfolk to the cemetery, known for the mollification of mortal powers as the house of life, and say Kaddish.

Meanwhile, as Shira sat shiva with the rest of the family, perching on a low stool for seven days according to the custom, in coarse clothing borrowed from her sister, without bathing or brushing her hair, lacking the strength to make a sound, and thus reciting her mourning prayers silently, just by moving her numb lips, in this endless period of mourning numbness she had the thought, which afterwards she considered over and over again, that if indeed what her father, mother, and the godliest of the godly Hasidim said was true, that whatever happened, it happened as it was meant to happen, because adult matters of life and death are sacred and mysterious, then perhaps, she told herself, all this nuptial haste had served to tie her not so much to life, Jewish life, any kind of life, as to death, which unlike life is not a Jewish thing, but universal and equal, for everyone, it occurred to her, Jew or goy, Ruthenian or Pole, even cows, goats, hens or cats die in the same way, alone and usually in torment, so perhaps the truth was that she had been married to death, that unlike her older siblings she had been sacrificed, perhaps because she was the last one, the youngest, but in fact, she told herself, she was still alive, death had not yet chosen her as it had chosen David, it was they, the living, who had given her away to death, she was still alive, only a few years had passed since her first blood, which though unclean, was still the blood of life, not like the blood that had burst from David's mouth, the blood of death, so if it was true that life and death were two sisters, like Shira and her older sister Hadasa, surely one should love them both the same, yet she could sense that unlike her and Hadasa, those two sisters did not love each other in the least, on the contrary, they tussled in mutual hatred, so perhaps, she thought, things were entirely different from how everyone imagined, maybe the wedding haste that had taken her nowhere but to a low stool in the corner of a dark room had stumbled by itself, maybe the cycles of Jewish life were spurred on by sanctity and tradition to win the race against death, which though pacified with ingratiating words, was not the sister of anyone living, and then she thought, and considered over and over again, that there was one more life, which did not belong to anyone except her, not a Jewish or a Gentile life, but her life, Shira's life, and she started looking for it in everything that had happened over the past year between her and David, that timid, unfortunate boy, in their mutual embarrassment, in those moments at the dead of night when he had tried in vain to become a father, though not entirely adult himself, and finally she found it, she found life in the soft touch of his fingers, in his whispers and his breathing, in the ticklish down on his face and between his legs, she found it in him, David, perhaps from the very start she had sensed that it wasn't life but death that dwelled within him, just as his family had sensed it, and had hastened, in the short time granted him by fate, to fulfill the most important, Jewish commandment, and yet she found life in what had succeeded in occurring between them, she found the spark that had survived David and remained inside her, in her room, her bed, her hands, on her skin, a spark that was warm and moist, and when, six months after the mourning period ended, Reb Eliezer made an offer for Shira to marry his youngest son, Boaz, for it is advisable for the younger brother of a Jew who has died without heirs to take his place at his widow's side, she did not feel fear, because she realized that during the toughest period of mourning, those seven days spent sitting on that stool in the corner with her eyes fixed on her own inner depth, she had already found and chosen other eyes for herself in that depth, and in them she had lit, like a spark, that sacred life for which she could not yet find a name, or maybe she was afraid that as soon as she uttered it, if only in her thoughts, she would commit a grievous sin, and they were his eyes, the eyes of Boaz, whom she had seen twice before now, at the wedding and after the funeral, she had kept them in her mind and would not let them go, and when at last Boaz drove up in a britzka with the wedding retinue, entered their house and stood before her to lower the veil over her face, she looked him in the eyes with her head raised and made sure that the spark was burning there, though she alone was aware of it, though it was lit by her hand alone, not his, and once they were standing beneath the chuppah, she knew what this spark, this life, was called.

As a result, Shira was not in haste. And when on the first Shabbat eve following their marriage Boaz put out the candle and came to sit on the edge of the bed, when she saw his hands shaking as he undid his shirt, she told him too, now that she'd been matured, not just by blood but also by death and the experience of mourning, mature though still a virgin, she told him: Do not be in haste. When he became intimate with her, the spark of life flared with such force that she was afraid a demon may have entered her, but no, she quickly thought through all the rites, all the signs that had been sent, and assured herself that no demon had access to her, this marriage joined her with nothing but life, adult and sacred, and thus for the first time understandable, she let life feel at home inside her, and she could tell that grace and good fortune were taking up residence within her. Once it was all over and the sheet was stained with blood again, this time the blood of life, and Boaz, a boy younger than she, began to whisper a thankful *Shema Yisrael,* with a damp hand she closed his mouth, as a way of telling him that now they were bound together by a vow that was even stronger than they had imagined: now they were married to life, greater than Jewish or Gentile, Ruthenian or Polish life, or any other life at all, life that stretched from the earth to the sky, to the bottom of the sea and the tops of the mountains, deep inside the heart, and the veins, and the bowels of everyone alive. She was no longer in any haste, not even to see their child, when at last she sensed, and she sensed quickly, that it was inside her, that it was growing, she just waited patiently for it to be born, matured by the trials she had been through.

Four years later, the support guaranteed by his father-in-law in the marriage contract, which allowed Boaz to devote himself fully to studying the Torah, came to an end, and he had to decide what next. During this time, every day except Shabbat, from daybreak to late at night, he had conscientiously spent hours and hours at the *beys medresh,* poring over the tractates of the Mishnah and the Gemara, the works of the great mystics and Kabbalists, Arizal, Ramak, and Ramhal, the books of the Zohar, *midrashim,* collections of *responsa,* lives of the Besht and other holy *tsaddikim,* and though he made excellent progress, though at Reb Gershon's request he engaged in debate with rabbis visiting Liściska or itinerant *maggidim,* and shone with mental acuity and knowledge, at the same time, in secret from his father-in-law, he subscribed to Jewish newspapers, published in both languages, sacred and ordinary, also Russian ones, for in even greater secrecy he was learning Russian, and, in the most profound secrecy imaginable, he was corresponding with Zionists who, despite certain statements in the Torah and the Talmud that in their view forced Israel to remain in exile to the end of time, dreamed of restoring the Jewish state in Palestine. Shira did not keep him company in his studies, such matters were not appropriate for a woman, she took care of the house and the children, once a week she baked challah, made cholent and lit the Shabbat candles, but she did see those newspapers, textbooks, and letters, kept under lock and key in the desk drawers and concealed in hiding places behind the books on the shelf, things not found in any Hasidic home, and certainly not her father's home, and she knew what they meant, so she was not surprised when one day Boaz solemnly told her: "The sacred knowledge is not enough," and then added, as if in answer to her question: "Neither for me, nor for the Jews," and then he announced that he planned to continue his studies, but not at the *beys medresh*, neither the one in Liściska or any other, in clouds of pipe smoke, fumes of hooch and honey, amid Hasidic dancing and humming, in the intoxicating yet closed circle of godliness that leads, of course, deep inside the human heart and deep inside the world, but after all, he explained to her, in this world "deep inside" meant just the same as "nowhere," the world was not heading deep inside but forwards, and if the Jews did not get moving, if they isolated themselves from the world behind a wall of religious volumes and a chorus of prayer-house singing, the world would at best forget them, and at worst trample them. So it always has been, he explained, they have trampled us, because we are strange, no one knows better than we do how to read, how to puzzle, how to think, how to split hairs, of all the nations we are the wisest, the most thoughtful, but the only books we read are religious works and ledgers of accounts. When Shira timidly asked what in that case he intended to do, whether he would continue his studies at a yeshiva in one of the neighboring towns, he sighed and said no, not at a yeshiva, though for the Hasidim a yeshiva is a school of heresy anyway, at the yeshiva he would go on studying the Talmud, he could at most train for a rabbinical exam, but he was as eager to become a rabbi as a *tsaddik*. "In other words, I do not want to go to a yeshiva at all," he said, in an even quieter tone than hers, as if uttering the most hideous blasphemy, "I want to do real studies, at a Russian university." "Goy studies," she whispered, at which he merely nodded, rather than saying it, even in a whisper: Yes, goy studies. Shira knew what this meant, she realized that he was sure to be condemned as an apostate, he might even be excommunicated and disinherited, and she knew what it could mean for her, for their family, but Boaz was saying all this without anger or rebellion, without contrariness or disdain, but instead with the calm conviction of a young sage. Finally, he added out loud, maybe to justify himself: "I do not have a calling to devote my life to studying the Scripture," so she laid a hand on his cheek and replied that she understood, and it was true, she trusted him, she accepted his extraordinary resolution like any other gesture on his part, soft and tender, youthful, and at the same time brave and manly. Calm took precedence over fear within her, because life was burning inside her, sacred life, she could feel it not just in herself, in Boaz, and between the two of them, but she could also see it embodied in their two little sons, healthy, bright and laughing, and she knew the name of this life, which in god-fearing Jewish families was never pronounced, perhaps it was considered too sublime to be called what happened between a husband and wife, though deep in her heart Shira was sure that some passages in the *Shir Hashirim*, such as this one: *Behold, thou art fair, my love, thy two breasts are like two young roes that are twins, which feed among the lilies*, or this one: *How fair is thy love, my sister, my spouse, thy lips, O my spouse, drip as the honeycomb, honey and milk are under thy tongue, and the smell of thy garments is like the smell of Lebanon*, and also this one: *I am come into my garden, my sister, my spouse, I have gathered my myrrh with my spice, I have eaten my honeycomb with my honey, I have drunk my wine with my milk*, and more obscure passages too, more piercing, though she had not yet guessed what they might portend: *By night on my bed I sought him whom my soul loveth, I sought him, but I found him not*, or this one: *I opened to my beloved, but my beloved had withdrawn himself, and was gone, my soul failed when he spake, I sought him, but I could not find him, I called him, but he gave me no answer*, thus deep in her heart Shira was sure that these passages in *Shir Hashirim*, despite what was taught by the rabbis, *tsaddikim*, and authors of women's prayerbooks, not only spoke of the marriage of the people of Israel with the Eternal, but also, perhaps chiefly, of what was happening within her, in Boaz, and between them, in their life, which was meant to be boundless. She knew the name of this life, and so she felt that if she said to him: "All right, if you do not want to become Reb Boaz, but a merchant or even an engineer, a doctor of medicine or of law, then I believe that God will bless you in this decision," she felt that if she said that to him, this hot, moist life would be speaking through her. Only later on, after everything, so she named it in her heart, after everything, for in fact everything had already happened in her life, so after everything, she thought, and then considered over and over again, that nevertheless she had been wrong, that words are always wrong, that only this hot, moist life, meaning love, for that was the name it bore, which she never uttered aloud, only love could not be wrong.

They were all wrong, she thought, as for the second time in her life she sat on a low stool in the corner of the room, and that thought was as loud as a scream, desperate, perhaps blasphemous, but the life that was burning inside her, the spark, though shrunk to a pinhead, yet still bright, was telling her she had a right to this blasphemy, because anyone who had lost everything, or very nearly everything, would be forgiven everything, or very nearly everything. Those who tried to console her by saying that the Almighty, may He be blessed, had favored her with the martyrdom of twofold mourning, thus He had marked her out for inscrutable purposes, and she should accept His judgment in utter humility, were wrong. Also wrong were those who claimed that the Eternal had punished Boaz for dissenting, like those who had defied His will in the desert, by casting a golden calf and worshipping it, for whenever a Hasidic son decided to become a merchant, doctor, or engineer, what else was he doing but choosing the golden calf, and after all, they whispered venomously, as if behind her back, though she could hear their whispers clearly, he who stays at home does not wear out his boots, and that is just how an apostate ends. Wrong as well were those who rebuked the venomous by saying: Stop it, an evil tongue is worse than an evil hand, and tearfully repeated the Hasidic words of wisdom: The saying is, do not pray and do not study, as long as you do not anger the Eternal, so how, they lamented, did such a very young, devout and upright Jew anger Him? Was it merely because instead of praying, studying the Torah, singing *niggunim*, and one day becoming a *tsaddik*, sermonizing and blessing Jews in need, he preferred to learn the trade of a merchant, a doctor, or an engineer? Can it be that the Eternal sent His avenging angel to Kiev, where Boaz had gone to inquire about attending college, and, unable to find him in the big city, the impetuous angel unleashed a pogrom there, so the goy rabble could trample and club him to death, as if by chance? Could the Eternal have not said to His messenger, just as He once told him about Job, that holy man from the Land of Uz: Lo, everything he has is in thy power, but do not lay a hand on him, or perhaps this: Lo, he is in thy power, but preserve his life? No, the angel was given free rein and used it to the full. It began with a pogrom that erupted in faraway Kishinev. Two days later, it was described in minute detail, with false sympathy, by *The Kievan*, a newspaper that had baited the Jews for many years. There was a vast swarm of Jews in Kiev, drawn to the place on business from all over Ruthenia, heedless of the fact that for the past quarter of a century, every now and then in the cities of the Empire somebody would seize a stone, an ax, and a cudgel, growl: "Damnable Yid!" and at the head of a mob go and even the accounts, in which to his loss slovenliness, deviousness, and drunkenness were at work, and to the Jew's profit the thrift and prudence of the eternal exile. The blacker the city became with gaberdines, *kashkets* and hats, the larger the crowd that thronged at the great Karpukhinsky synagogue on the Shabbat, the more Jewish merchants traded corn and dried fruit and nuts at the Rye Market, the less fire was needed to ignite a conflagration. Whenever one erupted, nobody knew where it had happened first, where the fists, sticks, and firebrands had come from, perhaps from the settlements of the working-class poor on the banks of the Dnieper, none of the Jews was sure, because for a couple of days, since the article in *The Kievan* had stirred the mob into action, snarling threats had been running through the city: "We shall deal with you even better than they did in Kishinev," and the Jews, already quite familiar with such promises, and aware that they were usually fulfilled, flitted along the walls of the houses with their heads down, and anyone who could sat in hiding, not going outside at all, but waiting for the snarling to fall silent. But Boaz knew none of this, he did not live in Kiev, where Jews were constantly threatened, cursed, or dragged off to the cells on any excuse, until they learned to catch the mood swings, like changes in the weather, to sense an imminent pogrom in the air like an approaching storm. Boaz was not capable of that because this was his very first trip to the city. At close of day, he alighted from the train, and then rode, probably in a droshky, to Khreshchatyk, where Reb Chaskiel lived, his cousin, who was at odds with his Hasidic family, and with whom he was to stay for the duration of his exams. Chaskiel had promised to come and fetch him from the station, but he had not appeared, so Boaz had reached the address he'd been given on his own, no, he had not reached it, because just then the fists and cudgels had forced their way into Padol, the district inhabited by Jews, and what cudgel or fist could have resisted the temptation, seeing a stray Hasid in the middle of the street, a skinny little youth, trembling under a long *bekishe*, clutching a leather suitcase, his astonished eyes staring from under his hat. But they were wrong, thought Shira, those who complained that it was unjust, such as her mother. Wrong too were those who justified the Lord of the world for extending His punishing finger and pointing out poor Boaz to the Gentile mob, such as Reb Eliezer, who, obdurate in his merciless severity, could not forgive his son for wanting to be Russified and for applying to a Christian university. Also wrong were those who lamented that not just the death of Boaz, but the entire Kiev massacre, in which at least a dozen people were killed, four times as many were beaten up, several dozen houses were burned down, stalls at the Rye Market were smashed, windows in the stores and the synagogue were broken, Jews' beards were cut off and girls were dishonored, just like the Kishinev massacre before it, yet another of the numerous pogroms that had run through the Russian and Little Russian lands like a forest fire on a torrid day ever since the Jews had been accused of the fatal attack on Tsar Alexander, though in fact of all the Russian and non-Russian rulers Alexander had been the most sympathetic to the Jews, for which they requited him with sincere reverence, so they were wrong, those who lamented that these pogroms were a sign that the Eternal had abandoned the Jews for good. So had said Reb Yakov, for instance, perhaps in a moment of weakness. But her father was wrong too, thought Shira, when on hearing Yakov speak these words, he had raised a bony finger and, shaking his beard, thundered at him that on the contrary, it was a miracle that despite so many calamities and misfortunes the Jews were still there, and indeed, it was a sign, but only of the fact that they truly were the chosen people. The tone of his voice and his raised finger alone would have sufficed to silence the debate, so Yakov had held his tongue, but Reb Gershon had gone on shouting, returning as if incidentally to Boaz, saying that if Boaz had sinned in any way, it was in refusing to take part in the Jewish mission to improve the world. And that all the greater honor was due to her, Shira, because her twofold widowhood was a sign of this most sacred mission, and of the suffering that was its inevitable price. The stern *tsaddikim* were wrong, always quick to judge a dissenter, and not just Reb Eliezer, for Reb Gershon too had cursed Boaz when he heard that he was planning to leave for Kiev, and what he wanted to go there for. "I don't want a Moskal in the family!" he had shouted. "You will cease to be a Jew! Get out of my sight!" He'd wagged a finger, taking no notice of either Yakov's calm appeals to restrain himself from uttering words that carried too much weight, or the lamentations of Hagit, who by turns begged her husband to forgive Boaz, and Boaz to change his mind and ask for forgiveness, nor did he heed the humble gaze of Boaz, who stood in silence with his head drooping, without at the same time nerving himself to make any gesture of apology or conciliation, nor did he notice Shira's sobbing, or even the moment when she finally fainted at the terrible sight of her family falling apart before her very eyes. Reb Gershon was wrong. Those who thought they knew the answer were wrong. Those who helplessly admitted that they did not know it were wrong. Those who asked it at all were wrong. All of them were wrong.

Life was not wrong, death was not wrong, tussling in mutual hatred, they were not wrong jointly and they were not wrong individually, but they spoke a language that none of the living was destined to understand, and he who judged that he did understand it incurred a penalty, in truth not always, because the word "always" was wrong too, but sometimes, according to some arcane decrees. The Scripture was wrong. Words were wrong. But Aronek and Itzok were not wrong, whenever they came home from the *kheyder,* where they were taught those erroneous words, and ran into the yard, and Shira heard their unerring laughter, greeted them with an unerring embrace, and felt the unerring warmth or the unerring chill of their cheeks. Their eyes, their fingers, and their tears were not wrong. Those people were wrong who whispered, ever more often and more boldly as the years went by, that she would be well advised to marry again, because the children should have a father, and she was still young. Those people were wrong who then shook their heads and said that the Talmud advised against it, because even if a widow has a roof of gold over her head, she is still a widow, and a twofold widow is a *katlones,* a murderess, and no betrothed could feel safe at her side. Those people were wrong who sent offers to Nachman the matchmaker, though more rarely than in the past. Those people were wrong who, at the sound of her name, crossed their fingers just in case, and hid their children behind their skirts, cape, cart, or fence whenever they saw her in town, to stop her from casting an evil spell. She, Shira, was not wrong, in her darkness, her ignorance, and her silence, because as she had once thought, and then considered over again, first of all a person learns to speak, but not until later to be silent, and only one who is silent is never wrong.

Frozen Spring—Jerusalem Returning

By Entela Kasi

Excerpt from a Novel

Translated from Albanian *by the author with assistance from Sarah Lawson*

"I need to forget everything," Hannah wrote to Johan as she passed through the last stone arch connecting the gardens of the Mishkenot Sha'ananim Centre with the narrow stone path of the Beit Israel synagogue. She continued to walk along Dror Eliel Street, then stopped for a while in Teddy Park, the green zone with fountains planned from its inception as an open space for children. She passed the intersection of Dohha Isaac and Al Batriarkeya Al Armaneya to enter the Old City through the Jaffa Gate. When she reached St. James Cathedral, on the road between the Armenian Patriarchate and the Orthodox Monastery, Johan called her.

"We can't forget, Hannah! We live to witness our memories. When will you return to London?"

"I think in two weeks," she answered.

"They're saying that the world will be closed down soon. There will be isolation and limitations in travelling, so please take care."

"All right, Johan. I am going now to the Armenian Gardens."

"When you simply say, 'all right,' I am afraid it is not so," said Johan.

"Kozeta is waiting for me there."

"Well, dear, how was the exhibition at Mishkenot?" he continued.

"Kozeta and Marianne said it was 'all right.' The pictures from 1938 of the house of Mohamed R., the elder, superimposed on the pictures from 1998 of the body of Med R., the nephew, made the visitors burst into tears. They are used to pain, but they weren't expecting this. The Righteous among the Nations massacred in the darkness of the Balkans—this reminded them of the Holocaust. "

"Listen Hannah, yours is not just an exhibition; it is history."

"Yes, Johan, it is. This evening I will go out for a glass of wine with Kozeta and Marianne. We will be near downtown, at Mishkenot. My room there is number 12. Pictures of Yehuda Amichai are in the lobby. He stayed there once to write. Outside the windows of my room is the Tower of David, all lit up. It shines all night and keeps me awake. I am as light as the feather of a bird."

"Listen, Hannah. If things get worse you should take the first flight from Tel Aviv to London."

"Johan, you know that I will be stopping in Tirana and Pristina, and in The Hague."

"All right, Hannah. You know what is best for us both," Johan said, and the conversation was closed.

"Shalom," she said.

Kozeta and Marianne were waiting for her in the Armenian Gardens. During the Prague Spring, Marianne had been in Jerusalem with her family. In those days she was a young woman and her father was working for the embassy of Czechoslovakia in Israel. Marianne recalled when her father made the decision not to return to Prague until the Eastern Bloc fell. When they returned to Prague, she'd worked for President Havel. She was the adviser on culture in the cabinet of the Czech president.

"Johan is scared this time," Hannah told Kozeta when they met.

"Maybe he is right this time. It seems that strange things are going to happen. Who knows what else is coming."

"What can be worse?" Hannah asked both women.

"After Med R. died, you do not take death seriously, is that it?" asked Marianne.

"Yes, that's right. After he left us, nothing else can ever scare me."

"You need time to get over it, dear," said Marianne. "The pictures in the exhibition were traumatic. Very painful for us all. We share the same stories and we become the stories we write. That's what my father would say if he'd seen the photos on the stone walls at Mishkenot. Do you remember the last time you were here with Med R.? It was January and I took your picture on Mount Herzl. He insisted, saying you very much wanted your photographs taken there. Med was a noble man. I have never understood your strong relationship, though. I still need time to understand what you both were to each other."

"If I tell you that we were like Constantin and Doruntine in the legends of the Albanians, can you understand that?" asked Hannah, looking at the walls of the Armenian Patriarchate. "I told Med R. I would go to Mount Herzl only with him. I told him that I would visit Yad Vashem only with him. And so we did. He kept his promise."

"But you didn't let Johan show you his letters," Kozeta said softly.

"Yes, this is true. I asked Johan not to show me Med's last letters. I couldn't face it. My illness has returned. Sometimes I do not feel my left hand. But it is different from 1989 in that now I can feel pain."

"Everything stems from your sadness, Hannah."

"Do you think it will return, Kozeta?"

"What are you saying, Hannah? Do you want to break my heart into little pieces?"

"I am afraid. Johan is afraid, too."

"Instead of talking about life, you talk about death. Enough is enough. I am with you for the first time in the land of your grandparents and you talk about death. This is not good, my dear. I am happy that in my old age I am here with you. We will have wine this evening. I will tell you many things you do not yet know. Do not make me sad, my dear."

"Dear Kozeta! How much Mother Thalin loved you!"

"She has inherited Rachel's nature," Kozeta whispered to herself and took Hannah's hand.

"My poor mother lost her mind when she was quite young," said Hannah. "I am afraid I am like her. She lost her mind after I was born. Poor Mama, my sad mama! My beautiful *amma*," added Hannah, as though whispering an old song.

"Hannah, she did not get sick because you were born, and she did not get depressed because of your birth. She got depressed because she was afraid for your father. They were both under surveillance. They were terrified. I was terrified, too. It was the peak time of terror in Albania in those days. All the artists were sent to prison or labor camps after the eleventh Festival of Music. Many of your parents' friends were arrested. The dictatorship in Albania was insane. Nazism and Bolshevism were the same as far as they could see. We who lived through it remember it well. Now the best thing is to forget a bit. Back then I could never have imagined that one day I would visit these holy sites with you. Now I'm here. Here we are, Hannah!"

"You are strong and beautiful, Kozeta."

"Where do you see beauty?" smiled Kozeta.

"The way I remember you. The same beautiful woman who was on television and the news. Your face is the same."

"I was younger and stronger in those days."

They were walking along the stone streets in the Armenian quarter of the Old City. Hannah stopped in front of Sandrouni Armenia Ceramics, one of the best known ceramic ateliers in the old city. She entered it and carefully approached the handcrafted plates displayed on a large wooden, pomegranate-colored table. The owner of the workshop, a man of at least eighty, started telling her about the skill of handcrafting porcelain, clay, and ceramics. The works she saw were stylized with carved arabesques, and to her they resembled the paintings of Chagall that she'd seen on the stone walls of Ljubljana Castle, when she and Med R. were there for a meeting of the Writers for Peace Committee in 2009. Med presented his diaries from the war in the Balkans to the public in that castle, at an event sponsored by the embassy of Kosovo in Slovenia. It was May, and she remembered everything vividly. They had their picture taken in front of one of the Chagall paintings. A grandson of A. Schultz the elder (A. Schultz, the younger, the architect) had taken the picture. This grandson wrote the story of his grandparents' family during the First World War, when they were displaced from Saint Petersburg to Stockholm when his father was a small child. This novel was considered one of the best in 1984 when it was published in Sweden—the best novel about both wars, the first and the second. Schultz the Younger had given it to her as a gift. She told him that one day it might be translated into Albanian. Med took care of the entire process, the book was published in Kosovo in 2010, and the writer came to visit. Those days were memorable.

"Med was always able to make things happen!" whispered Hannah to Marianne while they were in the atelier.

"Yes, he was like that," she answered.

"You know, Mother Thalin used to keep some porcelain bowls like these for Pesach."

"Yes, I remember well."

"She also had some porcelain plates like these small ones on our wooden dining room table."

"Yes, I know," said Kozeta. "She used them for celebrations when relatives visited her for different feasts."

"I would like seven of these porcelain plates," Hannah told the old master craftsman, gazing at the colors and the carved letters on them.

"If they make you happy, I am honored," said the old man, coming to the wooden table where all the handicrafts were displayed. "Where are you from?"

"Albania," said Kozeta.

"Albanians saved Jewish people during the Holocaust. We know the story very well," said the old man to the three women.

"My grandmother Thalin was Armenian and my grandfather Jacob was Jewish," said Hannah.

"They were saved by Albanians from Kosovo in Prizren, a beautiful little town there," Kozeta said.

"You are one of us, daughter," said the master craftsman, and his eyes took on another color, somewhere between shadows of grass and grey clouds.

"Yes, indeed," Hannah answered, lifting a porcelain plate of deep blue. "I am Albanian, Jewish, Armenian, and recently an Englishwoman, as long as I remain married to a rabbi in London."

"There are many of us all around the world."

"The same is true of us," added Kozeta.

"Charming lady, your mother!" said the old master craftsman to Hannah, looking at Kozeta.

"This beautiful lady is, shall we say, my other mother. Yes, she is very charming."

"Pardon me, my dear. Maybe I'm overstepping the limits of our conversation, but I very rarely see Albanians in these streets of our old town. I would like you to remember me with these pomegranate-colored porcelain cups. They can be used for wine during Rosh Hashanah or Pesach. I want to present you, Hannah, with seven of these cups. So you will remember me and my atelier in the Old City."

As he was wrapping the cups carefully, she gazed at his hands, unable to say a single word. The three women were all looking at the old man's hands. Suddenly there was the sound of a crack. Hannah had dropped a porcelain plate onto the stone floor. She suddenly thought of crises like the war in Kosovo. The seconds passing felt to her like hours.

"Don't be alarmed, Hannah. Okay, my dear? Everything is all right," said Kozeta, taking Hannah's hands in hers. Mother Thalin on such occasions would say that the evil eye is at it again. Hannah felt her fingernails press against her palm, tightly and painfully. Kozeta was massaging her hand and fingers gently. After some minutes Hannah whispered with difficulty a half "We." Then she added a half "re," then an *m*, and at last she pronounced with effort the entire phrase, "Where am I?" Then she asked, "Where is Med R.?" and "Where are we?" Her eyes looked as though they'd been flooded by a high tide during an unexpected thunderstorm. "Yes," she added, "across from the Armenian Church. The monastery is nearby."

"Yes, Hannah," said Kozeta. The master craftsman brought a cup of pomegranate juice.

"Perhaps you are a little tired, daughter," he said. "You will feel refreshed with this juice. We call it 'the juice of life.'"

"Thank you for your kindness. I'm sorry to bother you," said Hannah after a couple of minutes. After she finished the juice, the master craftsman accompanied the three women to the stone pavement of the Armenian Church opposite his atelier.

"Do remember me with these cups and plates," he said to her. "These are my gifts to you. I am an old master craftsman, and I'm happy that I can give you some little symbolic heritage of ours. Take care and stay happy." He went back into his atelier. Hannah had the impression that he continued looking at them from inside the blue glass windows.

"Zalman Shazar was the third president of Israel," said Marianne as they continued walking through the Old City.

They sat at a table near the Jewish Quarter, in one of the many restaurants there. "Mishkenot is near the Zalman Shazar Centre. When we visit there later, you will see all the pictures on the walls."

"If you feel tired, we can postpone our visit for another day," said Kozeta, looking at Hannah.

"Don't worry, everything is all right," Hannah answered. It was late afternoon. "Of course, we'll visit Shazar's house today. I feel fine. Thank you for lunch, Marianne. It was delicious."

"It was just a light meal," answered Marianne. "but I am happy you liked it." She went on, "Shazar was the first Minister for Education and Culture. Golda Meir describes him well in her book. She quoted him as once saying: 'There are no typewriters here. Well, we will write by hand. All the children of Israel from the age of four to eighteen will be offered education granted by the state.' In the year 1947 he and his wife Rachel participated in an Arabic language class for teachers of Hebrew. The picture I was telling you about yesterday evening at Mishkenot is from the Jewish National Fund Photo Archives, through the Office for Public Communication of the government at that time." Marianne finished the story as they approached Zalman Shazar's house.

The stone slabs of the entrance pavement were the same as those in the streets of the Old City. They had a unique color, somewhere between white and light beige. The same color as Mother Thalin's braids wound around her beautiful head. The shade was between baked wheat grains and hay. This afternoon Hannah was dressed in a long, olive-colored dress made of soft cashmere, decorated carefully from the neck to its hem with light olive branches and leaves. She'd bought this dress in one of the women's handmade-clothing shops when she was with Med R. in the Old City for the first time. Hannah had put on her head the pomegranate-colored scarf that Med gave her when they went from Mount Herzl to the shops along the walls of the Old City.

The garden of the house was full of flowers. Everything glowed in the sunset. In front of the garden the walls of the Old City seemed near.

"Shalom! I am Rachel," said the woman at Zalman Shazar's house. "I'm sorry I could not join you yesterday evening at the opening of your exhibition at Mishkenot. I returned late yesterday evening from Lebanon. Please feel at home. I am very happy to welcome you here."

She invited the women into the house, and suggested they sit on the sofas in front of the big windows.

The house was completely white inside.

Place of Birth: Report on the State of the Union

By Norman Manea

Excerpt from a Novel

Translated from Romanian *by Jean Harris*

Headed by Chief Rabbi Dr. Niemirower of Bucharest, Rabbi Zirelsohn of Chishinău, and Rabbi Dr. Burstein of Botoshani, eighteen of the most illustrious rabbis looked into the case.

THE REPORT from 1928 summarizes the "serious investigation" undertaken on December 31, 1928 by delegates I.M. Wechsler and Suchăr Feller on the last day of the year 1928, and thus on the eve of the New Year's celebration. A profane holiday, the New Year—so thought the ignorant, ready for merry-making and another joyful year. The day marked an anniversary, in fact: the anniversary of a *bris*—"a circumcision, gentlemen!" delegates Wechsler and Feller were ready to shout. The circumcision of the Jewish boy, Joshua, a week after his birth: this is what your New Year commemorates. Before becoming the Savior, Jesus, the boy circumcised 1,928 years ago, had become the rabbi Jehoshua. Jesus Christ was not Roman after all, or Romanian, or German, or Russian, or Spanish, as the multitude would believe. The honorable delegates, who had come to Botoshani to bring peace and concord to the disturbances of their co-religionists from Burdujeni had no time for digressions, however. They would return to Botoshani for New Year's Eve.

We summoned Mr. Zalic Gruenberg together with the four members that make up his committee. We have likewise called Mr. Herman Horowitz, with the four members of the rival committee. We have requested that they give us their registers and detailed minutes. We have likewise informed the serious people who desire the serenity and prosperity of the city of Burdujeni. So began *THE INVESTIGATORS' REPORT.*

The Sound and the Fury of daily life! Beginning, naturally, with moral and civic exigencies. The Jewish population of an average, small, Eastern European town was really sufficient unto itself. It didn't care about New Year's Eve. It didn't want to hear about delicious, cooked pork; it defended itself against the pagan merry-making of the New Year that could turn against it at any time, which, as newcomers and aliens, the citizens well knew.

Mr. Zalic Gruenberg brought us all the record books and the register containing the minutes, as well as receipts for monies paid out. Mr. Horowitz and his committee, however, do not have record books or minutes. We established that the Jewish school is closed, abandoned to ruin, and subjected to public charity. We asked Mr. Horowitz about the goal of his committee. He answered: the removal of Rabbi B. Basches. For this reason, his group has taken on a ritual kosher slaughterer named Haim Litener and has named him rabbi, without his having the certificate required for this rank. We further found that eighteen of the most prominent rabbis, headed by Chief Rabbi Dr. Niemivower of Bucharest, Rabbi Zirelsohn of Chishineau, and Rabbi B. Burstein of Botoshan, have looked into the conflict and punished the slaughterer, H. Litener.

They were in a hurry to return to their homes before the holiday, which hovered (as always) dubiously in the air. In spite of that, the honorable investigators did not limit themselves to a summary evaluation of the situation.

The purpose of their trip had been "to introduce peace and concord to the city of Burdujeni." Thus, they proposed pacification measures to be instituted in the new calendar year which was just about to begin:

A new election, presided over by a committee composed of a communal adviser and a member of the Israelite Community of Botoshan; after the election, the penalties inflicted on the slaughterer Litener to be lifted, the said individual to be rehabilitated and returned to his position, strictly limited to kosher slaughter, while Rabbi B. Basches should go on functioning as Chief Rabbi, an office that he occupies with dignity as a learned author of an important book.

In an attempt at impartiality, Messrs. Wechsler and Feller wrote their report in an impersonal way, as was appropriate in the case of such a grave errand with such serious consequences.

Could it have been possible somehow that Mr. Senator Wechsler was a relative of the poet Fundoianu, born in Iashi under the name Benjamin Wechsler and destined to die in The Great War of Extermination at Auschwitz under the French pseudonym Benjamin Fondane? In the next decade of unabated local conflagrations related in Messrs. Wechsler and Feller's *REPORT*, Fundoianu's poetic lines—*And there will come an evening/And I will leave this place*—might have sent a warning and a summons that would be important (and not only in Romania) if it were read with attention.

—

The letter, dated February 28, 1929, sent by the representatives of the local Jewish community to The Worthy Union of Jewish Communities in the Old Kingdom[1] reports on the misdeeds that continued at Burdujeni:

Mr. Horowitz' group, composed of individuals with personal ambitions, did not want to hear of free and fair elections. We had a sad experience when we convoked the population for just such an election, presided over by no less than the city's mayor. The chief of the local garrison took part, as well![2] *Mr. Horowitz, the innkeeper, first enlivened the group with drink before they arrived at the voting place. The Horowitz gallery then broke through the velvet ropes and, rushing into the voting hall, provoked so formidable a scandal that the authorities, in spite of all attempts to restore order, found themselves forced to leave in disgust.*

The mayor and the chief of the garrison are unable to quiet the combatants' fervor! Poverty, suffering, humiliations, and danger seem less urgent than discord with its irresistible energy. Everyone is "someone" in the metropolis of Burdujeni—each a value and a principle in those (still peaceful) years before the time of wrath.

The conclusion comes on a note of high lamentation, both moving and rhetorical:

If this is the state, in point of fact, we respectfully ask you to allow us this question: Are we *able to hold free elections? In this state of spiritual hostility?*

The wise heads of Burdujeni are not satisfied with the description of events. They add too—as did delegates Wechsler and Feller in *THE REPORT* delivered on the last day of the year 1928—proposals for a more peaceful dialogue, a re-beginning:

---

1 In Bucharest, that is, the capital of the Kingdom of Romania, which united Moldavia and Wallachia in 1859 (Translator's note).

2 The garrison chief's participation was shocking in its day. Ordinarily, the garrison was assigned to protect the Jewish population from antisemites. On this occasion, Jews needed to be protected from themselves.

The existing interim committee should continue to administer the affairs of the Community until riled spirits have calmed down.

On April 22, 1929, an important personage leaves Bucharest: Mr. Horia Carp, journalist.

I conveyed myself on April 2 of the Common Era to Burdujeni, and I asked the two parties to present themselves, each with a delegation, the new arbiter reports. The armies each send five representatives to the negotiations, but an initial incident disturbs the parity:

The delegates from the Horowitz group asked that Mr. Calman Rabinovici, a stranger to the place, be admitted to attend the discussions. This individual would be the group's secretary. The Gruenberg group declared themselves opposed. For this reason, the delegates of the Horowitz group withdrew, so that only Mr. Horowitz remained at the discussions. The attached protocol, through which both groups oblige themselves to accept the decision of the undersigned, is signed by all the delegates of the Gruenberg group while only Mr. Horowitz signed on behalf of the other group.

The talks went on from 3:30 p.m. until late at night without the arbiter's reporting the hour when they concluded—probably out of embarrassment.

Suddenly the Gruenberg battalion "feels weaker. It has only eighty partisans," while the Horowitz division seems also to have "other" unspecified "reasons" for compromise which only the peculiar secretary "from outside" knows—maybe. Ready to get along, even if temporarily, *each of the battling groups holds to the commitment it has made to its rabbi or* dayan *[which is to say, judge, whose powers are limited to rabbinical court]*. The Horowitz division accepts an agreement through its chief, present at the talks; the rabbi will maintain his function, as will the *dayan*/ritual slaughterer Litener as his subaltern. The conciliation seems reasonable while *the merited sacrifice of ritual slaughterer Litener would be reason for eternal unrest and dissension,* as it would imperil, too, the situation of Rabbi Basches, in danger of being fired after the elections by the Horowitz group, found to be in the majority.

My moral conscience rightfully keeps me from giving a prize to a person who, in my conviction, remains the only party guilty of divisiveness. However, to assure the situation of Rabbi Basches, and to bring peace and good understanding to the breast of the Burdujeni Community, after painful and intense reflection within myself, I have decided, and I ask you to bring this decision to the knowledge of both groups, declares the Arbiter of the Peace Conference.

The four provisions of his final decision are clear and indisputable:

1. The interim Gruenberg committee will close its books on April 30, the date when it will dissolve itself and cease activity. It is proposed to the Horowitz group that they introduce several persons from the Gruenberg group in the list of candidates for the new committee.

2. Rabbi Basches remains the only rabbi of the community "with all the rights that flow from this position of dignity," with his current salary and with the mention that in the future his salary must always be greater than that of the ritual slaughterer. Rabbi Basches, a sage, a *talmid khokhem,* is asked never to interfere in public organizational policy, and to preach understanding among his congregation.

3. To avoid the susceptibilities of the Horowitz group and not to offend the self-respect of the old slaughterer Litener, seventy-four years of age, this gentleman shall maintain his title of *dayan*, but only as an honorific, without the right to exercise it.

There follows the foreseeable grave tonality of the conclusion which dramatically allies the Ancestral Law, individual ethical conscience, and the ideal of brotherhood:

In this decision is inscribed the teaching of my conscience, and I hope that the two groups will understand the fraternal thought that guides me and will accept this decision as they are obliged to do.

The envoy to the Worthy Union solemnly concludes his mission to the negotiations at the Jewish metropolis at Burdujeni in 1929. A "fair" decision: one, it might be said, that even the American Congress would not repeal.

N.B.: In a community of two hundred and forty families, the reasonable group is "weaker," naturally; it does not exceed eighty families. Immediately after a group constitutes itself as a committee, a unity, there appears a countergroup, the dissident interim committee. Coalitions, calumnies, conflicts—naturally, as in the rest of life! Instructive for the observer and for posterity: false "unanimity" is lacking.

Delegates from Botoshani or Bucharest, or even from Jerusalem, cannot establish eternal peace; at most, conflictual, negotiable "democracy."

~

Subsequently, the documents, as well as the historic reality of Burdujeni, continue the never-concluded History:

In the year of grace 1936, in the month of July, under the sign of Cancer and the Crab, when the vulnerable newborns of the tricky summer constellations wrestle with the uncertainties of beginning, Burdujeni holds its electoral campaign, now regulated by the Jewish community's tri-annual electoral calendar. The State of the Union has evidently improved.

On July 28th at 4 p.m., the leadership committee of the Israelite Community of Burdujeni was to be confirmed for a three-year term. The elections had already taken place on May 24, 1936, and they'd been validated while the inevitable "contestation of results" had been rejected.

Contestation had not been lacking, thank God, but it had been analyzed and rejected this time, by the Worthy Minister of Religions, no less. The Prefecture of Suceava County had consequently given its approval by means of the Order of July 27th, since on the following day, at the location of the Israelite School, which was also the Community Seat, the committee was to meet so as to constitute itself an elected body.

The characters from 1928–1929 no longer appear. Only Mr. H. Halpern, one of the five "partisans" designated in 1929 by the Gruenberg group for negotiations with the fierce Horowitz, walks back on stage, pacified by the prestige and fatigue of age.

It is found that the number of elected members necessary for the constitution of a body legally in conformity with the community council is present. Mr. Herman Halpern, who is chosen unanimously the President by Right of Age, formally presides over the constitution of the group.

Unanimity! But only for a President by Right of Age, a temporary presider in an honorary position. For an hour or less, the old H.H., in only a "formal" sense, will conduct the process.

Mr. Herman Halpern, taking over the function of President by Right of Age, thanks the members for the honor they have done him. He brings to the attention of those present that a candidate from list N.1 has addressed a request that the constitution of the committee be delayed for the reason that Mr. Litman Landau, head of the N.1. candidates' list, is missing from the locality.

The voting system seems to have evolved. There appear to be two lists, probably to keep the factions content. The absentee, head of list N.1, seems to be a serious candidate for chiefdom.

As a result of the discussion that took place, it was decided that this question be put to the vote with secret balloting. The result was seven votes for constituting the body and three for delay.

The absence of the redoubtable L.L. would incline the balance in favor of the senior member, H.H., but there are at least two recalcitrants with knowledge of the past. They have not forgotten that the Sanhedrin of the ancient Hebrews would annul the death penalty (which it pronounced extremely rarely anyhow) only when the decision was taken unanimously. If unanimity cancels even death, which even The One Above cannot annul, what about its power to cancel a poor temporary position made to the measure of earthly temporalities? Not for unanimity, it might be said, was the chosen people chosen! Unanimity is suspect. Mr. Herman Halpern might be unanimously chosen President by Right of Age, but when it comes to being the President of the United Factions of Burdujeni, things won't work out unanimously—not ever, not no how! That would be an affront. It would mean we should consider the members of the Worthy Community dopes, or worse than that!

The Israelite Senate of Burdujeni elects, then, "through acclamation," two vice-presidents—a procedure probably motivated by the fact that there are two VPs, and there's no danger of their being in agreement. The voting continues, however, with real seriousness when it comes the turn of the cashier and controller.

A close, really Jewish fight for the job of controller! To summarize the proceedings: Although there had been three candidates registered, there was also, however, on the part of the voters, one very "non-Jewish" abstention (if only to make stereotyping impossible).

~

The chosen one, however, Mr. Shulim Braunshtein, seemed to anyone who knew him the least suited to that traditional post.

It shows even in the calligraphy of the minutes, where it is not hard to recognize the beautiful handwriting in Eminescu's style,[3] with the superb curves and variations of Shulim the bookseller, son of the bookseller Avram Braunshtein and brother of the "lady bookseller de luxe," Janeta, called Sheina, which is to say Gorgeous, Mamma mia. After the war and after Transnistria, where his parents died, which is to say my grandparents, the temporary "controller" from Burdujeni, frightened of the popular democratic paradise installed in

3 Mihai Eminescu (1850–1889), a writer in several genres, generally considered Romania's most important Romantic poet.

Romania, would carry on his profession as bookseller and newspaper warehouseman in Israel.

His sister, Janeta Braunshtein, had met, several years before the elections of 1936—also on a July day, on the Fălticeni Suceava bus—the elegant and sober accountant from the sugar factory in Itscani, who would become her husband. Mother would bear Janeta's new name, Braunshtein, adopted through marriage, until 1988, when she was buried in the place where she was born.

~

In the great fratricidal and factional struggle of the agitated 1928–1936 period—when, to the rising East and to the setting West of Burdujeni, the future planetary fire storms smoldered—the elections of July 1936 attest, in writing, to the presence in those places for an age, or more (who can tell?), of the numerous Braunshtein family.

They had spread out over the whole country, these people named Barid, Riemer, Leibovi, Kotter, Braunshtein, Segal, Pisani: members and descendants of the clan. Janeta, Rebeca, and Shulim, and Abram Braunshtein, their father, were located there, in the self-same place, consumed by a feverish normalcy that would soon shatter under the wrath of which Wechsler-Fundoianu-Fondane had felt a presentiment, along with so many others. In 1936, the year of my birth, they had sent their candidate to public office. Uncle Shulim, with his neurotic kindness and his desire to appease everyone, did not seem at all suitable for the much-disputed function of controller. A conscientious man, however—that, yes. Shulim Braunshtein, the bookseller, had presented himself at that meeting, despite the fact that his sister, then convalescent, still found herself in danger of death. She had just given birth to a boy, about a week before, on July 19th: a difficult birth in which mother and child had stood under the sign of death.

~

On the date of the meeting, July 28, 1936, the covenant of mutilation had been committed already, though. The *bris*, the circumcision, had been carried out. The deep, irrevocable sign of old Abraham, whose name my grandfather bore with modesty and pride, had been dug into Grandfather's own body; the covenant with God had been imposed on me without my being able to protest other than through inarticulate roars. The ugly mite had decided with difficulty to abandon the placenta. When he left it, the reason for his hesitation was plain to be seen: he hadn't much chance of survival. So he had to be kept for days and nights in an incubator to catch his breath, if he had any. The family no longer hoped for anything beyond saving the mother. Yes, the mother had escaped with her life. She had not recovered, though; the danger had not in fact, disappeared. Only old Avram could not contain himself for happiness. He was a grandfather again—and through Sheina, his favorite daughter. And a beautiful one—everyone knows Sheina derives from *schön, Schein, scheinen, Schönheit.* Grandfather was the only one who believed in the new citizen's survival. Convinced that a new Noah would live, he wanted him to be named after his brother, Noah, who'd died not long before. "If he's got nails, he'll live," Grandfather Avram remarked calmly and in his low, soft voice.

Surprisingly, the starveling in the incubator already had nails. Little, bitsy, minuscule, invisible—the nails, though, of survival.

Sonata in Auschwitz

By Luize Valente

Excerpt from a Novel

Translated from Portuguese *by Claudio Bethencourt*

1. Berlin, April 1999

It is a special date for the Germans. After decades, Berlin is once again the capital of Germany, now reunited. It is a special day for me, too. I'm going to meet my father's grandmother: my great-grandmother Frida. The re-inauguration of the Reichstag, the German parliament, happens to be on the day of my arrival.

It is not the first time that I've been to Berlin, although it feels like it. Right after the fall of the Berlin wall, I and some other students from Lisbon's Law School made our way to this city. Our professor from Criminal Law organized this informal trip because he is keen on the German legal system that has greatly influenced the Portuguese one. He used to call me "*Hafner*," the little German. At that time, I was barely twenty and such words neither bothered me nor affected my existence. I've never told my father about that. Under no circumstances was I to speak about his German past. I never dared to joke with him about that.

My father claims to be a full-blooded Portuguese man. He loves this country more than anyone who was born here. He was only five when he came to live in Portugal and he quickly assimilated the country's language and culture. He claims not to remember a word of German. Actually, he has never been keen on learning it. He met my mother in college in the early sixties and was smitten. She fell in love with him, too. They graduated from law school, fought side by side against Salazar's military regime, and got persecuted and exiled to Mozambique, where my brother and I were born. He in 1968, and I in 1970. They named me Amalia in honor of my maternal grandmother. They were not fond of *fado*, the traditional Portuguese music. I, on the other hand, love to listen to the melancholic guitar tunes expressing pain and sorrow. Ironically, I learned to appreciate this kind of music thanks to Amalia, my grandmother.

She also taught me how to play the piano, one of my greatest passions. We came to Portugal in 1974, a few months after the Carnation revolution. It was around Christmas. My father got naturalized and was able to exercise his voting rights.

I never had any contact with my paternal grandparents, Gretl and Helmut. We settled in Lisbon whereas they lived in a small town in the Algarve. In fact, the first and only time I met them was when we returned from Maputo. As I recall, my brother and I were building a castle on the living room rug when someone's fist slammed down on a table. A few minutes later, my mother quickly rushed over, picked us up by the arms, and whispered: "Wave goodbye to Grandma and Grandpa, we are heading home." Had it been any other occasion, we probably would have pouted, but at that moment we realized something serious had happened. We just got up and left. Never again did we see our grandparents Gretl and Helmut. I erased their images from my mind. No one ever dared to speak a word about that day.

As I mentioned earlier, no one ever speaks about the past in my house. From a very early age, I realized that Germany and the Holocaust were simply topics not to be discussed. It was not exactly taboo, but it was unpleasant. At school, there were no Jews. In fact, there are very few in Portugal. When my history teacher introduced the topic of World War II in class, I simply opted to stay away from it, and spent my time playing the piano, listening to music, and organizing school protests. My father, unlike other parents, encouraged me to defend my anarchistic ideas.

My dad is not aware of my rendezvous with Frida. She is turning one hundred years old in a few days. It must be exciting to have lived in the twentieth century and to reach such an old age. We spoke over the phone and arranged to meet in an elegant neighborhood in Berlin, at the bar in the Kempinski Hotel, on Kufurstendam Avenue—or simply "Kudamm" —the most exciting street on the east side of the city. I get there two hours in advance. I have enough time to go for a stroll in the wide avenue filled with designer stores, restaurants, and cafés. I look forward to seeing the sunset. Our meeting is scheduled for seven-thirty. My first trip to Berlin with my college mates flashes through my mind. I was standing in that avenue, Kudamm, in July 1990. It was an exciting trip in the heat of summer. Berlin was the capital of techno music; the techno beat was the vibrant sound in the night clubs. A wall that had been standing in the middle of the city for decades was torn down, reunifying the two sides. None of that interested me. All I wanted to do was rave the night away in the warehouses and abandoned factories that were sprawled around the city. I remember dancing all night with hundreds of people. The town was in a party spirit nine years ago. I was young and didn't have a care in the world. I was oblivious to the past.

I came back to Portugal and realized my life was rather dull and boring. I thought of living in Germany. Maybe studying music and taking a break from law school. German techno had been influenced by contemporary composers such as Stockhausen. It was different and innovative. I grew up playing classical music. I decided to apply for my German citizenship. My short field trip to Berlin had made my father resent me. He was antagonistic to my visiting Germany. I did not need his permission since I was a legal adult; however, his financing was crucial. Finally, my mother intervened and persuaded him to pay for my trip. He never gave me a good reason for not wanting me to go to Berlin. Four days in Berlin? To him, it seemed we would surely get wasted in bars, stay up all night, walk around like zombies the next day in guided tours. In the end, we would come back exhausted, longing only to sleep. We could do the same in Lisbon for less money, he reasoned, after writing out the check and then slamming the office door.

He was right. That is exactly what we did. But after coming back to Portugal, I had an overwhelming urge to live in Berlin. I don't know why. I never shared that with him. I kept my plans secret. I started taking German lessons. After studying the language for about a year, I managed to master it. I haven't stopped speaking it since. Back then, I also developed a keen interest in issues of human rights and the migration flows that resulted from the Eastern European countries opening up. I realized that my dream of giving up everything for techno music was nonsense. I really enjoyed playing classical music. But had to admit I loved my country and wanted to fight for a fairer and more egalitarian government, just like my parents did.

A decade has passed since then. I graduated and moved to a new apartment where I live alone. I got a master's and a doctorate in international law. I set up my own NGO geared towards refugees living in countries with conflicts in Africa. I am always flying to various locations, but I haven't been back to Berlin. I have returned to Germany on at least two or three other occasions, to attend conferences in other cities. My piano is still part of my daily routine and I play it whenever possible. Music is still a great passion in my life. My life, consisting of intellectual work and a few love affairs every now and then, would have remained the same had I not arrived in my parents' home unannounced one day. It was less than a month ago on a beautiful afternoon in March.

Despite not living there for a number of years, I still have the key to my parents' apartment. It is good for all of us. I watch over the property while they are away, and they let me have access to the nest whenever I need it. That afternoon, I just dropped by to see if I could find a book to lend to a friend of mine. I don't even remember the title. It was past four o'clock in the afternoon and I knew that no one would be home. My parents live in Campo de Santana, and their office is a few blocks away on Avenida Liberdade. They usually have lunch there. Cicera, the housekeeper, invariably goes to the apartment three times a week. She would come every day in the past—I mean when my brother and I still lived with our parents. Her routine is still the same: she meticulously vacuums the rooms, dusts off the furniture, and uses the dust cloth to wipe the books. Barto, our dog, passed away three years ago, but we can still feel his fur resting in each corner of the rooms. Cicera was not supposed to be working that afternoon.

I rushed into the apartment as I was in a hurry. The quiet living room helped me relax my breathing. "Hello, is anybody home?" No answer, nothing but silence. I went straight to my former bedroom. The apartment is quite spacious. There are three bedrooms and an office attached to the living room by a big exterior sliding door. The spacious common area is isolated from the bedrooms by a corridor. A telephone extension is located in the hall. As soon as I spotted the receiver, it reminded me that I had to make an appointment with my gynecologist. I had to reschedule my appointment for another day. As I picked up the receiver, I heard my father's voice. I realized he was in the office and had not noticed me come in. The office door was shut. My immediate reaction was to hang up the phone, but I hesitated for a few moments. My fingers got numb and I held my breath. My father was speaking in fluent German with a woman on the other end of line. It was my grandmother Gretl. He only addressed her by her first name.

The conversation between them was void of emotion. The tone was polite. Every now and then, the conversation would pause. I suddenly placed my hand over the phone mouthpiece to prevent them from hearing my breathing. Despite my fluent German, I was puzzled. The conversation did not make sense to me. What was happening? Who were those people I had never heard of? "Ingeborg the wife of the industrialist passed away and had no kids. Frida was alone," said Gretl, gradually disclosing the information. Her voice did not express any emotion whatsoever, and Herman seemed equally indifferent to her words. "Ingeborg was the one who emotionally supported Frida all these years." She proceeded: "Now there is only you." He remained quiet. Finally, she raised her voice as if she had lost her patience. "Herman, Frida is about to turn one hundred and she wants to see you." He gave her a curt but controlled response, as if he were speaking to one of his clients–it was quite different from the burst of anger he showed to me and my brother. My father replied: "I'm sorry Gretl, I have nothing to do with these people. I am not part of this mob." Gretl responded immediately. "Mob? How dare you speak like that! Frida wants to see you! You will never get it, will you? We are not to blame for anything! Your grandpa and your dad were officials! They just followed orders! They fought to build a better country for you." My father paused and replied: "I don't wish to argue that. Tell Frida the truth. Just say we are no longer in touch and that I abandoned the family. Just make up an excuse." However, Gretl insisted: "I just called you because Frida contacted me after all these years. She has been restless. Every night, she has a recurring nightmare about Friedrich and does not want to die before she speaks to you about him." Gretl continued in a hostile tone: "You claim to be a staunch ally of humanitarian causes. Have mercy on someone who is probably going to die soon! You think it was easy for me to pick up the phone and call you? My only son, who has not spoken to me in over twenty years? Who thinks I am to blame for a past I did not choose!" There was a brief silence after her words, but to me it seemed like hours. My father sighed and replied once again in a low but clear voice: "Gretl, I am not going to look her up, and that is that. My family is my wife and kids."

Before he hung up, Gretl made a last attempt. "Do whatever you think is right. You don't listen to others, but only to yourself. At any rate, you have to write down her number. She still lives in Berlin. Please write down her phone number. I'm going to let her know exactly what you told me. Here is her phone number in case you change your mind." She started dictating the number, pausing every now and then to make sure he was taking a note of each digit. I wasted no time and grabbed a pen from the drawer and wrote it on the back of my hand. They bid each other farewell in a frigid manner. They did not ask how the other family members were doing or mention whether they would contact each other again. I waited for them to hang up and then followed suit.

My first impulse was to get into my father's office and lash out at him with a bunch of questions: "Who are you, really? Why did you hide your German past? Why didn't you tell us about Frida? Who are Ingeborg and

Friedrich?" But I restrained myself from doing that. I simply picked up my bag and quietly left.

A month has passed since that afternoon, and here I am in Berlin. I am about to meet Frida in a few minutes. My father never found out that I was in the family apartment that afternoon. He has no clue that I called his grandmother and set up a meeting with her. I rush towards the Kempinski Hotel, hoping to reach there in a few strides. The closer I get to the hotel, the more I am gripped by fear. But I am not turning back now. I long to know the past, even though I know it cannot be changed.

2.

The Kempinski Hotel was a landmark for the city of Berlin. It was also a landmark for Frida. It stood on the corner of Kufurstendamm and Fasenenstrasse, a few meters away from her former house. She still spoke about this site as "her building" although she no longer lived there. Despite the bombing in World War II, it was one of the few constructions that remained intact among the rubble. This is where Kudamm is now. Now Frida lives nearby in a more modest residence. It is about two hundred meters from the hotel's entrance, next to the railway lines. She doesn't mind that. She just wants to be close to "Kempi," the place where, before the war and the city's downfall, she used to enjoy herself. She still goes there once or twice a week to have lunch. It is a way to revisit her past, a reminder that the world was the block where she lived.

Frida was sitting at the table in the corner when Amalia arrived. She spotted her granddaughter at once. She was nothing short of exquisite–a graceful, delicate beauty. Her resemblance to Friedrich was striking. True, her great-granddaughter's features were identical to hers, as well. She stood up, leaning against the table. They greeted each other with a handshake. Actually, Frida wanted to embrace her, but restrained herself.

"You are Herman's daughter." She spoke with a tremulous voice. "I'm sorry that the last time I saw your father he was barely five." She paused for a moment. "You might even be a grandmother, too. . . . Do you have children?"

Amalia shook her head as she moved towards the chair opposite Frida. Frida touched her gently and pointed to the chair next to her. "Sit next to me. Age takes its toll on sight and hearing."

Amalia sat down and grinned slightly. She complimented Frida's looks. Now they had broken the ice.

"Your phone call caught me by surprise, especially after Gretl told me that Herman would not contact me. How is your father doing?"

Amalia opened her backpack and pulled out a recent family picture. Frida immediately pulled out the magnifying glass that was in her purse and followed Amalia's finger moving around the picture.

"This is Herman," said Amalia. She pointed at the tall, gray-haired man on the left side of the picture. "The woman standing by his side is Helena, my mother. This is me, and this is my brother Miguel. My brother has a son called Pedro."

She remained quiet for a while. Amalia's German was perfect. They soon ordered two glasses of red wine and something to eat. Their conversation flowed smoothly on trivial topics.

"Your German is fantastic!" Frida mentioned.

Amalia spoke about her keen interest in the language, her previous visits to Berlin right after the fall of the wall, her work as a lawyer, her passion for music, and finally her life in Portugal. They had barely started drinking when Frida told her about the Kempi's history. This hotel was the biggest restaurant in Berlin before the war. There were at least four hundred seats to accommodate patrons. The reconstruction in the fifties turned the location into a luxury hotel on the west side of the city. Despite the city's division, the wall had not yet been erected at that time.

"This was a sign of Berlin's rebirth from the rubble," she added.

Frida spoke of the bombings as something out of a history book. She did not mention the horror, the anguish, the relief that she experienced to be alive and intact after each attack. The buzz that echoed in her ears, the momentary deafness, the soundless screams, the begrimed faces and agonizing looks. She did not speak about the rapes that occurred when the Russians took over the city. She simply pointed out statistics.

"There were over three hundred bombings. Initially, they were restricted to military sites. As the war unfolded, there were civilian ones, as well. Berlin surrendered in the beginning of May, a few days before the final capitulation on May 8th."

She paused for a moment. That day would always remind her of her husband and what he had done. However, that would be discussed another time.

"The devastation on all sides was palpable," she continued. "The population had left the city over those six years. The main Allies, the United States, Great Britain, Russia, and France, decided to divide the city into four sections and manage them jointly, but that did not work. In the beginning of the sixties, the wall was built, making a clear division between the socialist and capitalist sides."

There was no dialogue. It was a monologue. Frida spoke compulsively. All of a sudden, Amalia realized that Frida was spewing facts straight from the history books to avoid any confrontation or silences during the conversation.

"Surely you did not come here to have a history class," she said in a sterner voice. She did not sound anymore like the lady of frivolous talk. "And this is not the reason why I tried to contact Herman after so many years."

Amalia bit her lips nervously and sighed heavily. And the more Frida gazed at Amalia, the more her looks reminded her of those of Friedrich. She really missed her son. Frida had to restrain herself from embracing and kissing Amalia. Instead, she held Amalia's hands and invited her to come over to her house. Frida insisted on paying the bill. Then they stood up and walked across the bar towards the hotel lobby. Frida nodded her head to the restaurant staff as she and Amalia headed to the street. Her right arm leaning on her cane while the left one leaned on Amalia.

~

At seven thirty-five, I find myself arriving at the Kempinski bar, five minutes late. The bar has just opened. The place is still empty except for the table against the wall.

There she is. She is turning one hundred in a few days. "A century," she told me on the phone. The image stuns me for a few minutes. I allow it to be etched in my memory. She hasn't caught a glimpse of me yet. I manage to watch her without her noticing me. The silver hair—definitely blonde in the past—is in a bun. I spot some strands of loose hair neatly placed. She surely fixed her hair this way. She's managed to keep good posture despite her age and there's a slight curve on her spine. She is wearing a pastel-colored outfit with a beautiful white scarf wrapped around her neck to match the tones of the spring season. An aristocratic air lingers around her and in her posture.

My father somehow resembles Frida. I do, too. Despite the fact that he is blonde and I am brunette, our facial features are quite similar. Once she spots me, she immediately stands up. I can hardly believe she is turning a hundred years old. I would have guessed she was in her eighties. She asks me to sit next to her. I promptly tell her she looks much younger than her real age. She says that the secret to looking younger is to start the day by having a glass of warm water with a squeeze of lime every day, but on an empty stomach. It is equally important to go for a forty- or fifty-minute walk, regardless of the season—summer or winter.

I cast a glance at her ear and spot a hearing aid attached to it. The fair skin with dark spots has wrinkles more from expressiveness than from the passing of time. Her skin looks so soft that it makes me want to touch it. Her strong voice muffled by a low pitch makes me pay closer attention to the way she speaks. The sound is audible. In general, people who have hearing problems tend to speak louder. Frida starts a conversation about general issues, and I only take part in it when she asks me something. I don't care for chat. My focus is on watching her. She is my great-grandmother. She is almost one hundred years old. I probably would have lived to be a hundred not knowing about her existence, had I not intercepted that call. I do not believe in coincidences. Frida is the guardian of my history, yet she relentlessly speaks about history. I can tell she is fully familiar with Kempi–this is how she refers to the hotel–by the way the staff treats her. They are so kind to her. I don't care what she talks about. My ears relish just listening to her voice.

The food in front of us is practically untouched. So is the wine. As she reports some of the events of her life, I can see the hint of sadness in her eyes, despite the impersonal manner in which she speaks. I wonder when we will actually get to know each other. Who are Ingeborg and Friedrich? Frida seems to read my thoughts. "You did not come here to have a history class. . . . Well, I did not contact Herman after so many years on a whim," she explains. She invites me to go over to her apartment in the neighborhood.

We ask for the bill. I reluctantly allow her to pay it. I help her stand up. She is thin and wears long pants and slippers to avoid any kind of accident. She is slightly shorter than me. I assume she was probably one meter seventy centimeters in height, or more, when she was young. As we exit the hotel, I let her hold onto my arm and take small but accurate steps. The other hand is equipped with a cane that helps her keep her balance.

She explains to me that she would like to show me something before we head to her house. "Do you know Paris? Kudamm is regarded as the Champs-Élysées for Berliners." She says this with a restrained smile as she spews out a lot of information regarding the wide avenue where, in the 1920s, Berlin's night life pulsated. She brags about the charming neighborhood of Charlottenberg, the urban zoo, and finally the Gedachtniskirsche, the church that never got to be restored. The ruins at the end of the street are a permanent reminder of the destruction caused by the war. "As if we needed them to remind us of the war," she says in a whisper. We spend a few minutes in complete silence, looking at the damaged tower. I want to know what's going through her mind. Frida actually saw the bombings; and such memories haunt her, as I heard from my grandmother Gretl on the phone, speaking of Frida's terrible nightmares. Who are these people who my father erased from my life?

I never dared to think of having relatives linked to the Nazi past. That may have been out of fear. Hearing my grandmother Gretl say that my grandfather was just a Nazi official who simply followed orders had not made me dive into the issue. But now that I stand before Frida, the "official" carries different weight and meaning. I am now side by side with my great-grandmother who lived and experienced the horrors of that war. Here lies my past.

The Washerwoman's Daughter

By Eliya Rafael Karmona

Excerpt from a Novel

Translated from Judeo-Spanish (Ladino) *by Michael Alpert*

"Where is my father's money?" said Léontine to her brother. "My father left a lot of money. He was a carpenter, very skilled, and when he died he left a large inheritance. What happened to all that money?"

"But I married you off, dear Léontine," said Merovak to his sister. "I gave you a big dowry and I found you a husband, as was right."

"It was worthwhile giving away so much money to get a thieving husband, a drunk of a husband, was it? It would have been better for you to find me a craftsman who knew how to earn his bread with the sweat of his brow and would always live honorably. But now, poor me, I'm always on tenterhooks. Every minute I think they've arrested my husband and have taken him off to prison and sentenced him. He's already served two stretches of a year each and God save us from a third one."

"Something's got into you today, Léontine. It's not like you. The husband I chose for you is a good young man. If I had given you a husband who worked with his hands, he wouldn't earn much and you would not live as well as you do now. What do you lack? He earns lots of cash and satisfies all your wishes as soon as you ask for them."

"That's true, but in the end, what will become of that thief? Isn't it jail? Isn't it punishment? And what good is it for me to have a husband if I can be sure that he's going to arrested and jailed when I least expect it? Really I don't understand your idea. The two of you could easily invest the money you have today in an honest business. You've been in that trade for so many years, and you've got money and you can begin another business. Stop that wretched thievery which will bring you down one day."

"My dear sister, do you think we can do something different now? Impossible! We are used to making several thousand francs all in one go, so we couldn't possibly start a business making small sums."

"Léontine, open the door!" A voice was heard from the window. It was Armand the thief, Léontine's husband, who was back from his latest job. The woman opened the door and the husband entered, puffing and exclaiming at the same time: "Léontine, be happy. You want to have babies and I've brought you a very beautiful one who will amuse you when I am away from home."

"Oh! A child!" exclaimed Léontine, taking it from her husband's arms. "Where does it come from? Did you steal it?"

"No, darling. Let's go inside and I'll tell you." The husband and wife went to the room with Merovak, who sat down beside his associate and brother-in-law. The latter said to him: "Merovak, God has brought us a child."

"How did this come about?" asked Léontine and Merovak in astonishment.

"Well, last night, I'd gone around to get some tools to get into the house of the famous Count Gustave Talmiri. The waiter in the café where we were sitting has a brother who works in the house, and he promised to introduce me to his brother. I think we can come to an agreement that this brother will open the door at midnight. These lads from the provinces haven't seen much money and when I promise to grease his hand with a few thousand francs he'll accept the arrangement I'm offering."

"Armand!" said Léontine. "You know how I worry. I beg you, tell me who this child is."

"Well, I had left the café to go home. It was already past midnight. In the streets I walked through, there was almost nobody. I was walking fast so as to get home quicker, when my eyes suddenly saw something white on a bench in the street. I was curious to see what it was. I went up to the bench and saw this baby, left there by heaven knows who. Now, my dear Léontine, change its clothes because they must be damp from the night dew. Put what you want on it and tomorrow I'll buy everything that the baby requires."

While the baby cried now and then, Léontine began to take off its swaddling clothes and the two men began to examine its face, for it was very pretty.

Hardly had the woman taken off the swaddling clothes when she felt something hard. She picked it up. It was a large, thick envelope with these words written on it in big letters:

TO THE PERSON WHO RESCUES THIS CHILD

The two men swiftly opened the envelope and found a letter and forty banknotes, each of a thousand francs.

"Oh!" cried Merovak, "we're rich!"

Armand put the money in his inside pocket and began to read the letter aloud.

"Dear Rescuer,

I leave my baby to the mercy of somebody, but I don't want it to be looked after for nothing, so with this envelope I am leaving the sum of forty thousand francs to maintain this child until the age of twenty. As soon as he reaches that age, I ask you to tell me by letter addressed to RD, Poste Restante, Paris. You will be rewarded for your care of my son. Certain as I am that this child will be well looked after and raised, I thank in advance the person who becomes my son's guardian."

"This is good," said Armand. "We will bring this child up properly. When he is twenty years old, if we are rich, we shan't tell him, and if we're poor it will be a good way of solving our problem."

He put away the letter carefully and the two brothers-in-law, Armand and Merovak, left Léontine to change the baby's clothes and began to talk about the matter of Count Gustave Talmiri.

"There isn't much to think about," said Armand. "He lives at number 19 Rue Aubert. Once we make the arrangement with the house servant, everything is easy. We'll wait for two or three days. That café waiter I told you about is going to introduce me to his brother, and I think I'll be able to carry out the plan successfully."

"Look at this beautiful baby," said Léontine to Armand. "Although he's wearing just bedsheets, he looks so pretty. Who knows how lucky he'll be?"

"Is it a boy?" asked Merovak.

"Yes, a boy, and just born. Of course, he needs to be fed so, first of all, go and get me a wet nurse, quickly, and find a nanny."

"That's my job," said Merovak. "I'll go and find you a wet nurse at once and tomorrow I'll be able to find a nanny."

"Since you're going out," said Armand to his brother-in-law, "get two *okas* of wine and an *oka* of ribs to roast. Last night we thought we had no money and poverty was staring us in the face. Now that the Master of the World has taken pity on us, we should eat and drink and praise His name."

"Bravo, Armand, I had the same idea. The innkeeper where we drink every night has got a delicious white wine. I'll buy some and we shall have a good time tonight."

Merovak left, and Armand and Léontine stayed indoors looking closely at the baby. "What name shall we give him?" the woman asked her husband.

"This baby has brought us a fortune, hasn't he, Léontine?"

"You're right."

"Well then, I'm going to call him Fortunato."

"It's rather a long name."

"Long or short, I like it."

"If you like it, that's what we'll call him."

Merovak arrived then with everything they had told him to buy.

The meat had just been roasted, and the three people whom our readers have already met sat down to eat heartily, drank deeply, and then went to bed.

A Place Nowhere

By Birte Kont

Excerpt from a Novel

Translated from Danish *by Nina Sokol*

It was the last class that Tuesday. Danielsen, our history teacher, entered the classroom and put down his briefcase. Went to stand in front of the lectern and looked across the classroom. Then he turned toward me and said loud enough for everyone to hear it, "You'd better skip the class today because we're going to be talking about the history of the Jewish people."

He didn't say that! Yes, he did! No, did he really say that?

In earlier times, I would immediately have gotten up from my chair. Would have bowed my head and dragged myself across the classroom hoping that the floor would open up and swallow me.

Now I dug my feet into the floor and moved all the way back in my chair, could feel the hard wood against my back. Then I folded my arms across my chest and gazed at the little man who looked like he had just shrunk and vanished inside his suit. And in a shrill voice that surprised me, I said, "I'm allowed to know what happened. I am, after all, Jewish!"

Then I suddenly realized it: the Jew in me had jumped out of my mouth and was now standing as large as life in front of the entire class!

No one said a thing. My heart was pounding. Everyone turned around. Everyone looked. at me. Marianne, who sat in front of me, placed her hand on my arm.

Danielsen looked at me through his round horn-rimmed spectacles and continued to clear his throat over and over. You could never be sure where you had him. When we hadn't properly prepared for the lesson he would bark like a little terrier. But he was also the kind who would say, with fervor in his voice and an eagerness that would make the spit fly from his mouth in every direction, that we were never to drink hot tea without first blowing on it! Marianne's mother, who was a nurse, had let it slip that he recently had been to a rather nasty medical examination.

My blood was boiling and for the first time I wasn't the one who looked away.

Then he turned on his heels and went up to the chalkboard and pulled down the world map:

Babylon. The Roman destruction of the temple in Jerusalem. The Jewish uprising on Masada. The Crusades and the banishment of the Jews from Spain. The pogroms in Russia and Poland. Hitler and Nazism.

Uncertainty could prick like the cactus on my windowsill. I had always carried this uncertainty in my body. A word here. A word there. Words that didn't make sense. Words that didn't have anything to do with me. Words that had everything to do with me? Uncertainty became certainty. Nightmare became reality. That had to be why it practically put my mind at ease to learn that Jews across the globe for two thousand years had been blamed for all the evilness that had happened in the world. That had to be why the knowledge that Jews everywhere had become everyone else's scapegoat gave me a feeling of near triumph.

But a second later that feeling of greatness reversed into the very opposite.

"For no other reason than that they happened to be Jews," Danielsen said.

Now he was referring to the Night of the Broken Glass. It had that name because the streets were flooded with shattered glass after the Nazis had ravaged Jewish shops and synagogues. Then Hitler and the Nazis seized power across Europe. The raids. The outbreak of the Second World War. The concentration camps.

Danielsen said that it was most likely due to coalition policies that what happened to the Jews in the rest of Europe didn't happen to the Danish Jews. "At least we know that almost all the Danish Jews managed to flee to Sweden during the autumn of 1943. And the fishermen risked their lives when they sailed the Jews across the Sound."

When the bell rang, Agnete, Marianne, and several of the others formed a circle around me. Her eyes shining, Agnete's lips moved as she tried to tell me something. But my thoughts had already left in advance and were on their way home.

Danielsen came over, too. He placed a hand on my shoulder and in a low voice asked me to follow him. I put the history book in my school bag, waved to Agnete and Marianne, and trudged behind him in the hallway. Some meters further on he opened a door to the back staircase through which I also slipped before the door shut with a clicking sound. All at once the steps out there seemed never-ending. I dragged myself up the stairs, leaned out from the banister, and looked up into a landscape of glass, steel, and concrete. Surfaces and edges, windowpanes and bars spread out, crisscrossing one another as in an abstract piece of art.

I winced, and when I turned my head and looked down into the abyss of the staircase my head began to swim. Still, I continued, placing one foot in front of the other, going up and up following in the heels of Danielsen. He stopped at a landing and opened an orange door which led to a passageway with more doors. They were blue. He selected one and I followed him across the threshold. Were there more levels of hallways and rooms one after another? The interior of the school, the assembly hall, from the ground floor all the way up to the glass roof with balconies surrounding it on every floor and doors leading to the classrooms, was like the stomach of a gigantic whale. This was where we would meet for the morning song. By and by we would separate between the ribs of the whale until the last bell of the afternoon would make us ride its wave and wash us back to the world. I was now in a small office. Danielsen pointed to the armchair by the window and asked me to take a seat while he went out to get something.

I looked around. There was a bright-colored poster hanging on the wall above the bookshelf. Chagall, it said in black letters. I recognized the motif. A couple floating as one body in the air across the roofs of the city's houses, away from Vitebsk?

Danielsen returned with two steaming cups of tea. He handed me one of the cups and asked me to be sure to . . . but I already knew that.

Then he sat at his writing desk and cleared his throat. He was sorry about the unpleasantness he had had to confront me with that day; he really had assumed that I already knew all about it. He blew on his tea and took a sip. But then he'd seen by the look on my face that it must have been the first time I had ever heard about it. He was sorry about that. And if there was anything he could do for me while he was still there at the school . . . He was waiting to get admitted—yes, he was soon to be hospitalized.

He had been talking into space. Now he opened a drawer and took out a notebook. Turned around and handed it to me.

I got on my feet and took the notebook.

He was still looking at me.

"If you could write a little bit down, in fact, that's what I usually do myself," he said, giving me a small smile, "just some scattered impressions. That which you heard today must have . . ."

He interrupted himself and remained silent for a little bit. Meanwhile I sat gripping the mug to warm up my freezing fingers.

Then he spoke again. As a history teacher he couldn't imagine parents—not to say anything bad about mine; they had no doubt had their reasons—he couldn't imagine parents who would allow their child to grow up outside of history, so to speak.

"Historyless." He turned the word in his mouth showing clear signs of unpleasantness, cleared his throat, and continued, "To be historyless! That is like a vessel without a compass. History itself has taught us that! And if there's anything you ever want to talk with me about, just let me know!"

The last words were said with the same fervor as when he spoke about tea.

I took a different route home. Everything was covered in frosty snow. The sunlight sparkled in the trees, through the hedges, and on the rooftops. The snow had transformed the residential neighborhood into a dazzling white fairy tale landscape. When we said goodbye, Danielsen had said he would inform my mother about what had happened today. He even had the feeling that my parents had been merely waiting for the right moment to broach the topic. And he said he hoped—giving my hand a warm squeeze—that his effort would prove useful and beneficial for the conversation that undoubtedly lay ahead between me and my parents.

Pogroms and gas chambers. The Jews' escape to Sweden. As I tried to transform the bustle of thoughts that filled my skull into questions I could ask, I crossed the park and was now standing in front of the stream. Something was lying on the lumpy ice and I had to squat to see what it was. It was a dead bird, a sparrow. It lay on its side a little distance from the bank. I reached out for the dead body of the bird. It had frozen into the ice. Only its head and one of its wings was sticking up.

That evening Father sat at the dining table looking at some of his old photographs. I walked over to him. Looking at the furrows on the skin of his face, I sought traces of the things I had heard about at school that day. Right now, it was all distant and unreal. In front of him lay a pile of photographs which he had spread across the table.

"Look!" he said as he pointed to a picture of some racing cyclists, "there I am, and can you see who the others are?"

"Isn't it Kay Werner and Evan Klamer?" I asked.

"Yes!" he nodded, smiling up to both ears. "And who is he? The one standing next to me and smiling?"

"It resembles Gunnar Nu Hansen."

"It is Gunnar Nu! Ah yes, that was a great period!"

Mother entered the dining room.

"Are you sitting there again looking at those old pictures?"

I turned around and looked at her. But there were no signs of history to be seen on her face, either.

Night after night after that, I waited for Mother and Father to call for me and say that there was something important they wanted to talk with me about. I would secretly study their faces for signs, for a crack in our everyday life. And Helle's. She had to know. My hope died each day that passed. Monday night Mother and Helle went to the hospital to visit Grandma. I realized that what I was waiting for would never happen.

But then Father called for me. I was to immediately come into the living room and, with my heart pounding all the way up in my throat, I ran in there.

He was standing in front of the TV, pointing at the screen and saying that something would be coming on which I *must* see: sex education.

Then he left the living room. A little later his footsteps could be heard going down the cellar staircase.

I trotted back to my room and sat down at my writing desk. Danielsen's notebook lay in front of me and on the first page I wrote in capital letters: *NORA!*

~

Tikøbgade Street, number 8, first floor to the left, Tove had said. That was where Nora lived with Mikkel, as the baby boy was called. It was in Nørrebro, according to the map. And I was now on my way there.

For weeks I had biked into Vesterbro. Always during the afternoon when people returned from work. I always made sure to be back home before my parents returned from the shop. The streets all looked like one another—narrow, dark and worn streets where the houses loomed, and where it teemed with dogs and cats, small shops, and all different kinds of people.

I wheeled my bike through the crowd, down one street and up another, dizzy from all the exhaust coming from the cars and all the noise. The clamor as from a thousand voices echoed in my head. I had a vague memory of where the street was but had of course forgotten the name of it. The only thing I had to go on was a mere mailbox. A mailbox where the "B" was missing.

Tilkøbgade was a dead end street. Number 8 was at the very bottom, by the elevated tracks which passed close to the house at the top. I parked my bike against an iron grille that surrounded a small garden for the apartment on the ground floor. Inside the grille a baby carriage stood on the grass.

I went into the hallway, took a deep breath, and rang the doorbell.

Nora's face lit up when she saw that it was me. But as she stood there in her tight brown dress, her arms hanging down along her sides, she practically became one with the battered, brown-colored door frames.

"Well, I'll say!" she said with a dry snap in her voice. "Sure, you're not too refined to come out here?" She leaned a little forward, pointing toward the baby carriage in the yard. "In your circles that sort of thing is gotten rid of!"

"Nora, if you only knew . . . they know nothing about me coming here, Tove was the one who gave me your address."

Then she pulled me inside and hugged me. "Sit down in the living room! I can hear Mikkel's awake, I'll just get him."

The living room faced the street and was airy. There wasn't that much furniture. Through the windowpane I saw Nora pick up Mikkel from the baby carriage. On a shelf next to the window there were a number of photographs. Next to a photo of Lasse there was one of Helle and me.

Mikkel had been given something to eat and was sitting on the floor playing. Nora and I sat down on the couch. I could no longer withhold the words. "Did my mother and father also go to Sweden?"

Nora nodded. "They were lucky. Not everyone managed to get across."

She lit a cigarette, blew out some smoke and said, "Shortly after the government was dissolved, the country was in a state of emergency. That was in 1943, at the start of September. At the start of October, the Germans let it leak out that they were planning a campaign against the Jews. There were raids, and a number of Jews were caught and sent to Theresienstadt. Your family doctor hid many Jewish families in his office at night. Including yours. And along the entire east coast of Zealand the fishermen organized major relief work by sailing Jews to Sweden, several thousands." Nora took in another whiff of smoke. "Then you could once again be proud to be a Dane."

"But how . . . ?"

"Your mother and father were told to drive to a harbor someplace up north. A boat would be waiting for them there. But when they got up there they got quite a shock. The fishermen weren't willing to let your sister go with them. You must understand that it could have jeopardized the lives of everyone on the boat. If they had gotten caught, that is. But your mother refused to leave Helle behind, she was only six months old. So they gave her an injection. But there were many who weren't allowed to take their babies with them. Your cousin Ralfi had to live with a Danish family who hid him."

"Cousin Ralfi had to be hidden? Do you know he died?"

Nora breathed in as she said yes.

For a moment none of us said anything. Then she continued, "It was all very dramatic. As they were crossing, the engine suddenly died and Helle woke up and started screaming. The Germans were in the vicinity, you see, so the others threatened to throw her overboard." Nora crushed her cigarette in the ashtray. She lit another cigarette and drew the smoke into her lungs.

"Yes, your eyes are so big, but they managed to get across, and later got to Stockholm. Then, after the war, it all came out what had happened to the Jews all across Europe."

"Where do you know all that from?"

"Your mother had been so strong and brave through the whole ordeal. But when the nightmare was over she broke down. The doctor sent her to a sanatorium, a place in Jutland. Meanwhile I moved in with your father and sister. She was about two years old. I got close to your father back then." She paused before continuing. "He hadn't had an easy life with his father, your grandfather."

"I never knew him."

"Did you know your father had an Orthodox upbringing?"

"My father?"

Nora coughed a few times and nodded. "When your mother returned from the sanatorium, they agreed to put it all behind them. The future was all that mattered. Your father built up a new business and your mother helped him. But she was still very fragile and I stayed with them for a while. Mrs. Sand also came over to help them get their day-to-day routine to hang together. Then you came, the new little hope of the family."

Nora sent me a little, crooked smile.

"But you weren't like your sister. And if anyone was having a hard time of it, then it was her. You couldn't help it, of course, but Helle felt that you took all the attention away from her, so your mother tried to compensate for that.

You were pretty and extroverted and she was shy and toothless. She has been jealous of you, always."

"Helle?"

"Yes, you were a rebel no one could get to shut up. You asked questions and demanded answers. No, they couldn't get you to shut up . . ."

"But how . . .?"

Nora took a last whiff of the cigarette bud and crushed it in the ashtray with an impatient movement of her hand. "What could you possibly know? No one ever told you anything." She took another cigarette from the package, held it in her hand as she sat looking at it. Then she lifted her gaze. "But that which had once been dangerous was no longer dangerous. Still, the fear remained in them. The fear that your mother fed your sister. In your mother's eyes, Helle would always be a vulnerable little baby whom she would have to protect with her very life. She has never properly let go of that."

I nodded. My whole body felt aflame. "I know that. Helle is my mother's right hand. And do you know what? Marianne from my class is going to sew my bat mitzvah dress. Last week I tried it on with the pins still in it. Mother and Helle came into my room and lavishly praised Marianne. But when I left the room with her and came back, I saw Helle bent over my writing desk. She turned around and said that Marianne had written my essay. Of course, I said that wasn't true but she kept saying that it wasn't my handwriting, I wrote in script writing. I said that I was practicing writing like Marianne, her "j"s and "g"s had loops, and you don't use that in script writing! And do you know what, Nora? She wouldn't believe me! I was so angry that I stamped my feet on the floor. But *I'm* the one who's helping Marianne with spelling and commas. Her grades in written Danish have gone up from a 7 to a 9 +! And the worst of it is," my voice cracked, "my mother . . . immediately took Helle's side. She didn't even ask me!"

Nora had been sitting, patiently listening, holding her cigarette in her hand. When I paused, she let out a sigh of frustration and lit the cigarette. Then she said, "That's nothing to make your teeth clatter. The most important thing is to have a clear conscience, that you can look yourself in the eye. Because if you can do that, then you can look the whole world in the eye. Remember that!"

Mikkel came over and whimpered. Nora put down the smoking cigarette on the edge of the ashtray and lifted him up on her knee. Cradled him in her arms.

"Incomprehensible, isn't it?" she said to him. "Here you are, this beautiful baby, and your father doesn't know you at all."

"Who is he, Nora? Mikkel's father?" I asked and couldn't make out the glance she gave me.

"I might tell you some day. But for now, all I'll say is that when Mikkel grows up, one day he'll have to make a choice. If he wants to amount to anything, then he should choose his father's surname. But if he'd rather live it up, it would probably be wisest to take an ordinary name like Jensen. There are advantages to everything!" Nora said and laughed. Then she grew serious again. "That story has done more damage to the soul than your parents would care to admit. I've always said to them that they have an obligation to tell you kids your family history. But they believed it was safest for you not to know."

When I got home I went to the bathroom. I turned the key in the lock that I was only allowed to lock if I wasn't going to take a bath. Safest for us not to know! My knees were shaking and I sank down on the bathmat. Could I trust Nora? Had my mother pushed Nora away because she had talked about the war? Or were there other reasons? When I asked Nora what was going on between her and Mother, she said, "It's not the first time we've been on bad terms. I've always been frank with her. But your mother's always come around again. And I'm sure she will this time, too, if your father lets her. I grabbed hold of her when you were going to the Jewish school. They shouldn't take you out of that school again! Nothing would be gained from that other than that you'd get confused. But your father insisted on it. You and your sister were to be nothing but Danish."

"But that's not how it is at all."

"But you have to understand that they felt they had to keep a low profile after what they went through. All they wanted was to forget about it. They partied. Good grief, how they partied! Your mother was out showing off her ocelot coat! But the fear was in their bodies and that wouldn't go away on its own."

Nora fell silent and shifted on the couch.

I said, "Whenever I come home too late, Mother always looks like I've risen from the dead. And once when *they* didn't come home at the time they normally do, I ran all the way down to the big intersection to look for them. What if they never came back home? When I saw Father turn at the corner I started to cry. 'How foolish! A big girl like you!' my mother said. Then I was ashamed of myself. They could drive off again, as far as I was concerned! And do you know what, Nora? When it's dark, Helle doesn't dare walk alone from the bus stop by herself. Then I bike down to the bus stop to get her."

"Yes, that's exactly what I'm saying. You're going to manage just fine!" Nora said, lit another cigarette, and sat for a long time staring at the smoke. Then she got up and walked out of the living room.

Shortly afterwards she came back with a bottle in her hand. Poured a little into her glass and emptied it.

"'I guess we can talk about it,' I said to your mother. But she wouldn't speak. She heard what you and I were talking about that night. But she's sure to come around again!" Nora said as though to convince herself. Put out the cigarette in the ashtray and poured herself another glass of schnapps.

"You know your father's principles, he won't budge an inch. But one thing's for sure, he's got the right connections! The next day he called your mother to say that there was a two-and-a-half bedroom apartment ready for me. And then she quickly got me installed in here. She washed the entire apartment, polished all the windows. Filled my refrigerator with food. Do you have any idea what it means for someone like me to be able to say, 'My refrigerator'?" Nora looked at me with starry, shining eyes. "Your parents have always helped me. I've always paid back every dime. But ever since I've moved in I haven't heard a word from your angel of a mother! But she'll come around again." Nora's voice had grown grainy.

I was to visit Nora again. Or come by her new job—she was working at the bureau of the Danish National Archives now. Then she'd help me look for information about my family, it would be good for me to know more, she thought.

But how was I to see Nora without Mother discovering it? My angel of a mother who, as she said on the telephone, had an eye on every finger. It made me think of "The Angel of Light," which was one of the songs we sang at the morning assembly. Didn't she know that? Didn't she know that her Jewish, non-Orthodox hands had been returned to favor by the Angel of Light? And that the diamond ring that always sat on her finger had an otherworldly shine to it? "Shining color from above?" It surrounded her hands and everything they touched. In my mother's presence I would get sucked in, in my mother's presence I was trapped in a teeny, tiny, idiotic, and ignorant present. How could I not see Nora?

Without thinking about it, I had begun to undress. Got to my feet and took off my pants, socks, and underwear. Left them on the bathmat and climbed into the bathtub. Turned up the faucets, didn't put the stopper in. I lifted the shower head from its cradle, leaned my head back against the cool enamel of the bathtub, and passed the jets of water across my body. The lukewarm jets felt gentle on the skin, like the brush of an angel's wing that made me forget everything, and little by little made me float.

I closed my eyes, letting the Water Angel take me upon its wings, all the way up to "The Angel of Light."

Helle studied psychology and for several days she had been looking at me in a strange way. So one evening when we sat down for dinner I decided that I might just as well make a clean breast of it.

"I've found out where . . ."

But Helle broke in, "Mother says that you've started talking in your sleep about angels, water angels. Have you started drinking holy water instead of water from the tap?"

"Mind your own business, you fat . . .!"

"Now, now, girls!" Mother entered with a bowl of cucumber salad and sat down at the dinner table.

Helle began helping herself to the food, but continued in that teasing tone, "And I guess you don't think anyone knows your little secret!" There was a pregnant pause. "But it starts with a 'J'—here there was another such pause—"and then comes 'P' . . ." My hand squeezed the fork so hard that my knuckles turned white.

I was lying in my room. Trying to settle down and read.

The sickle moon came into view above the apple tree. I stared up at the star-filled darkness and thought about Nora. When we talked, it had all made sense in my mind. Now it was strangely unreal, as though it had absolutely nothing to do with me. Was Helle really jealous of me?

I let my fingers slide across the wall where I had fastened a postcard from Lasse with some thumbtacks. A square with plane trees. A landscape of lavender fields. He had been confirmed. In France it was called a "communion." He had sent a picture of himself where he was standing in front of the church with his broad shoulders and looking handsome in his navy colored suit. He was staying at a place for the treatment of polio and rehabilitation. His father was teaching at a school close by. Lasse wanted to study literature, he said.

The last time I took the bus to his house was shortly before I turned fourteen. The farewell made me choke. I fixed my gaze on his shirt pocket as we tried to talk as though he wasn't moving to France. He was looking forward to it.

"I'm going to see the house where Marcel Proust lived. It's a museum now. Blue. The house is in Illiers Combray." He pronounced the name in French, "Illeeyers-Combray." And with an awkward movement he placed his hand over mine. "You should come down and visit us."

But that would be inconceivable, Father said.

Nora's words returned. In my mind's eye I saw a boat that sailed from a harbor. A wake of foaming whirlpools. A sense of drowsiness settled over me, a warm wave that rolled through me. And as the warmth spread through my body, I felt something take shape in my skull, something I was to do. But just before I grasped what it was, I had fallen asleep.

Tormented, I opened my eyes. The sun was stinging. I got up and dressed. Took a mouthful of tea and walked with Agnete to school, but I didn't really wake up until later in the day.

It was Saturday afternoon. I parked my bike in the carport and locked it. When I went inside the house, Mother came out to the hallway. "Where have you been?" she asked, overly nonchalant as she looked at her reflection in the mirror and straightened her hair with both hands.

"Just out biking."

"You're lying!" She turned around and looked at me with a strange sort of delight shining in her eyes. "You were at Nora's. We saw you and followed you in the car. It's not the first time, is it? Is it?"

I looked at her without blinking. I had been to visit Nora four times, and I intended to continue doing so.

"But today was the last day you're ever visiting her, just so you know!"

I ran to the bathroom. Slammed the door behind me and turned the key.

Smash!

I decided to start with the mirror. But when I peered into it I sneered at myself. I was just about to cry.

The Researcher

By Michel Fais

Excerpt from a Novel

Translated from Greek *by Mina Karavanta*

Lieber Anschel, Lieber Franz,

I am sorry for the sudden bout of intimacy, sorry if I tired and inconvenienced you, sorry if I said anything that might have hurt your feelings or upset you.

I have been reading your work since I was twelve. If it means anything to you. I switched straight from *Mafalda* to you. Straight on. A kind of Mafalda that stood between Prague and Komotini. A six-year-old lonely girl who at times felt she was called Yulie, at times Milena, and at other times Dora. This could possibly cheer you up. I started with *The Metamorphosis.* I shed light on the pages with a little flashlight in the tent of a youth camp by the sea. The boy I had fallen for was totally ignoring me, and the so-called group activities were utterly boring, until my mother—I'd rather be silent about our Kafkaesque relations—brought me some children's books. She finally returned to Komotini with the children's books, leaving to me the book she was reading.

I was born fifty-two years after your death in a border town in northern Greece. A provincial society that, despite all the makeup of prosperity and development as time passed on, remained a depressing mud town of Christians and Muslims, but also of inconsolable Jewish ghosts at its deep core; once a fortress, a walled town of the Ottoman Empire, that once belonged to the administrative district of Andrianopolis.

For years I felt like something between an ashamed girl and a trapped animal.

Do you think that this is due to, among other things, my unfulfilled initiation ceremony into adulthood? The passage from the children's world to the adults' world that never took place because of a tongue-twister that troubled me since I was a child.

To this very day, I feel the haunting shadow of a perpetually postponed bat mitzvah.

I am sorry for being so intimate at this very last minute. I owe you a lot. I will restrict myself to the most important thing. To what usually quietens down this addictive trouble of writing.

Writing what you cannot write is maybe the only way to write.

Fallen Angel (Anschel) of Prague, I have gone to extremes for you. I have masturbated, I have been intoxicated by your texts. I have thought of jumping over the balcony with your books in my arms. I have gotten into fights with my colleagues at the university at conferences and symposia, especially with those who regurgitate the theses of various Kafka experts. I have even badly hit one of my boyfriends by throwing your diaries at his head. I am ashamed. I have even drawn your astrological chart.

Cancer with horoscope on Leo. Moon between Gemini and Aries. The prevalent planets are Hermes, Sun, and Mars. Your number is 3, which shows—shall I go on?

The only extremity I have not committed yet is to travel to Prague. I have dutifully followed your example with *Amerika,* the *missing* continent of the *missing* Karl. As soon as my book comes out, I will visit Prague. And I will stay for as long as I can afford it. By myself. In your town, engulfed by your town. To be precise, I will imitate you. I will walk on your footprints.

Wandering in Prague both appeased and excited you. After it first familiarized you with your singular fragmented being, as well as with the shattered pieces of the world around you, it also involved you in an ongoing game of no return, through the seduction of fatigue and withdrawal—since, even though you were convinced you had not left your room even for a minute, you found yourself wandering around in your birth town like a cursed man, as if you were a homeless person, a somnambulist or a dead man. Someone, anyway, who had for a long time lost his sense of the private and the public sphere, as well as of the real flow of time.

Enough!

I will stop ridiculing myself, will stop looking for your footprints in your now touristy town. No, I will not visit Prague. Never! You can never do an autopsy on the urban, existential, sexual, and historical nightmare that sprang up in the head of a writer at the turn of the previous century. You do not attempt an autopsy on something that is irrevocably buried—*dust, always ash, always shadow*—and, despite all this, unimaginably indelible and alive.

At any rate, Prague did not exist even when you lived in Prague.

I am thinking, I am on the verge of reaching the conclusion that, to me at least, the most reliable research methodology for your work is sleep, hypnosis, self-hypnosis, illusion, the experience of leaving one's body, virtual reality. A passionate, an excitable, simulation of death. Mainly through these spurning, unreliable, and most of all unreasonable and unprofessional tools did I approach you—an incommunicable approach. My method is the method of sleeplessness. Neither yours, nor mine, but of your texts. Writing keeps you awake. Your lids are heavy with sleep and yet remain open, your limbs are fatigued and yet stretched, your consciousness plunges into the abyss and yet remains alert.

Deep down I approached you in a homeopathic way. Live by the dream, die by the dream. Let's not repeat your famous diary saying . . .

Needless to say, I do not deny the huge benefit of having spent endless hours in libraries or on the internet, immersing myself in huge bibliographies, going over documents, passages, words, and titles, comparing dates, biographical and narrative details, while also distilling interpretative convergences and divergences of emblematic, radical, conventional, even inadequate and maladroit researchers—all of which have their place in the Kafkaesque Babel.

Yet every morning I would wake up, in the midst of my sleep, while sleeping, whichever way I was sleeping, with the same impossible question: recomposition or decomposition?

In other words, do you recompose the past of your object of research to delineate it convincingly in the present, or do you become decomposed in its place so that you trace it back to its time, to the people who shaped it, to the thoughts and the images that possessed or pacified it?

This is the crucial question to which I measured myself as your researcher. To confide in you that I have dreamt of you is an exaggerated exaggeration.

I'm sorry, sorry, sorry. Sorry for everything.

Next time I will be cautious. I will be succinct and to the point. Which means, I'll be silent.

If needed, I will restrict myself to your death throes:

"Yes, this way, this way is good" (according to Brod).

"I am leaving though" (according to Klopstock).

Or maybe rely on sister Anna's dazed gaze with "it is finished?" I am wondering, will there be a next time?

I will tell you something that I don't know how you will take. Something that has been my burden for a long time now. You can call me anything you want. Superficial and erratic, even paranoid, or obsessed. I cannot hide it from you, though. I find it impossible.

I ignore what you find out and how you do so. Even we can barely tell the difference between the event and its distortions despite the immediate access we have to facts. What can I say? Maybe sometimes the irrevocable distance, being informed after the event, is more accurate and sober than the information that the immediate experience provides.

To make a long story short. You may have been informed about the dreadful trials and the bitter end of your last love, Dora. Roaming the entire scene of horror of the twentieth century. Nazism, Stalinism, destitution, isolation. Her daughter, Franziska Marianne Lask, lived a hard life just like her mother.

This is the one I want to ponder. To insist on. With insatiable determination.

She may have been the daughter of the German communist Lutz Lask, who lost his life in Siberia, just like many of his kind who fled to the great Soviet fatherland in '36, but anyone who met Franziska (calling her by just the first of her two names honors your memory) talked about a creature who looked like you, not only in spirit but also in appearance. As if Dora, who had one of your big, framed photos on top of her bed, had not got pregnant by the head of *The Red Flag*, but by the author of *The Castle*. This girl, who lost her birth father at the age of six, was raised under the weight of your traumatic absence in her mother's life. She became the child you did not have with her mother. What a difficult father, what a difficult fatherly ghost . . . On top of having a mother too obstinate and adamant about refusing to appropriate an inch of your posthumous fame in order to alleviate the destitution that burdened her and her daughter. A mixture of communism and Hasidism. An unlikely cocktail! The outcome: the mother died when she was barely forty years old (August 15, 1952) of kidney failure in a hospital in east London. Unknown and lonely.

Eighteen-year-old Franziska Marianne loses the ground under her feet. Without any flair for the melodramatic: she is deprived of the necessities to bury her mother, your beloved Dora. This afflicted by misfortune creature who suffered all the disasters of European history in the second half of the twentieth century, the daughter you never knew, the daughter who was born outside your orbit, your real daughter, your main inheritor, exhibited signs of schizophrenia. It is said that she heard voices and sounds while experiencing delusional situations. Exactly the same way—and here I am thinking aloud—several protagonists or narrators of yours did. Except that, and you know this firsthand, the fictional characters go in and out of their invented darkness. Whereas Franziska Marianne, despite the efforts of several Jews in London (including your own niece, Marianna Steiner), became alienated from everyone. She disappeared off the face of the earth. She became a beetle, a weasel, a mole, she became a hunger artist. Without return, though. She was brought back to "reality" by the police, who had been notified by her neighbors. It was October 12, 1982 when the police and the locksmith broke into her apartment in Muswell and found her decomposing body in her bed. She had died of starvation at the age of forty-eight.

Enough with the enigmatic Kafkaesque deductions, though.

At any rate, Kafka's enigma is that there is no enigma. To be precise, an enigma is a state balancing on a tightrope between a condition of hilarity and a zero ground. There might be no tightrope, let alone a rope. And the rope, whether tight or loose, might represent one's desire to suspend oneself in the lightness of terror.

Anyway. I've stretched this too far. Too far. Let's get to the point.

On Facebook I coordinate a closed, small group that consists of your most dedicated readers. We have called it "Hotel K." It involves not only academics and researchers. Amongst the members of the group, there are writers, artists, architects, lawyers, students, and bibliophiles who read you systematically, without ideological misconceptions or fixations. Men and women of all ages. Random individuals from across the planet. A network of persistent and open-minded readers of your work. We exchange news, thoughts, articles, of our own and others, photographs, and anything else that might concern your world in the passing of time. One day a photographer from Buenos Aires uploaded a photograph of Franziska Marianne at a young age. He was preparing a photo exhibit, the theme of which was the women in your life. I had never seen the picture before. There was an online moment of embarrassment. Dead silence. She and I looked alike like two peas in a pod. I don't want to say how beautiful she was. To be precise, she was a noble mixture of her mother's gaze and yours. I was paralyzed. It took me three months to reconnect with "Hotel K."

I am certain that, aside from being called stupid, I run the risk of being accused of vanity.

I here enclose her photograph (alas, in poor resolution) and mine at a similar age. You can take a look and draw your own conclusions.

At that moment I wrote a note in my journal: *From Mafalda to Franziska . . .* There are modernisms and modernisms. Fortunately. The plural here has always been the curse of obsessed readers. In fact, your modernism upsets expert readers, not programmatically but in action. It paralyses them, it freezes them in time, as it quietly and insidiously draws them into a conflict zone of reversals, controversies, and doubts. Without exaggeration: you attract, as much as you repel, your interpreters. Especially those who approach your work fully armored with adamantly concrete and inflexible theories. As you demonstrate with every aspect of your writing, interpretation is that which does not exist in reality. This is against the reading spirit of our times, when we are forced to read the interpretation of interpretations often rendering the text absent. As you demand that we allegorically return to the animal, so you ask that we really return to the text. To a text that we must silence in order to relate what is non-relatable. Exactly the way he did. "He who was pulled out, He who was saved from the Waters, He who pulls out." The slow-tongued Jewish preacher, Moses. He who, together with his dispossessed people, crossed, among other things, the linguistic desert of his time, until he spoke a dialect that pulls out salvaged meaning—a dialect that consolidates a return to, and refuge, in time: an uprooted return, an uprooted refuge.

I think that, maybe because of this distant memory, the characters in your stories suffer from having either no sense, or an overwhelming sense, of self. Because of this invariable self-sameness, they are more accountable—one can totally argue this—to an internal plot that often delays, defers, becomes abstract, nearly undermines, or becomes indifferent to the external plot, the action of the story. The result of this organized chaos is that your characters do not display a concrete psychological identity. As if, deep down, they are not individualized acts but reflections of a cruel and uncertain epoch. Hence they often appear to be controversial, fluid and centrifugal; an epoch whose temporality is indefinite, though: does it belong to the past, the present, or the future? What is most certain is that you are drawn by faces that are most real and intimate, that experience situations that are truly unnatural and unfamiliar. And because you map their passions so coldly (the way a researcher performs an experiment) but also so comically (in the same manner an actor bursts into laughter instead of bursting into sobs or crying out), a sense of comic abyss is conveyed to the reader.

Please, count me in as one of the characters in your story. The most insignificant one in one of your most incomplete stories. Like the flash of a character that remained a spark.

This is more than enough for me. This is my only ambition in life. The highest one.

(I am really wondering, come to think of it . . .) Can this underweighted, unmapped, nearly embryonic figure bid you farewell as a quasi-heroine and not only as a lifelong reader of yours? In other words, to address you with a repetition of hearing, of seeing, and—why not—of touching?

(I am wondering, truly wondering, wondering about myself writing whatever I am writing to you. And yet I go on. I have an excuse, though. At the back of my mind, there is the thought, not entirely unfounded, that, at the end of the day, I am not your fatigued researcher who is writing to you, but a disheartened heroine of yours, and, above all, a disheartened woman. And be prepared for everything when dealing with a disheartened woman . . .)

I hold on to the memory of the most indelible farewell you have ever been given. The sweet-scented farewell of Dora who stood by you like a mother, a sister, a nurse, and above all, like a woman fully in love. I refer to the bouquet of wildflowers that that dedicated Polish Jewish woman laid on your chest just before you shut your eyes forever.

And then, of course, I refer to her formidable silence about you. To her persistence not to cash in on an inch of your memory. On the memory of your short-lived and so valuable, common life.

Nabokov, speaking as a writer-entomologist, made his declaration about *Metamorphosis*: It is not about a cockroach but a beetle. I wonder, will a Nabokov expert on your plants be discovered? And more specifically, a writer-botanist who will determine the specific kind of flowers in the bouquet that Dora laid on your breathless chest in your final hour? There is still some confusion regarding the matter. Did it consist of peonies? Lilies? The lemon yellow and poisonous laburnum? Or something else?

I also hold onto the memory of Milena's eulogy that was published a short while after your funeral (*Narodni Listy*, 6.6.1924). I read the closing section: *His work in its entirety describes the horror of mysterious misunderstandings and unjustifiable guilt. He, as a man of so many ethical reservations that he stayed sleepless even when the others, the deaf ones, felt safe.*

Could I possibly add mine . . .?

(I am surprised at the thought, I belabored this point and I am writing it to you . . .)

Ninety-six years since your death. I do not know if it is exceptionally later, untimely in the present or, on the contrary, rushed and premature. Since we are not talking about just anybody. We are talking about a consciousness like yours, whose relationship with time suffered from a long-lasting stagnant anticipation. I do not know if what I thought of as a retrospective endowment of your absence, as a little stone I would crave to lay on our tombstone, is considered something indecent or blasphemous.

Whatever is to burn, is as if it has already been burned, we read in the Talmud. So I blurt it out . . .

Black
Black
Black
Black
Black
Black
I go back to
I go back to
We only said goodbye with words
I died a hundred times
You go back to her
And I go back to black

So, what I have thought as my own insolent farewell (farewell in a manner of speaking, since not a day passes that something of you does not upset me) is one of my favorite songs by a favorite singer of mine.

You would have liked her. Perhaps she would have made you anxious at first. But I am certain that not only would you have flirted with her, but you would also have made her yours. I am not saying you would have saved her from drugs and alcohol or saved her from the fatherly labyrinth or the seduction of wild lovemaking. I do not know if she would have had the patience, the time, or the interest in responding to your long and soul-consuming letters. At any rate, she was in a rush. Her internal speedometer constantly went over the red line. Twenty-seven years was the maximum she could last. She would probably have sent you an email or an SMS. And I believe that. I am almost certain. For her eyes—her sad, ferocious, unprotected eyes—you would have gotten over your fear of technology.

The lines I enclose in this letter are from the song "Back to Black" and the singer is Amy Winehouse. A slow, mournful, passionate song. It came out in 2006 and had an incredible world impact. Do not panic! You also fell victim to your global impact—even if you did so in absentia and retrospectively; to your Kafkaism that has for decades wrenched you as much from your mass popularity as from our hermetic isolation. On the one hand, the t-shirts, the plates, and cups with your face printed on them, and, on the other hand, the hyper-theorized analyses of your work, the self-referential painting exhibits, the exaggerated theatrical performances—I do not want to frighten you more, but what is about to happen, always in honor of your work and your memory, in 2024 will be beyond words.

The more I think about it, the more I believe that Amy would have been your beloved one. One of your beloved ones. You would have been struck with awe. Especially if you saw her on stage. Her movements, her performance, her sensual presence that she was at times self-conscious about, other times sarcastic about. To my mind, the Winehouse phenomenon would have something to say to the Kafka phenomenon. This controversial Jewish girl from North London, of Russian Polish origins, who dressed in an old-fashioned way, had a grand hairstyle and a chaotic tattoo for a body, and a mythical contralto voice that mixed and matched musical and performative elements of jazz, soul, pop, swing, funk, gospel, even hip-hop—a mixture you would not find that unfamiliar, if we judge by the fusion of linguistic and stylistic elements in your writing, always in favor of integral clarity.

I do not know if the big clock in the square of the Old City of Prague, on the eleventh of June 1924, stopped at exactly at 16:00, the time when they buried you, by actually lifting you to the attic of your last hexagonal residence of grey travertine. There, in the last Kafka residence, where your father, your mother, and three sisters, on rotation, migrated from the floors below, I do not know if, on that bleak day, the drizzle interrupted the monotonous Kaddish prayers. What I know, though, or rather am certain of, is that Amy would have been the perfect performer of the Yiddish songs that you so much liked in interwar Prague.

For this reason, Franz, do google "Amy Winehouse Back to Black" and then plunge into the wild velvet of her voice . . .

(I will delete this I don't . .

Luck

By Irena Dousková

Story

Translated from Czech *by David Livingstone*

Abram Abramovich and Ivan Ivanovich sat exhausted on a damp, uprooted tree which they had just rolled off the road. They sat in silence, each at one end, as far away from one another as possible. They needed to catch their breath but had nothing to say to one another. Not even their long-shared journey had served to bring them any closer from the way it had been before, for years of their lives, living on the same street, in the same village.

Ivan Ivanovich, a burly, fair-haired man, whose left leg had remained practically lame after an accident long ago, was almost thirty years old. The consumptive, pale, and gaunt Abram, a Jew, was approximately ten years older. If not for the war, if not for their extreme need, they would never have set off together and wouldn't have talked at all, apart from the essentials, as was the norm. The village, however, was dying of hunger. Ivan's lovely wife, Katya, and his elderly infirm mother were just as badly off as Abram's Sara and their five children, and just as poorly off as all the remainder of the fifty inhabitants of Berezovka, whether they were Russians or Jews. They were used, of course, to hardship, having always struggled to get by. Life had been difficult under the czar and it continued to be tough with the Bolsheviks. There did not seem to be any other possibility in this abandoned, damp corner, in this undulating landscape, which was insufficiently fertile, where practically wherever one walked, the earth seemed to be collapsing under its own weight, as if soaking up water. From time immemorial, only mosquitoes seemed to prosper here and only God knows when and why a village had been founded here. It had happened, though. They were used to it, they knew how to live with it. That was earlier, however. If at least, before, there had been a glimmer of hope, now there was none. There was only war. The German army had crossed through a huge chunk of land like a knife through butter, bringing and leaving behind only one thing: death. Death, death, and only death once again. Death in one hundred different ways, one of them being hunger. But what choice do you have?

When things began to get truly grim, someone had come up with the idea of this journey. It was supposed to be business, not particularly advantageous, but necessary, if they wanted to survive. Winter was approaching. The villagers gathered together what they still had left. Each gave a few items which should fetch the highest price. The price of food. They chose Abram, who had some acquaintances in the town, as Jews always do. At least that's what people say. They chose the cripple Ivan, that was clear as well, he being from a horse family, there being only two horses left at this point in the local kolkhoz. They weren't friends? They didn't like one another? All the better—at least they'd keep one another honest. They'd be keeping an eye on each other. They could be sure of that, both the Russians and the Jews. When all was said and done, there weren't all that many adult males left in the village anyway, so they didn't have much of a choice.

They had set off with an old, creaky wagon and with one of the two remaining horses. There was no time to lose. The fall had already colored the oak trees in red, and a wind was rising above the meadows. Soon the wind would gather in strength, bringing with it black-greyish clouds and the rain. The ever-present groundwater would then connect up with the water from the heavens, and not only the meadows, but all of the roads, would turn to mud, making it impossible for a tractor, if someone actually had one, let alone a wagon with one horse, to pass.

The journey was a long one and far from pleasant, but they had met with luck, one might say. They hadn't encountered anything much worse than hunger and cold. Ivan could manage horses like a part of his own body and after seven days they finally arrived in the town. They were forced to resort to their hiding place only once. Part of their miserly treasure had been used as a bribe to a meddlesome and thieving policeman who was on the verge of making trouble for them. They would miss that ring in the end, but it could have turned out worse. Both were certain of that.

Ivan was particularly annoyed that the Jew had spent part of Friday evening along with Saturday morning in the synagogue. In his eyes, it was an unnecessary waste of time which should have been dedicated exclusively to their affairs. He had to admit, however, that in the end Abram still managed to carry out their business, and the desperate transaction which they had made the trip for was also accomplished. Only one or two of those acquaintances had been found in the end, out of those whom Abram had relied upon. The rest had vanished in thin air. A former classmate with all of his family had apparently moved away and it hadn't been completely clear if it had been by choice. And the brother-in-law of his wife's brother-in-law? His acquaintances shrugged their shoulders and, with their fingers on their lips, shook their fearful heads from side to side. Papa, Generalissimo Stalin, keeps an eye on everything. He has eyes everywhere, eyes and ears. Lots of ears. He guards everything. Everything? Not exactly everything. The Germans have taken over for him and are almost here. He couldn't guard the Germans, so he guards us even more. Nobody knew anything with certainty, and it was better not to ask. He didn't ask.

They sold what they had, or better said, exchanged them, and placed the modest-sized pile of rare goods onto the wagon, in a prepared ahead of time hiding place between old rags and several bundles of hay for the horse. It went slowly, however. Ivan knew that he wouldn't have been able to arrange it any better; he probably wouldn't even have got as much as they did. They set off on the return trip at the break of dawn, Sunday morning. Not much had changed, but their mood, without having said anything, was slightly more positive. They had accomplished their task, done as much as they could, and were now returning home. Ivan continued to stare at the Jew with suspicion as he—morning, noon, and evening—would pray, or whatever he was doing, gibbering and chattering while comically rocking back and forth. Perhaps he's not even praying, and if he is, who knows to whom? If he were calling upon the Devil instead of God, who would be the wiser? Who knows what he's actually doing? Ivan certainly didn't. He would stare at the way the Jew chewed his bread with onion or with garlic, nothing else at all over the entire period, each time turning over and investigating everything in his hands three times to make sure (the Devil knows what). All this, instead of being grateful that he had at least something to stick in his mouth. And his constant washing of his hands before every meal, like some kind of aristocratic lady. All this constant foolishness, all these delays. All in all, an odd black bird that Abram. Just like all of them.

Well, not exactly all of them. Ivan knew a number of Jews, that's true. That people's commissar with a pistol at his hip, who had been in the village twice, he was also a Jew. He certainly didn't pray, not that one. And he certainly didn't resemble quiet Abram. Nor did that Samuel Hirsch, the former owner of the textile factory and the richest man in the village up to the revolution. His bones had been probably gnawed on by wolves long ago in Siberia, but Ivan still remembered him vividly from his childhood. He, along with the farmer

Voznecky, were the only ones in the village to have a carriage. He would proudly—it appeared to Ivan—put on airs riding in it along with his fat wife and their three pretty daughters. Ivan only actually saw him once, perhaps twice. The man hadn't done anything to him, but he would remember that look of his forever, whereas Samuel Hirsch understandably wouldn't remember snotty-nosed Ivan. He didn't even notice him, didn't even spare one little look at him. He was a zero, nothing, empty air. That was a sufficient reason for hatred. No, that one didn't resemble this pauper Abram at all. Each of them was different and it was hard to decide which of them was more contemptible. Ivan didn't like any of them. Perhaps only those three daughters of Hirsch, but those were women and they didn't count.

Abram, in contrast, observed the Russian with unmitigated distaste: the way he constantly scratched his bare chest and elsewhere with his dirty hands, the way he wouldn't wash even when he had the chance, and the way he stuffed himself. Yes, stuffed himself, there was no other way of describing it. He would stuff himself and gobble down everything which he could get his hands on, stinky lard, unripened apples. He belched and farted and would drink liquor in the evenings. Only in the evenings, not during the day—that had been their agreement from the beginning, and to give the Russian credit, he had tried to more or less keep to it. Nevertheless, it was unbearable at times. He would keep silent and frown, in almost a threatening fashion, and when he did say something, it was even worse. The filth which would flow from his mouth as soon as it opened—all those vulgarities, the dirty and sleazy jokes! Abram was ashamed that he had to put up with it, that he had to listen to something like that. And Ivan had found a girl, a skinny tramp, on Friday night. Abram hadn't even been spared their shameful animal squealing. And the Russian had a wife at home, a young and pretty wife. Abram knew her. Her name was Katya, a kind-seeming person at first glance, proper and quiet, with gentle eyes. Ivan should be ashamed of himself!

Abram hadn't said anything. What could he say? It wasn't his concern. Everything he was forced to see and hear deeply repulsed him, however.

And then with that horse! The man's behavior with the horse irritated the Jew more than anything else. The Russian called the horse "Mishko," like a person, and behaved towards it as if it were a person, with everything which that entailed. He called the horse not only "Mishko," but also "brother" and "turtle-dove" and "my darling," and he would constantly caress and hug the horse. He would place his hand on the horse's thin shoulders with his rough, dirty fingers entangled in the mat of its light-colored mane. He would speak to that horse, whisper to it, explain and promise something in a soothing, persuasive voice. In the evenings, he would even stick his face next to the horse's and more than once, when he had drunk a bit, he would, God knows why, begin to weep out loud and shamelessly while hanging onto the horse's neck.

Abram didn't like it one bit. A person is a person and a horse is a horse—and that's the way things are. He had never even touched that large, seemingly calm, animal, being actually a little afraid of it and preferring to respectfully keep a distance. It was another thing, however, which bothered him even more. It would happen, and this on a daily basis, and God knows how many times, that Ivan would beat the horse. He would actually brutally whip it or hit it with his cane, while at other times he would pound it with his hand, often clenched in a fist. It never took much, and Ivan would explode into flames like a bundle of straw, screaming and storming, losing control of himself and letting out all his fury on the horse. On that same horse whose mane he had shed tears into during the night. To his brother, to his turtledove, to his darling. When this happened, Abram would cringe helplessly, overcome again and again with horror, pity, and the depth of the impassable chasm which can separate man from man. At this, he would suddenly realize that people and animals are of the same essence and can actually dissolve into one another.

They continued on their way. The journey grew shorter with each of them minding his own business. Despite their mutual dislike of one another, which they were well aware of, their shared goal kept them in check. At one point, however, things began to grow tense. They had stopped for the night near the road at the edge of the woods at a point where a structure had originally stood. Now it was only a ruin with a few bare walls and fallen roof timbers. Even this, however, at least provided the illusion of shelter although they were planning on sleeping outside anyway. There was also a well. They had spent the night here before, on their journey to the town. Ivan took care of the horse, and they made a fire and sat in silence around it. After a short period of time, a dark figure emerged from the shadows of the ruins. She appeared before them even before they'd noticed the noise she made. They were startled. A piece of dry bread stuck deep in Abram's throat; he coughed and the onion which slipped out of his hand rolled away into the dark. Their fear was only temporary, however. It was a woman. Actually, more of a girl—dirty and disheveled and even more petrified than they were. She could have been around fifteen or sixteen years old. She spoke up, told them her name was Nina, but who knows if she actually said Nina, as she spoke so quietly and hesitantly, one could hardly understand her words. They began to ask her questions, but she only answered confusedly. She was trembling all over, with her hands pressed to her chest while gazing fixedly at the ground. Her eyes betrayed her, however. Despite her shame and fear, her pale eyes would lift every so often and focus, against her will, on the half-eaten slice of bread in Abram's hand. He finally understood, invited her to sit at the fire, and shared his food with her. She gobbled down everything which they gave her but remained on edge. She cried out something about the Germans, about shooting and the dead, about villages burned to the ground somewhere nearby. Perhaps. She seemed to be saying something like that. They could only guess from her disconnected speech, often interrupted by tears.

They told her she could travel with them and she seemed to accept their offer. It was difficult to communicate with her. Her limited vocabulary and obvious trauma—from God knows what terrible experiences—had seemingly turned her into a half-animal, a timid forest creature. She refused their offer to lie down with them on the blankets around the fire pit and returned to where she had slept before: between the four bare walls and the fallen timbers. She was apparently sleeping on a few handfuls of damp straw in one of the corners. They didn't try to stop her.

Abram fell that night into a deep sleep. His evening prayers, voiced with a heart full of fears which he could not suppress, had not been a great success. Despite this, with the help of God, he had finally fallen asleep. He was awakened by noises, the origin of which he was unable to immediately determine. It took a little while for him to come to his senses and realize where it was coming from and what was actually going on. This only served to increase his horror. The despairing scream and tears were coming from the ruins. The scream of that girl. Abram looked around him and, though it was almost pitch black, noticed that the blanket next to him was empty. There was no doubt as to what was going on. There was no doubt as to the identity of the rapist. Abram stood up. He walked uncertainly towards the ruins. It was against his conviction, against all of his established customs, which urged him not to get involved with these people. He wasn't thinking of this, however. He wasn't thinking about what would be appropriate, or about what Ivan would do to him. He only stood up and headed in that direction. The screaming was unbearable. The quiet which suddenly followed was little better. He had taken only a few steps when the furious Ivan flew toward him from inside.

"What are you doing here?" he screamed. "What the hell do you want? Do you want to watch, Jew?"

"Where is she?" Abram asked as calmly as possible.

"She ran away."

"Where? Where could she go at night?"

"How should I know? She'll come back in the morning, don't worry."

"And if she doesn't?"

"If she doesn't, she doesn't, the Devil take her. I don't give a damn!"

"How could you do this, Ivan Ivanovich? What kind of man are you?"

"Do you think I'm going to confess to you?"

"You have a wife at home—"

"What business is that of yours, you . . . you kike! You . . .!" And suddenly he was squeezing him around the neck.

"Nothing, nothing at all," groaned Abram, readying himself for a blow.

Surprisingly, the Russian let go of him.

"I just don't understand it. I can't understand you," said Abram.

"I can't understand you, either. And how could you, anyway? Have you ever been interested in us? Me, or her, does it even matter? The same, miserable, Russian rabble! Or isn't it like that? Don't try to pretend."

"I could say the same thing about you."

"I doubt it."

"Perhaps, it's not the same thing. We, at least, don't kill your children, don't rape your women, neither our own, nor yours."

"Because you can't!"

Abram only waved his hand in disgust. Are they any better than the Germans? he thought to himself. But he didn't say it out loud.

Ivan seemed to have heard him, however. "I didn't want to hurt her," he said. "I wanted to comfort here, bring her pleasure."

"Pleasure!" Abram couldn't help himself from laughing. "Do you think that gave her pleasure?"

"You!" the Russian began again threateningly. "What do you know about pleasure?"

"*Borekh hashem*, I have five children, don't I?"

They dropped the subject. Ivan wanted to ask what the connection was, but he didn't, although he didn't know why. You're talking about something else, he thought, and was certain of it. Having said that, those five children were there. Four of them were even boys. He knew them, they weren't so bad, not yet. He'll definitely ruin them. Make them into the same black birds as he is himself. He doesn't know how to do anything else. But they weren't that way yet; they were cheerful and bright. They were alive and kicking. Ivan, that giant of a man on the verge of thirty, didn't have any children, God knows why. It didn't make any sense.

"If she doesn't come back and go with us, she'll probably die somewhere," Abram couldn't help mentioning when he had buried himself once more in the blankets. And whose fault is that going to be? He decided against saying it aloud.

She didn't return. They didn't speak all that much in the morning, but both postponed their departure as long as they could without putting it into words. They needed to do this or that, should they give the horse something more, should they take more water? All in vain. She didn't appear. They had to set off without her, and the horse, that third silent wretch with protruding ribs, received a good beating that day. When the yellow moon came out that night, round and seemingly full, some horsehair on the horse's neck, moist and salty, looked like a handful of seaweed or algae.

Another day passed and still another. They didn't even sleep the final night. They continued with their journey. They were too excited to rest. The third day, at early dawn, they approached the place from which they had departed. The October morning fog initially prolonged the illusion that they were back home. Then the sun came out. Frozen with horror, they climbed down from the wagon, both the Jew and Ivan, the latter suddenly ludicrously awkward. They were standing in the middle of the ruins of a fire. There was nobody and nothing, only sooty remains. Nothing, only silence screaming at the skies.

Night descended. They sat next to one another on a tree trunk, drinking a bottle of vodka. They hadn't even bothered to make a fire. Abram got up, approached the horse, and threw a blanket over it; Ivan had forgotten for the first time. Abram remained standing and, as always, began to recite the prescribed evening prayer.

"You're praying? Your children are dead and you're still praying?"

There was not any anger there, merely vast astonishment. Abram did not answer. He raised his arms helplessly. What shall I do? (he asked his arms), tell me what I should do. Steam rose from the nostrils of the horse. The horse was exhausted and had injured its leg. It shut its eyes and, despite the horse blanket, shivered slightly. Ivan caressed it.

"It's had enough," said Abram. "We should . . ." He didn't finish his sentence. "You could eat the meat and take the rest with us on the journey."

"On what journey? Where can we possibly go?"

"I don't know." He shrugged his shoulders at Ivan.

Abram threw a blanket over him just as he had with the horse.

"I couldn't put it in my mouth," he remarked. "It will rest, you'll see. Perhaps it will be better by the morning," he told Ivan.

As if it actually mattered.

Abram woke to a cold morning with a terrible pain, a scream, and blows raining down upon him. A German soldier was pointing a gun at him and kicking him incessantly. Ivan was no better off. Five Germans were standing in a circle, one of them apparently an officer. Abram didn't know, he couldn't even make a guess, how long it lasted until they finally let him stand up with his hands above his head.

First they shot the horse. Two Germans looked it over and one said the horse was kaput; then they shot it. Ivan silently crumpled to the ground and, for a second, Abram thought they had killed him, too. They quickly made him stand back up. With kicking and punching.

"That girl," Ivan whispered, "it's good she ran away. I . . . didn't do anything to her. Yes, I wanted to, but she screamed, fought with me . . . I let her run away."

"That's good."

More and more blows, and constant screaming.

"Where are they?"

"Who?"

A blow from the butt of a rifle.

"You Jewish swine! Are you going to tell us?"

Finally, Abram understood.

He didn't know. He really didn't know. They weren't here. They had only arrived from the town yesterday. They hadn't been here for a week.

A blow after each sentence. The Germans searched the wagon.

"Food. Only a little food," one of the soldiers announced.

"They don't seem to know anything," the officer stated. "We can end it."

"What do they want, Abram?"

"They're going to kill us."

"I know. But what did they ask about?"

"They didn't get them! They don't know where they are."

They made them stand against the wall of a burned house.

"Abram?"
Abram realized that, for the first time, Ivan had addressed him by name.
"Abram, a miracle . . .?"
"I don't know," Abram smiled. "Perhaps only luck. Incredible luck."

Where Were You When Darkness Fell

By Mario Levi

Excerpt from a Novel

Translated from Turkish *by Leyla Tonguç Basmaci*

Entry into Hell

There was a dream that followed me ruthlessly for years. It took me a long time to come to terms with what I saw, or rather with what I was forced to reveal to myself. What's more, I am not even sure that I have succeeded. All that is left within me is simply the echo of those voices and of that laughter. In my dream Lee Van Cleef, the unforgettable villain of westerns, dressed in that long black coat of his, looks at me with his eagle eyes and that smile that predicts terrible things and with his long-barreled gun he suddenly shoots my father, who is at a short distance from me, in the forehead. I can still see my father collapsing in pain and the red hole that appeared in the middle of his forehead. Where were we? Why were we there? What was it that was wanted or expected from me? The place where we were looked a lot like one of the beaches we went to in my childhood. But it was so quiet, it could have been a horror film. Maybe it was the early hours of the morning. There was no doubt that it was the right time for an execution. On the vast beach there were only a few people and they were far from each other. I remember that there was a man who looked at me with reproach, with contempt, and even with ridicule, and that an old woman whose skin was tight from too much sun, who looked very much like one of the women whom my grandmother met with on certain days of the week, to play cards, hastily got up from her place and said, "*On l'a tué le pauvre!*/They have killed the poor man!" about my father, who was lying on the ground. The woman wasn't interested in me. It wasn't clear whom she had said these words to, in that endless void. A little further away, three men were sitting together and laughing among themselves. They didn't seem to have either seen or heard what had happened. But I was there. I was full of fear, but I was also trying to smile at Lee Van Cleef, who was continuing to laugh and to blow off the smoke coming from the barrel of his gun. That was all. Then I woke up.

I had this dream about ten years ago. My father had died a long time before. At first I couldn't make any sense of why I had seen him like this at our first meeting after so many years. But then it dawned on me: it was actually I who had committed this murder. But because I hadn't actually managed to do it, I made the worst villain in my memory kill my father, who breathed down my neck with his influence and presence in my later years, at every step I took, or wasn't able to take. What's more, when we watched those films together, in a very distant past, this villain was among the characters that affected us the most. It had been such a long time, so many people, feelings, words and images had gone by. All the deep feelings stirred up by those details mattered greatly to me. What that old woman said, the way she expressed it, the way that man who kept smiling stared at me, the distance and indifference of those other men, and the fact that I stood there without moving, without saying a word, with that evil feeling inside me that I couldn't come to terms with. That fear . . . Yes, I was afraid, once again, I was afraid. I was afraid of showing and revealing "too much" of myself. I have inherited the ruins of a history that was full of deep threats that have instilled this fear in me, that have anticipated and nurtured my reticence. This history, whether I liked it or not, drew me inside, and it was also the history of my loneliness, which I outlined—which I couldn't avoid outlining—with my own steps, out of my private moments of darkness, of my sexuality, of what my face—that I never liked seeing in the mirror—reminded me, and it was also the history of my languages that taught me who I was, of my country, of my ancient city. Was there no cause for why those men in the distance should have been indifferent to this murder? Had that woman, with that typical behavior as an "outsider," shown that reaction for no reason at all? And that man, that man who looked at me so judgmentally? Who was that man? Was he one of those people whom I had to confront under different disguises, at different stages of my life, from that hell that I built out of those whom I alienated, one of those people who always managed to intercept me somewhere or other with their threats, whom I just couldn't get rid of, whom I perceived as my enemies and couldn't avoid? Or maybe . . . was I that man? These questions could lead me on to other questions and other probabilities. But I couldn't go any further. That murder was more than enough for me. I had finally managed to kill my father. . . .

The next morning, I remembered him, not in the way he looked when he was in his shop, which was practically his temple, but through those words that I hadn't been able to expel from the depths of my mind for so many years: *You are going to be nothing but a scoundrel!* When I thought of the values on which he had based his life, being considered a scoundrel by him shouldn't have affected me very much. What's more, in my view, being associated with a lifestyle of that kind could even have justified my rebelliousness. Both the words that would make me enjoy my rebellion to its full extent, and the feeling of rejection that would make me believe in myself even more were present. However, when I looked at the whole thing from another point of view, whatever I did, no matter how much I tried to convince myself, I always ended up being hurt because of that feeling of not being taken heed of, which I just couldn't cope with. Not being taken heed of, that's it. I think that that was what upset me the most for such a long, long time. After all, is there anybody who doesn't want to be noticed in one way or another? Is there anybody who, after having felt the pain of striving to get noticed, can emerge unscathed from such a clash, such an internal struggle? I had only recently graduated and I was doing whatever I could to reject the life that was offered to me, or rather that was being imposed on me. Submitting to it in a sense would mean accepting death.

To be defeated, to surrender, and worst of all, to compromise. At that time, neither my feelings, nor my political views would have permitted this. Because those days drew their strength from the spirit of change, and even from the spirit of change through destruction. When I went to London on the pretext of pursuing my education, with what little I obtained from turning into cash the gold coins that I was given at my bar mitzvah and that were diligently kept in a black velvet pouch in a drawer at home for "important occasions," my lifestyle there was what my father expected of me: I loafed around and deluded myself with a number of daydreams, and this was part of that rebellion, it was one of its requirements. Both my parents had vehemently opposed the idea of turning those gold coins into cash. I felt provoked by their opposition. I wanted to hurt them, and I also wanted to experience the feeling of being able to get up and go without my father's support. In other words, I had reasons that in my view were very valid, for telling them that that was the most "important occasion" for me. They therefore weren't able to come up with any serious objections. It wasn't such a huge amount of money anyway; in a city where not only reality but also illusions were expensive both to buy and to sell, I calculated that it would see me through only for six months. After that . . . After that all I needed to do was daydream and enjoy the exhilaration that would accompany those dreams. When I began to run out of money, I would throw myself into an adventure I couldn't even imagine, and with the belief that I had to cling tightly to the conviction that I could save the day as I wished, I would earn my living working at a number of jobs, as a waiter, a dishwasher, a member of the cleaning staff at a hotel, as a cashier at supermarkets open all night, regardless of whether they belonged to Arabs. I would show people that I could survive even in foreign lands, and then, when the time was right, I would return with that feeling of victory that I needed so much. But I didn't know when the time would be right. Maybe I wouldn't return. Like many relatives of ours, I had become fascinated with the idea of rejecting values and I had fallen in love with the fight that this passion drew me into. But it took me only a few months to realize what a mistake I had made. The reality of the situation was very disheartening. The London School of Economics, where I attended a certificate program, was so full of right-wing lecturers that it turned me off completely. And the money that I could earn working in restaurants run by Cypriot Turks could never ensure that I exclude my father from my life for good. What's more, there were other disappointments, too. The England that I was forced to see wasn't a country of houses with beautiful gardens. Moreover, not everybody in this country was fluent in English and the number of unhappy and bitter people was much higher than I thought. This could be seen clearly even in the London Underground. The West that I saw there was a weary, ruthless, very dark West hidden behind a layer of luster. A West that crushed foreigners and killed them in different ways.. That was one of the greatest breaking points of my life. And within that time, I also realized that I wouldn't be able to live without Istanbul. Anyway. . . . This intense disappointment that revealed me to myself so openly that I couldn't ignore it is now part of a very distant past. That was when I returned. I simply came back, or maybe I ran away once again. It was as if in London I had left behind a dream based only on lies. Maybe I had buried other possibilities, but I was unaware of what I had destroyed and how. Unaware of how dearly I would pay later on for this silent murder. In those days I was so far away from that encounter and that conflict that would so deeply unsettle my life. My family had reacted happily, but in different ways, to my return. Of course, I couldn't in any way share any of that happiness. My mother believed she had to relentlessly repeat that her prayers that I marry a "local" girl, "one of us," had been granted and as this adventure had finally come to an end with no great tragedy, she did whatever she could to pull me into her own world and into the settled life that she believed in and that was required by tradition. I don't doubt that she had no malicious intentions when she expressed her feelings. But because of my sense of not being visible enough and not being noticed as much as I wanted to, I often felt like slapping her with all my might, or, to put it bluntly, beating the hell out of her. Or maybe it was not her that I wanted to beat the hell out of, but those values that she just would not give up. My father, on the other hand, contented himself with simply watching these scenes and smiling, without saying a word. Naturally, he was enjoying this victory. I could not tell him what I had left behind. I myself didn't know exactly what it was. But I felt a deep ache, a sense of resentment. But I couldn't explain this feeling to him. We had never talked of any significant issues. It was probably because of this that I persevered in my efforts to justify their idea of me as an "elegant" scoundrel. One morning, a short while after I had returned, I went to the shop and I told him that I wanted to open up a small restaurant. A small, warm, cozy restaurant. Just like the life that I dreamt of. I no doubt hoped that he would help me financially. However, his father had produced cologne for years and years, and he himself had sold supplies such as freckle medication, sulfurous soap, talcum powder, depilatory wax, Chinese condoms, Brilliantine and shaving brushes. He was a merchant who had always kept his accounts in order and who prided himself that none of his promissory notes had ever been subject to protests, so it was not possible for him to understand such issues, let alone invest in them. So he had seized another occasion to strike me where I was most vulnerable. Instead of money I received advice, and instead of words of support, I listened to another of those sermons that I knew so well. I had wasted my time studying economy all those years. The streets were better than a university, to learn a trade. If I persevered like this, I would come to no good and I would always do my best to ruin him. What's more, he had said all of this in Ladino. In other words, both his anger and his concern were very genuine. Whenever he was very mad he would prefer this language. Just as when he was very happy and he was forced to share a secret. He believed that the words of this language made him more sincere and effective. But I didn't care. And I didn't care that he had once again flung into my face that I was a scoundrel. What saddened me that morning when I left the shop was not what I had heard, but my own desperation. The fact that I was so desperate that I still needed him to fulfill my dreams.

I could have subjected myself to this conflict in other ways. I could have chosen a life where I had a higher price to pay. But every age and phase believes in its own truths. Nowadays I find it easier to accept this fact. Over time, like so many of my peers experiencing such rebellions, I too laid down my arms. It didn't take me long to see the void before my quest. I began going to the shop, at first convincing myself that I could postpone my life and my hopes for a while. My father didn't expect more than that from me anyway. He had this business that he had worked so hard to create from scratch and I was his only son. It was as simple as that. In the frame of mind that I had managed to adopt, I began to believe that if I chose the alternative presented by my father, life would be much less problematic. Sometimes I had difficulties in recognizing myself and in living with myself. That was when solutions that I came up with due to my youth, in other words tranquilizers, came to my aid. The way I saw it, I had a long, long life before me and when the time came, I would feel stronger and be able to confront it. That's when I would fulfill my dreams without asking for anybody's help. I was at an age and time when I couldn't understand the real significance of "now." This meant that things could be postponed. Maybe this, too, was a sort of evasion. An evasion that I took refuge in knowingly, but that I wanted to believe would strengthen my ties with life. I was stuck between choices and obligations. Maybe I had lost the will to fight that I once had. Maybe . . . Maybe, it was because of this feeling of defeat that I wanted to build myself a safe haven where I could feel more secure. Sometimes despondency can act as a tranquillizer.

But my visits to the shop then were different from my visits when I was a student. Now I was able to see other people, and what's more, I wanted to see them. I wanted to believe that I could perform new plays with other people and that I could acquire mastery in these plays. I had ended up severing, or rather having to sever, my ties with the characters of that play that I was gradually drawing away from, with my friends, those people who had enabled me to view those days with an exhilaration that seemed endless. Everybody had gone their own way. I had no choice but to believe that they too, like me, had followed the path of their new lives, and to hope that they at least found themselves on those paths. I hadn't heard from them for such a long time. My evasion in those days required that there be a distance among us. What I was endeavoring to live with was a sorrow whose existence I had always felt, but that I could never come to terms with properly. I had no idea where my friends were, who they were with, what they were experiencing. To tell the truth,

I didn't even want to know. I had convinced myself that I could only survive by severing my ties like this. But it was difficult to explain this when I remembered what we had shared and what we had left behind. After all, everybody had made up their minds to choose themselves a path and to walk alone on that path. That's what life required us to do at that time. I had no doubt that they too thought of me from time to time. But I also had no doubt that they would not call me. The protagonists of that wonderful troupe we called "Team of Artists," whose stories I still carried inside, had to be the protagonists of an imaginary play that would not end, whose curtain would not come down for a very long time, maybe not until my very last breath. Just as I wanted to believe in my new play, I had to believe in their plays, too, wherever they were. That was why I felt both a bittersweet joy and the will to live when I imagined them experiencing all they could on the paths of their own lives.

In reality, it wasn't easy to endure that feeling of defeat. The struggle was over. It was as if a truck had hit us. At least that's how I felt. There was again talk of change. But this change was very different from what we once imagined. It was disappointing, it hurt. But we had to continue living. A new pack of hungry wolves had descended onto the city. Anybody who was still alive, who had survived, would see what they had to see. Anybody who had found themselves an exit would do what they had to do, they would take whatever they could from the struggles, the legacy and the ruins of the people they believed in and whom they had buried not only in the land of this country but also in their own emotional history. The wounds would then be dressed once again, of course. They would be dressed, but they would never heal, and anybody who chose not to forget would still feel their pain. I could see this even then. . . .

It wasn't easy to do the military service under these conditions. But there, too, I understood once again what a strong weapon keeping silent was. But that's a time of my life that I'd rather not remember. I don't want to remember it, although I learned that I need to solve some issues on my own and that at very difficult moments people are able to find an incredible power of endurance within themselves. My adventure as an "outsider" continued there, too. But it was a very painful adventure. And it forced me to come to terms with certain truths. Remembering even this much hurts me. Luckily that nightmare didn't last too long. The law had enabled me to spend only a short time in the company of weapons, which were something that I could never approve of. When I came back, I felt as if I had returned from a completely different world.

Thus, in spite of all my resentment and my dreams, I was able to adapt more easily to the shop and to the shopkeepers in the neighborhood. Over time I managed not to stand out with my diversities. Watching the other players, I even learned to act like a good backgammon player and to put on different acts when with bank managers, porters or shopkeepers. More importantly, I even managed to play by the rules and manage that shop where I once was only a visitor and that I once was so foreign to. What's more, I improved myself so much that sometimes I couldn't even recognize myself. No trace was left of the old modest and shabby shop. Or of the old goods that were more and more incompatible with the needs of the time. Now we import perfume essences for industrial companies. I am the only owner and the manager of the shop. My father died of a heart attack a long time ago, sitting at his desk, when we least expected it. I didn't cry that day. We had to organize his funeral in a hurry. It was a Thursday and the ceremony had to take place the following morning because the Sabbath began on Friday afternoon. We could have waited until Sunday, but for some reason my mother insisted on completing the whole thing as soon as possible. My father needed to rest in his last place of repose. I don't think that what she said had anything to do with religion or with traditions. I think that she didn't really know what she was doing because she couldn't bear his death. But to me it didn't make much of a difference. All I could do was stand by as events unfolded. It was as if the person we were going to bury was not my father but somebody else. That's how indifferent and distant I was to what was going on. The necessary procedures went more easily than I thought. I wasn't sad, all I felt was a little bitterness. A bitterness that I would make sense of later on and that I would be able to place elsewhere in my life. Maybe that's when I first thought of my own death, maybe I thought that we hadn't settled our accounts, or maybe, although I couldn't confess this even to myself, I felt the pain of growing a little older, of being forced to do so. I now was a man without a father. Whether I wanted it or not, I could feel a sense of bitterness. The ceremony was well attended in spite of the haste and worry. Seeing those people, I had to recognize that he had led a righteous life both in his eyes and in the eyes of others. Following the seven days of mourning I collected his stuff at the shop. It was that day . . . That was the day when I unexpectedly burst out sobbing. In one of the desk's drawers there was the leather–covered, small, brown notebook where he meticulously wrote what he owed and what he was due. That's where time had stopped. The notebook was like a summary of his life. I think that that was the day when I finally buried my father.

The change in the appearance of the shop accelerated further from that point on. Nowadays there is only an image, a small corner, to remind people of those old days. That's where the bell jars containing the lemon and lavender cologne my father enjoyed producing are kept. I've put the notebook next to those bell jars. Some people see them and remember him. I've never asked myself why I did so. If I had, I'm sure I would have had to face many unexpected answers. I may have wanted to remind myself that he is dead and that his life consisted only of those few small calculations. Which means that a need for revenge is also in question. On the other hand, after all this time, when I think that, like many of his peers, he lived in line with what he believed and he fulfilled his time on this earth with patience, fully aware of his destiny, I have to confess that my heart softens and even breaks a little. But whatever I do, that distance between us that always hurts me still doesn't become any shorter. If that distance hadn't been what it was, would I have been able to take another path in life? Who knows? It's too late, far too late to ask this question. And it is too late to say that I now understand very well Uncle Seyfettin, who seemed so dejected at my father's funeral and who strengthened my ties to the shop at that very difficult time when I was attempting to walk amidst ruins and find myself. What with his intellectual side and his many diversities, Uncle Seyfettin had always been a kindred spirit. He was probably the same age as my father. He had always succeeded at displaying sorrow and irony simultaneously. That's how he was, whether he announced that he had been declared an irregular Freemason, or that he was a Bektashi[1] elder, or that his wife hadn't been on speaking terms with him for many years. His long story had now become very meaningful for me. Maybe one day I will manage to remember him and cherish him the way that he deserves. That day, at the funeral, when I asked him why he looked so dejected, his eyes filled and he said, "It's you I'm worried about, rather than your father's death." At that moment I hadn't been able to understand what he meant. I was bored. I wanted the ceremony to be over as soon as possible. I was thinking of the match with Beşiktaş that would take place that weekend and I was mad at my father because he had died at such a time and I wouldn't be able to go to the match because of this sudden period of mourning. That is why it was only years later, when the time was right, that I was able to understand what Uncle Seyfettin meant. He was worried about me because, in spite of all my small victories, with this death I would have

1 Bektashi elder: Bektashism is an Islamic sufi order founded in the thirteenth century.

had to resign myself to this life, from which I would always feel alienated. Anyway . . . I'm used now to deferrals and to being too late. Otherwise, how could I explain these silent murders that I have committed in different ways and in different places? How can I stand so close to that thin line between life and death? These questions belonged also to my play, to that play. I believed so fervently in that play. . . .

Words, Colors, Shadows

My name is Isaac. I have always been proud not only of being from Istanbul—which provides a sense of belonging whose binding power I have expressed at every possible occasion and which is engraved deep down in my personality—but also of being a fan of Fenerbahçe,[2] which has given me many moments of exhilaration up to now. Outwardly I never made any great efforts to choose or to obtain these identities. There is a reason why I say "outwardly." It is true that people discover themselves within one existence or another or as a result of a coincidence. If my forefathers had not been expelled from Spain, if they had not chosen to come here, if they had not chosen to share their history and their destiny with the people of this city for five hundred years . . . If, during those days of my childhood, when I was trying to find myself, my father hadn't told me that he was a fan of Fenerbahçe and he hadn't told me of the goals scored by Lefter. But the real choice revealed itself years later, in the insistence on staying in the same place. Though you pay the price, you still can't bring yourself to leave. Because in time you learn to love yourself more, you find yourself credible and you appreciate yourself because you stay on. As a person who experiences the unforgettable legacy of his history, who always opposes all types of racism and is open to all types of freedoms, I have always felt very angry to be forced to share the same language and borders of this country with people who choose to pursue nationalism by presenting anybody who is different from themselves with the choice of either loving this country or leaving, but especially when I lived abroad and I remembered that anti-imperialist struggle full of suffering, I was always proud of this land body and soul. Although I believed more in cultural climates and geographies than I did in homelands. Although I knew that laying claim on a country was no different from getting bogged down in a hollow type of nationalism. Although

2 Fenerbahçe: a Turkish professional football club based in Istanbul.

I witnessed, or rather I was made to witness, that I was not considered a real Turk simply because I was Jewish. In other words, in this country to which I'm attached primarily through my feelings, according to some I'm a Turk, and according to others I'm a Jew who bears the identity of the Turkish Republic. I now have so many memories and testimonies that have caused me to experience my being an "outsider" in different ways. I don't need to make a special effort to use the word "outsider." This is not a word that I use but that the law uses from time to time and therefore that I, too, whether I want it or not, end up having to use and to feel. Isn't it very meaningful that real estate belonging to Minority Foundations are seen as "foreign property"? As for the fact that those who are born with these "diversities" are still considered "banned" by the state and "objectionable," like political convicts, that's something I don't even want to think about. Because probing such issues may expose you to "undesirable" results, deriving from the fact that what you said was found "excessively" inquisitive or meddlesome, in a way that would confirm the saying that "sheep that stray are caught by wolves," or would justify people who tell you "not to meddle in such things." Our history is full of examples of people who paid very dearly for their "mistakes." It is easier to walk on slippery ground as long as you remember these examples.

On the other hand, when I look back at my life, I see that I have established my closest friendships and even sentimental relations with people who did not care about such diversities and who, from where I stand, were born "more Turkish" than I. This is one of the most meaningful sides of my destiny in this geographical region where I am. Otherwise, considering all the probabilities and risks it involves, I wouldn't have wanted to bring up my story after all these years. I had clung so tightly to it. The city too, which had enabled me to build myself, which held me through all binding power and did not let me evade it for another emotional climate, expected me to produce this story out of my experiences. Experiencing Istanbul is different from living in Istanbul. In order to experience and to feel Istanbul's diversity, you need to be able to hear its different voices. That is the only way to preserve the city's depth. The story I experienced was my history, my language. What's more, I needed this story in order to save my life. The feeling of being an "outsider" that can't be prevented, that you don't choose but are made to choose, the threat of having to pack your stuff at any moment, with the belief that you will never be able to be part of the real center and that you will be stopped at a certain point, was also present within the shadows of this story. Although the resentment deriving from those diversities that could not always be expressed was much less painful than what could be experienced in some of those countries that claim to be civilized and have been attempting to export civilization to this land for so many centuries. I can see and understand the reality much better now. But I still don't feel like forgetting completely what has happened or eliminating it from my life.

What's more, I experienced all of this even though in the eyes of many Jews I wasn't a good Jew. For example, I don't respect Sabbath days. I haven't seen anyone who truly respects them in this city. The Kiddush prayer is not recited at our home on Friday evenings. Of course, I have no reason to criticize those who do. Seeing that some people believe in "something" that strengthen their ties to life and that they can refer to and experience as they wish makes me even happy, at times. But it is a bittersweet happiness. Because by now I am so resentful that I cannot experience such purity and innocence anymore. Having lost my larger family a long time ago, I still celebrate Pesach with friends of mine. But the choice to do so is based on the need to relive my childhood, rather than to fulfill a religious duty. And traditions are thus passed on to others. If such things matter anymore. Chela, my wife, with whom I have shared almost thirty years of my life, who has always adhered to traditions and who has even taken strength from them, and whom I sometimes see as a symbol of submission, has always cared more than I about these issues. That is why her struggle to raise the children in line with the values surrounding her and enabling her to exist, and with the expectations of history, has never surprised me. But has it served its purpose? Nowadays it is a little difficult for me to answer this question. Because following the recent events, my life is in great turmoil. A scene that is not in the text, that hasn't been written and that I never thought would be written in those long, seemingly calm years, has completely changed the course of the play. A messenger came on stage at an unexpected point and said the line that invited me into this story. The journey could only begin as the consequence of such an encounter.

Once I used to believe that there was a destructive, deadly side to traditions. I can still feel hints of this belief. The difference in between derives no doubt from my having lost to a great degree my harshness and my will to fight as a result of what the years have imposed on me and what they have taken away. When and where did I lose my will to resist, to rebel? Who knows. Why should I even try to remember? I think that at some point I gave up playing the dissident. Maybe I was afraid of becoming even more of a minority. In the beginning I was very worried that this renunciation would be perceived as cowardice by some. This choice didn't befit the role that I had chosen for myself, to strengthen my ties to life. But I don't care anymore. I don't care that the "rebel" of once has come to this or that he has imprisoned himself. Every life has its own truths, which are subject to change and to destruction at any moment. With the passing of time, truth can be seen and experienced in a different way. One can draw new and unsettling meanings from changes and from looking at things from a different perspective.

Over the course of these changes and in the belief that I was embracing the idea of being a "local," like many of my peers who have chosen to experience their Jewishness together with a quest for freedom, I have learned to refer to the synagogue as *hebrah*, where I go only for weddings, funerals, bar mitzvahs, and on Yom Kippur, to avoid a guilty conscience, rather than to have my sins absolved. To think that for years I avoided using this word. For years. As if I was evading a curse that I didn't believe I deserved. The fact that I once avoided using the word *Yahudi* and preferred to hold on to the word *Musevi*, which seemed more "gentle" and "innocent," could also be sought in this evasion. No doubt there were reasons for these internalizations. I can still remember words that were said a very long time ago, and what those words made me feel. The fact that I can still remember them is meaningful as it is. One such incident happened at school, at the state school that I attended. As in all other state schools, our class was very crowded and contained many students from many different parts of society. When I remember our teacher, I realize that she was one of those women who carried the many issues and resentments of her personal life into the classroom. By now I can feel more benevolence than anger in the face of such hurt. Circumstances annihilate different sides of different people. But my present perspective on my experiences is not sufficient to cover up or make me forget the mortification that I felt whenever we made a lot of noise and she shouted, "You've turned this place into a *hebrah*!" I can't make up my mind whether she liked this sentence so much because she was ignorant and unaware of certain subtleties, because of her secret sense of discrimination, or because of her helplessness, because of the inability to find more suitable words to express her anger. Whatever the reason, those words were the first to make me feel in real terms that diversity that I didn't want to carry or that I was forced to carry as if it was a secret illness, and that discrimination that has always been ignored. There were other Jewish children in our class. None of us ever ventured to react to these demeaning words; we wouldn't even have dreamt of doing so and we preferred to join the others who were sniggering, but with a feeling of bitterness. That's what we had been taught to do. We needed to keep silent and keep living. In reality it was a very painful experience. No matter what people may say, its impact lasted for years and years. It is that experience that lay behind my reasons for not using the word *hebrah*. But in that educational journey where time smoothens our rough edges, I learned to reconcile myself not only to the hurt, but also to the feelings that these words evoked. What's more, over time I have got used to the attributes of cowardice and of stinginess that are associated with this identity that I was born with and that I have not chosen. As part of my daily life, I have met many people who wouldn't dream of making such associations, who consider them shameful and who see them simply as a source of friendly and innocent jokes and banter. The better you get to know yourself and others, the better you can judge the appropriateness of leaving some people alone with their imperfections, dilemmas and predicaments. It's like a sort of training for wisdom that seems unpretentious but that contains a secret assertion. Training for wisdom that anybody who is forced to walk on slippery ground has to undergo, whether they like it or not, and that within this struggle to maintain their existence they scrupulously pass on to their peers. I now know that this training is part of Jewish tradition. But of course, it was impossible for me to be aware of this truth in my childhood. But lessons had already begun. For example, when I first heard that we were stingy, I was so surprised and dejected that I ran to my grandfather and asked him to "reveal the truth of the situation." His response to my question, "They say that we are stingy, is that true?" was a warm, maybe slightly bitter, smile and a simple but equally formidable sentence, that I can still remember so well, filtered through that fine tradition of irony: "No, we are not. We are simply a little frugal." And when I asked him about his views on our cowardice, again he smiled at the association of this attribute, he shook his head slightly, he thought for a while and then he murmured, "Maybe a little prudent." It has taken me a very long time to perceive the depth of irony and even of melancholy that these answers contained. This is the destiny of certain words. It's only when the right time comes that we are confronted with their real impact and what they actually represent. You can't expel them from your life because by now you have found your place on that perspective of life. It takes a lifetime for a legacy to achieve the value it deserves. That is why destroying or disregarding a language is akin to murder.

When I remember those incidents, a feeling of insecurity pervades me once again. Yes, a feeling of insecurity. Although I believe that I am more entitled than most other people to say that I am a local in this city, or rather its owner. How many people now living in Istanbul can pride themselves with a five-hundred-year-old past in this city? But even when it comes to this truth, my past is still full of contradictions. I can remember the days when my grandmother spoke with her friends in Ladino, because she knew no other language, and she was ridiculed by many people. In those days I used to feel embarrassed to stand near her, I wanted to belong somewhere else, where I wouldn't have to experience or reveal my diversities. How unfair I was. That's what children are like. How could I have known that the real issue lay elsewhere? My grandmother and her friends hadn't made a conscious choice. In the years when they were students it would have been out of question to attend a Turkish school. What's more, they didn't feel such a need in those restricted circles where they lived, in that language world that had been preserved for many centuries and within those self-sufficient communities. They didn't even need to read that much, as part of that modest lifestyle where they were trained to become mothers only. Those were the days when people led a confined life and they experienced a different kind of alliance, solidarity, and mutual need, without being aware of other possibilities. Anyway . . . It's all over and gone now.

Nowadays I only remember these things when somebody brings them up. And I keep telling myself that other issues and truths are of greater significance in life and in this country. In this land where we live, there are so many so many intricate questions that can't be answered and can't be spoken. We are trying to survive in such a difficult region. There are so many people who don't permit those they have alienated to survive. If we set all of this aside, I still think that regardless of which part of the world they live in, all Jews are bound to feel the worry of being ostracized, of being subject to attacks and even of being annihilated. Was this one of the consequences of that feeling of long exile that was engraved deeper than what was transmitted through our religion and prayers? Maybe. Maybe this concern, which was maintained in a variety of climates, shapes, and amounts and through a variety of deaths, but which also strengthened people's ties to life, was a different form of the struggle to survive. I have never been able to eliminate this possibility from my life. That is why, deep inside, I have always shared the feeling of people who find themselves to be part of a minority or are forced to see themselves as such. There is a threat; people built it or were made to build it. There are also the dark traces of civilizations built on ruins and on murders, right by an abyss that was always ignored. Those in exile survived in the depth of that darkness. I had seen both what I could see and what I didn't want to see. Because that was what history taught us. History taught us this. I have never been able to forget those words. But then, what's left over from all that happened? What's left over? Everything is transient. Everything comes to an end. The graves are deep inside us. It's very difficult to answer these questions. All I can say is that all communities that have lost their self-confidence or are not able to come to terms with their sorrow, perceive as threats all the differences they encounter or that they are forced to feel by others. Just as most people who are not able to get rid of their predicaments and their feelings of defeat, or to reconcile with themselves, would perceive them. But when we think of the coexistence of these diversities, no one is actually threatening anybody else. Everybody wishes to live their own life, or what they consider as their truths. It's as simple as that. What the protagonists of this long play, which I have been performing for such a long time and at times have been observing silently, have felt and experienced during the course of events amply confirms my belief. The real truth lay in those emotional contact points. Diversities merged within those emotional contact points. The art of marbling could only be created within that water and with those colors. Those colors existed only because they tinged each other and they couldn't be separated from each other. When I want to believe in this probability, I remember that my grandmother, who was more devoted to her religion than any of us, shared so many things with her religious Muslim neighbors. This was my longest play and the one that I could never give up. Because I am Istanbul. Because my mother comes from a family that has lived in Istanbul for five hundred years. When I go on stage to tell this story, this is the history that lies behind me. My country and my emotional geography are engraved the deepest among the stones of history.

Those Faces Now Smile Inside Me

In that shop at Bahçekapı we used to talk about things that people who are bored with their work or with their lives talk about. We used to talk about politics, football and—as if we were very knowledgeable about it—women, but to tell the truth, the walls that some people built because of religious diversities never occurred to any of us. Like most of his Jewish contemporaries, my father adhered to the Democratic Party with all his heart and soul. In his opinion, the hanging of Menderes[3] was the biggest political murder and source of shame in this country's history. In later years he voted for Demirel and for the Justice Party. He absolutely hated İnönü. His hate, of course, derived from İnönü's policies concerning the minorities. That was a time when people were forced to acknowledge and to accept that in spite of all their good faith they were not considered true citizens of this country. But it wasn't possible to either forget or forgive what happened. Over the course of the years, I have felt this resentment deep down inside me. I couldn't help feeling sorry about what they had to experience. Over the course of the years, I have seen that this dark period, the time of the "National Chief"[4] that some people take pride in remembering and in reminding others about, is the most ruthless and fascist period of this country's history. So many mistakes were made that resulted in the people becoming alienated from the state. And we too had to join in at some point of this course of events, of this struggle for a more righteous country, that we believed in with our heart and soul. What a period that was. I now remember what happened with a bitter smile. A bitter smile. Partly because I can view from another perspective the child who experienced those days with such excitement, and partly because over the years I have realized that that excitement was real and that that rebellion was very pure and honest when compared with that filthiness. Because from time to time I feel sad about that child. Because I'm also proud of him. Because I miss that purity, that defenselessness and vulnerability. Because I can't explain anymore to anybody that the protagonists of that play are the real protagonists of my country. I was a sophomore then. I had worked hard to organize the shop staff against my father, the fascist boss! What a comedy. That shop had a total staff of four! One can therefore remember the play as a drama, or rather a tragedy. But now, after all these losses and after having had to come to terms with reality, I enjoy sitting among the audience and watching this comedy again.

The comedy had in part been written by the protagonists of the play, of which I was unwillingly a part. Kemalettin Bey of Findikzade was my father's driver and he did not cease working although he was close to his seventies. Let alone giving up working, he said that he saw work as a kind of religious ritual,

---

3 Menderes: Adnan Menderes (1899–1961). First democratically elected Turkish Prime Minister between 1950–1960, he was executed in 1961 by the military junta.

4 İnönü: İsmet İnönü (1884–1973). Prime minister and president of Turkey, known as the "National Chief." His party lost the first free elections in the republic's history.

but I think that he pursued this life because he had no other life, or because he was continuously evading something that I couldn't understand or name. Kemalettin Bey, with his meticulously clean but very frayed white shirts, his ties that were out of fashion and old but extremely tasteful, his dark suits, the lunchboxes that he brought from home, and his way of speaking that made me think that he had jumped out of one of those old photographs of Istanbul, was as right-wing as my father. He had worked for many years in the Justice Party's Istanbul office and at every opportunity he would feel the need to say that all left-wing people were traitors who received financial aid "from abroad." As far as I knew, he too had practiced commerce in the past and after having gone bankrupt he had begun to earn a living working as a driver for my father. Where and how had they met? Through which circumstances had he come to the shop? I never knew much about such details. My father didn't seem very keen to tell. My father tended to keep to himself the secrets of people whom he cared about and I respected him for this. That's why I didn't probe the subject too much, besides which there was no need to do so. All I knew was that their association, or rather their friendship, dated back to a long time before. I was little, I can barely remember those days. There was no shop yet at that time. All we had, to enable us to view the future with some hope, was a small room in one of those decaying commercial buildings in Eminönü which was used partly for storage and partly as a shop. My father bought a van to sell perfumery goods to pharmacies in Anatolia around the same time when Kemalettin Bey came into our lives. My father said that he began to work with him because he didn't want to be on his own during those long trips. For some reason I never forgot those words. What he said could have been interpreted in many different ways. Who knows what they had shared on those roads, what and who they had talked about. Whenever I think about how close they were, I feel that they must have seen that van as a mobile room that held their secrets. That room played an important role in my life, too. In my relationship with my father, it was as if many things—which I wanted to remember under different names at different times—began and ended there. The story of that ending still saddens me. But for them it was different. They had reached a point where, after all those roads and those journeys, they couldn't even think of going their separate ways. Ultimately, in spite of all the changes that took place, they didn't split up, they didn't go their separate ways. When my father opened the shop in Bahçekapı, the Anatolian phase of his life came to an end. And there was no need any more for that tired old van that had covered thousands of kilometers. That was the time when our financial situation began to improve. On my mother's urging, we even bought the flat in Şişli where we lived as tenants. Had it been up to my father, he would have never made that "stable investment." In his view, money needed always to be in cash, it needed to be invested in commercial activities and, most importantly, it needed to be movable. You never knew what the state might want to seize and when. I don't blame him for these thoughts. The legacy of our collective memory amply justified his concern. All of this aside, he never liked to be flashy. He would resent people who lived in this way and he would say that they chose this lifestyle because of their inability to cope with their predicaments. I think that many people from his generation thought the same way and they felt so throughout their lives. Behind these efforts not to exhibit oneself too much lay the threat of history. Although we were wealthy enough to easily buy one of the better models of Mercedes, we had to make do with a Peugeot 504, which for some reason was known as the "Jewish Mercedes." With the purchase of a car, the issue regarding Kemalettin Bey was solved. My father claimed that his own irascibility, caused by his diabetes, would not permit him to drive, and he asked Kemalettin Bey to be his personal driver. Thus began a new stage in their association and in a way that befitted their friendship. I understood this subtlety better over time. What I saw now was a man who did his best not to treat his long distance driving partner as a conventional driver, who took pains to sit always in the front seat and who didn't let him open his door. In this relationship, it was as if my father sought a brother, whose absence he felt from time to time.

Monsieur David, who dealt with the bookkeeping, was another hopeless case. He too was a Jew who led a modest life and learned to make do with what he had. He had never earned great amounts of money but he had always considered wealth as the most unwavering indicator of success. This was a very sad contradiction. It was as if throughout his life he had been drawn by the prestige deriving from wealth that he himself had conceived, rather than by money itself. Is that why he voted for the Justice Party? Who knows? He had managed to save a little money and after work he acted as a moneylender. My father, who always considered this a dangerous, cursed profession that was practiced by people who lacked commercial skills and moral principles, frequently expressed his disapproval, but as he paid him a very small salary he would overlook the fact that he inflated some expenses and pocketed some money, and that he committed this "crime" which actually enabled him to stay on. They had reached an agreement on a small, innocent type of complicity that shopkeepers knew so well about. They had established a system. No one could complain about the situation. My father knew that he could trust him completely regarding some open accounts. Moreover, moneylending increased Monsieur David's self-confidence. But to tell the truth, no one ever thought that this profession would slowly prepare the grounds for his death. One day he lost a considerable amount of money because of the son of Monsieur Daniel from Izmir, a producer and wholesaler of shaving brushes, who suddenly went bankrupt; Monsieur David went into a diabetic coma and, to our surprise and dismay, a short while later died of a cerebral hemorrhage. My father, without thinking of how much Monsieur David had wanted to succeed in this field and how much he cared about those small amounts of money, said, "*Izmirli bueno no ay*—No person from Izmir can be good," referring to the man who had been the cause of his death. This was another way of saying, "Nothing good can come out of Izmir." I don't know whether he had meant Jews from Izmir or all people from Izmir. It wasn't worth asking him or trying to find out why he had developed such a fervent view. When I tried to understand this death, what interested me more was the tragedy of this man who had made himself such a prisoner of money. This incident aside, I have always loved Izmir because of my memories of it and the people I met there. And now, after this long story I experienced, I love it even more. Anyway. Over the course of events, you learn to leave the people around you—those who in some way touch you—alone with their obsessions. It is enough to remember that there is bound to be a valid reason behind every word and behavior—it enables you to endure certain disappointments more easily.

My father's cousin, Mordo, who as far as I know was four or five years older than him, was a man with a poetic soul who was afraid of his own shadow and who, same as Kemalettin Bey, had landed, or rather taken refuge, in the shop after having gone bankrupt. Whenever we talked about political issues, he would look around with fear in his eyes and tell me to lower my voice. He believed that walls had ears and that the most unexpected people could turn out to be members of the secret police. The story of his bankruptcy was very sad, it was yet another case of somebody who got caught up. That's all I was able to find out. Because he used to tell us over and over again, sometimes with the addition of a few small lies, what had happened to him, the event that had caused him to become so destitute. I would, of course, eliminate the lies from his story. At times it was the places that changed, at times what was said, at times the clothes worn, and at times those "private moments." He had a very rich imagination. Judging from what my father said, that's what he was best at in life. This was a disparaging statement, if not humiliating. But I have to confess that it was this side of Mordo that I loved the most. From time to time his story would be embellished with small lies, but the main structure never changed.

My memories regarding that period of the shop consisted of these voices, faces, hopes, and expectations from life. Truths or fallacies. Intimacy or loneliness. Realities or illusions. Of course, it was a comedy that I should try to get the protagonists of this play to side with me. A comedy that ruthlessly revealed how life passed me by. But this was what I was going to do. Like everybody else, I too was in search for myself. I didn't know what I would encounter. But it couldn't have been any other way. The ability to continue to walk required not to know. Isn't that why darkness seemed deeper than light? Isn't that why nights were more bewitching than daytime? In those days I couldn't have known that those voices and those faces that I endeavored to leave behind me were inadvertently preparing me for another play. Some peace treaties are said to prepare the way for new wars and the path that I had undertaken was just like that. The breaking point that took place inside me was just like that. . . .

Red Cavalry

By Isaac Babel

Three Stories: Crossing the Zbrucz, Gedali, and The Rebbe

Translated from Russian *by Boris Dralyuk*

Crossing the Zbrucz

The sixth division commander reported that Novograd-Volynsk was taken today at dawn. The staff has moved out of Krapivno and our transport sprawls in a noisy rearguard along the highway that runs from Brest to Warsaw and was built on the bones of peasant men by Nicholas the First.

Fields of scarlet poppies blossom around us, a midday breeze plays in the yellowing rye, and virgin buckwheat rises on the horizon like the wall of a distant monastery. The quiet Volyn bends. Volyn recedes from us into the pearly mist of birch groves and creeps into the flowery hills, its feeble arms getting tangled in thickets of hops. An orange sun rolls across the sky like a severed head, a gentle light glitters in the ravines of clouds and the banners of sunset flutter over our heads. The scent of yesterday's blood and dead horses seeps into the evening coolness. The blackened Zbrucz roars, twisting the foamy knots of its rapids. The bridges are destroyed, and we are fording the river. A stately moon lies on the waves. The horses sink up to their backs and sonorous streams trickle between hundreds of horses' legs. Someone is drowning, loudly disparaging the Mother of God. The river is strewn with the black squares of carts, filled with rumbling, whistling, and songs that thunder over snakes of moonlight and glistening pits.

Late at night we arrive in Novograd. In my assigned billet I find a pregnant woman, along with two red-haired, thin-necked Jews; a third Jew is sleeping, huddled up against the wall with a blanket over his head. In my assigned room I find two ransacked wardrobes, scraps of women's fur coats on the floor, human excrement, and shards of the sacred plate that Jews use once a year—on Passover.

"Clean this up," I say to the woman. "You live in filth, hosts . . ."

The two Jews spring into action. They jump around on felt soles, picking debris off the floor. They jump silently, monkey-like, like a Japanese circus act, their necks swelling and swiveling. They spread a torn feather mattress on the floor and I lie down, facing the wall, next to the third, sleeping Jew. Fearful poverty closes in above my bed.

Silence has killed everything off, and only the moon, with its blue hands clasping its round, sparkling, carefree head, tramps about under the window.

I stretch my numbed legs. I lie on the torn feather mattress and fall asleep. I dream of the Sixth Division commander. He's chasing the brigade commander on a heavy stallion and plants two bullets in his eyes. The bullets pierce the brigade commander's head, and both his eyes fall to the ground.

"Why'd you turn the brigade back?" Savitsky, the Sixth Division commander, shouts at the wounded man—and here I wake up, because the pregnant woman's fingers are fumbling over my face.

"Pan," she says to me. "You're screaming in your sleep, thrashing around. I'll make your bed in the other corner, because you're shoving my papa . . ."

She raises her skinny legs and round belly off the floor and removes the blanket from the huddled sleeper. It's a dead old man, flat on his back. His gullet is ripped out, his face is hacked in two, and blue blood sits in his beard like a hunk of lead.

"Pan," says the Jewess, giving the feather mattress a shake. "The Poles were slashing him and he kept begging them, 'Kill me in the back yard so my daughter doesn't see me die.' But they did it their way—he died in this room, thinking of me. . . . And now you tell me," the woman said suddenly with terrible force, "you tell me where else in this whole world you'll find a father like my father . . ."

Gedali

On Sabbath eves I am tormented by the rich sorrow of memories. Long ago, on these evenings, my grandfather would stroke the volumes of Ibn Ezra with his yellow beard. The old woman, in a lace headdress, would conjure with her gnarled fingers over the Sabbath candle and sob sweetly. On these evenings, my child's heart would sway like a boat on enchanted waves. . . . O the Talmuds of my childhood, reduced to dust! O the rich sorrow of memories!

I roam Zhitomir and search for the shy star. By the ancient synagogue, by her yellow and indifferent walls, old Jews are selling chalk, bluing, wicks—Jews with the beards of prophets, with passionate rags on their sunken chests. . . .

Here before me is the bazaar and the death of the bazaar. The fat soul of abundance is killed. Mute padlocks hang on the stalls and the granite pavement is as clean as a dead man's bald pate. It twinkles and fades, the shy star. . . .

Success came to me later, came just before sunset. Gedali's shop was tucked away among closely packed rows of stalls. Dickens, where was your shade that evening? In that old curiosity shop you'd have seen gilt shoes and ships' ropes, an antique compass and a stuffed eagle, a Winchester hunting rifle engraved with the date 1810, and a broken stewpan.

Old Gedali paces around his treasures in the pink emptiness of the evening—a little shop-owner in smoky glasses and a green frock coat reaching down to the ground. He rubs his little white hands, tugs at his little grey beard and, bowing his head, heeds the invisible voices drifting down to him.

This shop is like the box of an inquisitive and serious boy who'll someday become a professor of botany. The shop has both buttons and a dead butterfly, and its little owner is named Gedali. Everyone's left the bazaar, but Gedali remains. He wends his way through a labyrinth of globes, skulls and dead flowers, whisks his motley brush of rooster feathers and blows the dust off the perished flowers.

We are sitting on empty beer kegs. Gedali twists and untwists his narrow beard. His top hat sways above us like a black turret. Warm air floats past us. The sky changes color. Up there, high up, delicate blood flows from an overturned bottle, and I am enveloped in the faint odor of decay.

"The revolution—we'll say 'yes' to her, but will we say 'no' to the Sabbath?" So begins Gedali, entwining me in the silk straps of his smoky eyes. "'Yes,' I cry to the revolution, 'yes,' I cry to her, but she hides from Gedali, and all she sends our way is shooting. . . ."

"The sun doesn't enter eyes that are closed," I answer the old man, "but we will rip those closed eyes open. . . ."

"The Pole closed my eyes," the old man whispers, almost inaudibly. "The Pole is a mad dog. He takes a Jew and pulls out his beard—eh, that cur! And now they're beating him good, the mad dog. That's wonderful, that's the revolution! And then the one who beat the Pole says to me, 'We have to take your gramophone in account, Gedali. . . .' 'But I love music, Pani,' I tell the revolution. 'You don't know what you like, Gedali—I'll shoot at you and then you'll find out, and I can't help shooting, because I'm the revolution. . . .'"

"She can't help shooting, Gedali," I say to the old man, "because she's the revolution. . . ."

"But the Pole shot, my dear Pan, because he's the counterrevolution. You shoot because you're the revolution. But the revolution is happiness. And happiness doesn't like orphans in the house. Good deeds are done by good men. The revolution is the good deed of good men. But good men do not kill. So the revolution is the work of bad men. But the Poles, too, are bad men. So who will tell Gedali where's the revolution and where's the counter-revolution? I once studied the Talmud—I love the commentaries of Rashi, the books of Maimonides. And there are other men of wisdom in Zhitomir. And here we are, all learned men, falling on our faces and crying out loud, 'Woe unto us, where is the sweet revolution? . . .'"

The old man fell silent. And we saw the first star cutting its path along the Milky Way.

"The Sabbath is coming," Gedali pronounced with significance. "Jews must go to the synagogue. . . . Pan Comrade," he said, rising up, the top hat swaying like a black turret on his head, "bring a few good people to Zhitomir. Oh, what a shortage we have in our town. Oh, what a shortage! Bring good people, and we'll give them all our gramophones. We aren't ignorant. The International . . . We know what the International is. And I want an International of good people—I want them to take every soul into account and give it a first-grade ration. Here, soul, eat, go ahead, get some happiness out of life. It's you, Pan Comrade—it's you who doesn't know what they eat the International with . . ."

"They eat it with gunpowder," I answered the old man, "and season it with the best blood. . . ."

And so she ascended her throne out of the deep-blue darkness, the young Sabbath.

"Gedali," I say, "today is Friday, and the evening is here. Where can I get a Jewish shortcake, a Jewish glass of tea, with some of that retired God in the glass? . . . "

"No place," Gedali answers, hanging a padlock on his box. "No place. There's a cook-shop next door, and good people did trade there, but nobody eats there nowadays, they weep. . . ."

He fastened his green frock coat on three bone buttons. He dusted himself off with the rooster feathers, splashed a little water on his soft palms, and walked off—tiny, lonely, dreamy, with a black top hat on his head and a big prayer book under his arm.

The Sabbath is coming. Gedali—the founder of a hopeless International—has gone off to the synagogue to pray.

The Rebbe

All things are mortal. Only a mother is destined for eternal life. And when a mother is no longer among the living, she leaves behind a memory that no one dares to desecrate. A mother's memory nourishes compassion within us, just as the ocean, the boundless ocean, nourishes the rivers that cleave the universe. . . ."

These were Gedali's words. He pronounced them with significance. The dying evening surrounded him with the rosy haze of its sadness. The old man said:

"The doors and windows have been knocked out of Hasidism's passionate edifice, but it is immortal, like a mother's soul. . . . Its eyes have been gouged from their sockets, but Hasidism still stands at the crossroads of the furious winds of history."

So said Gedali, and, having finished his prayers at the synagogue, he led me to Rebbe Motale, the last rebbe of the Chernobyl dynasty.

Gedali and I went up the main street. White churches glittered in the distance like fields of buckwheat. A cannon wheel groaned around the corner. Two pregnant Ukrainian girls walked out of a gate, their necklaces jangling, and sat on a bench. The shy star lit up amid the orange battle scenes of sunset, and peace, a Sabbath peace, descended on the crooked roofs of the Zhitomir ghetto.

"Here," Gedali whispered, pointing to a long house with a broken pediment.

We entered a room that was stony and barren, like a morgue. Rebbe Motale sat at the table, surrounded by liars and the bedeviled. He wore a sable cap and a white gown bound with a rope. The rebbe sat with his eyes closed and his thin fingers fumbling in the yellow down of his beard.

"Where has the Jew come from?" he asked, lifting his eyelids.

"From Odesa," I answered.

"A pious city," said the rebbe, "the star of our exile, the involuntary well of our calamities! . . . What is the Jew's occupation?"

"I am putting the adventures of Hershel of Ostropol into verse."

"A great task," whispered the rebbe, lowering his eyelids. "The jackal whines when he is hungry, any fool is fool enough for despondency, and only the wise man rends the veil of being with laughter. . . . What has the Jew studied?"

"The Bible."

"What does the Jew seek?"

"Joy."

"Reb Mordkhe," said the *tsaddik*, shaking his beard, "let the young man take a seat at the table, let him eat this Sabbath eve with other Jews, let him rejoice that he is alive and not dead, let him clap his hands when his neighbors dance, let him drink wine if he is given wine. . . ."

And Reb Mordkhe scurried over to me—a timeworn jester with turned-out eyelids, a tiny hunchbacked old man, no taller than a ten-year-old boy.

"Oh, my dear and so young a man!" said the ragged Reb Mordkhe, winking at me. "Oh, how many wealthy fools I have known in Odesa, how many poor wise men I have known in Odesa! Sit down at the table, young man, and drink the wine you won't be given. . . ."

We all sat together—the bedeviled, the liars, the loafers. In the corner, moaning over their prayer books, stood broad-shouldered Jews who looked like fishermen and apostles. Gedali dozed against the wall in his green frock coat, like a gay little bird. And suddenly I saw a young man seated behind him, a young man with the face of Spinoza, with Spinoza's mighty brow and a nun's sallow face. He was smoking and quivering, like a fugitive captured after a chase and brought back to prison. Ragged Mordkhe crept up behind him, snatched the cigarette from his mouth, and ran back to me.

"That is the rebbe's son, Ilya," Mordkhe rasped, approaching me with the bleeding flesh of his mangled eyelids. "A damned son, the last son, a disobedient son . . ."

Mordkhe shook his fist at the young man and spat in his face.

"Blessed be the Lord," Rebbe Motale Bratslavsky's voice rang out, and he broke bread with his monkish fingers.

"Blessed be the God of Israel, who has chosen us among all the nations of the earth. . . ."

The rebbe blessed the food and we sat down at table. Outside the window, horses neighed and Cossacks shouted. The desert of war yawned outside the window. The rebbe's son smoked one cigarette after another amid the silence and prayers. When the supper was over, I was the first to rise.

"My dear and so young a man," Mordkhe muttered behind my back and pulled at my belt, "if there were no one in this world but evil rich men and poor tramps, how would holy men live?"

I gave the old man money and went out into the street. Gedali and I parted ways and I walked on to the station. There, at the station, on the agitprop train of the First Cavalry Army, I was awaited by the glare of countless lights, the magical glimmer of the wireless, the stubborn running of the printing press, and an unfinished article for *The Red Cavalryman* newspaper.

Acknowledgments

Acknowledging and thanking all those who have contributed to the creation of this book is a real pleasure. This book would not exist without *Jewish Fiction .net*, and *Jewish Fiction .net* would not exist without its amazing team of volunteer manuscript reviewers, who generously devote their time to evaluating the mountain of submissions we regularly receive, and who were instrumental in initially selecting the stories for *Jewish Fiction .net* that are now in this book. *Jewish Fiction .net* has three reviewer hubs—in Toronto, Houston, and Jerusalem—and I am profoundly grateful to the volunteers in all three places who have worked over the past thirteen years to help produce our first thirty-four issues. To our current team—Dr. Bernice Heilbrunn, Dr. Carol Ricker, Dr. Charlotte Berkowitz, Dr. Julia Mazow (who, uniquely, has been part of *Jewish Fiction .net* since its beginning), Dr. Sheila Deutsch, and Sidura Ludwig—I extend my warmest appreciation and admiration for the intelligence, thoughtfulness, care, and seriousness with which they approach each and every story they review. I feel incredibly fortunate to be engaged with these individuals in this project, which is a labor of love for us all.

I am honored and delighted that this book is coming out with the excellent publisher, Academic Studies Press. My heartfelt gratitude to Senior Editor Alessandra Anzani, whose professionalism, as well as her commitment to, and excitement about, this anthology, have made working with her, as well as her whole capable team—Kira Nemirovsky, Alana Felton, Becca Kearns, and Matthew Charlton—a very positive and enjoyable experience.

I am deeply thankful to my fellow writers in this anthology, and to writers of Jewish fiction in general, both for their work and for the special community we share as writers. To the translators in this volume and beyond, I extend great appreciation because without them, these important works of literature would be inaccessible to me and to so many others.

A special thank you to Dr. Barry Walfish for steering me graciously through the fascinating but complex issues of transliteration related to this anthology. His erudition and thoughtful advice were invaluable to this book.

Thanks are due to Naomi Schacter of the National Library of Israel for inviting me in 2021 to give a webinar there about *Jewish Fiction .net*—an event that helped crystallize the idea of creating this anthology.

Fluttering in the pages of this book is the spirit of the recently deceased Israeli poet Hava Pinhas-Cohen, the spearheader of the brilliant "Kisufim" conferences in Jerusalem which brought together Jewish writers from around the world. Hava's vision of an international community of writers of Jewish literature coincided closely with my own (she expressed this vision through her conferences; I through Jewish Fiction .net), and this gave us a special rapport, which both inspired and reinforced me in my work.

I am indebted to the members of *Jewish Fiction .net's* illustrious Advisory Council for their help and guidance—a special shout-out to Thane Rosenbaum for the active role he's played, especially in this journal's early years—as well as to the generous individuals whose donations, of whatever size, have kept this unfunded, free-of-charge journal afloat for all these years. Thanks also to Lipa Roth for his unflagging moral support and practical assistance to *Jewish Fiction .net.*

Warm thanks to my son, the talented Joseph Weissgold, for his helpful and original suggestions regarding the cover design of this book, and for his creative involvement over the years with *Jewish Fiction .net*, including his design of its logo and website.

Last but not least, I thank my husband, Dr. David Weiss, who has been, throughout the creation of this book, an anchor, cheerleader, coach, and loving friend. I am the fortunate beneficiary of his wise counsel and enthusiastic support—not only for this anthology, but also for *Jewish Fiction .net*, and indeed for all my creative work, including my novels and stories. To him I am grateful more than words can say.

Nora Gold

Contributors

The Editor

Dr. Nora Gold, previously an Associate Professor, is a prize-winning author and the founder and editor of the prestigious online literary journal *Jewish Fiction .net,* which publishes first-rate Jewish-themed fiction that was either written in English or translated into English from twenty languages, and which has readers in 140 countries.

Dr. Gold received her PhD from University of Toronto, spent ten years on faculty at McMaster University, and left this position in order to have more time for her fiction writing. Her first book, *Marrow and Other Stories,* won a Vine Canadian Jewish Book Award and was praised by Alice Munro. Her second book, the novel *Fields of Exile* (the first—and to date, only—novel about anti-Israelism in the academe) won a Canadian Jewish Literary Award and was acclaimed by Cynthia Ozick, Ruth Wisse, and Irwin Cotler. Her third book, *The Dead Man,* received glowing reviews and a Canada Council translation grant, resulting in this novel's publication in Hebrew in Israel. Another book of Gold's fiction, *In Sickness and In Health / Yom Kippur in a Gym* (two novellas), will be published in Spring 2024.

The Authors

Shmuel Yosef Agnon (1888–1970) was born Shmuel Yosef Czaczkes in Buczacz, Galicia. He left there in 1908 for Jaffa, having published seventy pieces in Hebrew and Yiddish, and never again wrote in Yiddish. In 1908, he published his story "Agunot" (*Forsaken Souls*) using the pseudonym Agnon, and in 1924 took Agnon as his family name. In 1912, he moved to Germany, drawn by its lively Jewish cultural life, and in 1924 returned to Jerusalem where he lived until his death. Agnon is among the most widely translated Hebrew authors, and his unique style and language influenced generations of Hebrew writers. He won numerous literary awards, including the 1966 Nobel Prize for Literature.

Isaac Babel, one of the most influential prose stylists of the twentieth century, was born in 1894 in Odesa, Ukraine, which was then part of the Russian Empire. The first major Jewish writer to write in Russian, he was hugely popular during his lifetime. He is best known for his story cycle *Red Cavalry*—set during the Polish-Soviet War (1919–1921), in which he participated—as well as for the cycles of stories fictionalizing his childhood in Odesa and Mykolaiv and mythologizing the exploits of his hometown's gangsters. He was murdered in Stalin's purges in 1940, at the age of forty-five.

Lili Berger (1916–1996), born in Malken, Poland, was a prolific literary critic and essayist, novelist, and playwright. She settled in Paris at the end of 1936, teaching Yiddish and contributing to important periodicals. During the Nazi occupation of France, she was active in the Resistance and was involved in the rescue of Jewish children from deportation. She returned to Warsaw after the war but left in 1968 during the great exodus, returning to Paris and resuming her literary activity until her death in 1995. Her many articles and essays were often about writers and artists, many of whom she had known personally.

Jasminka Domaš lives in Zagreb. She is a member of PEN and of the Croatian Writers' Union. She is one of the founders of the Jewish Religious Community Beth Israel. Between 1995 and 1998 she collaborated with the American Foundation for Virtual History, founded by Steven Spielberg. She has written texts and screenplays for over ten documentary films, mostly dealing with the Holocaust. She has also written several books of poetry, novels, books on Judaism, and short stories. One of them, "Omnibus," has been included in an anthology of stories by Jewish female writers from some thirty countries of the world.

Irena Dousková is a novelist, poet, playwright, and screenwriter. At home and abroad, she is best known for her tragicomic trilogy: *Hrdý Budžes, Oněgin byl Rusák,* and *Darda.* She is the author of eleven books of fiction, and more than one hundred thousand copies of her books have been sold in the Czech Republic alone. Her books have appeared (or are due to appear) in eighteen languages. Irena Dousková was born in 1964 in Příbram. She graduated from the Faculty of Law at Charles University but never entered the legal profession. She has worked for the most part as a journalist, as well as a librarian and a dramaturge at a cultural center. Since 2006, she has made a living from writing books, dramas, and film scripts. She lives in Prague.

Michel Fais was born in Northern Greece (Komotini) in 1957 and lives and works in Athens. He has published seven novels, four novellas, two short story collections, two plays, and two photographic albums. The editor of the literary supplement of the *Efimeridaton Syntakton* newspaper, he teaches creative writing at the Greek Open University, the University of Western Macedonia, and the "Sxoli" Creative writing seminars by Patakis Publishers. In 2000, he was awarded the National Short Story Prize. His work has been translated into six languages, his plays have been staged, he has co-written screenplays, and has had solo photography exhibitions. In 2021, Yale University Press (the Margellos World Republic of Letters) published his *Mechanisms of Loss,* translated by David Connolly.

Varda Fiszbein was born in Buenos Aires, Argentina, and now resides in Seville, Spain. She is a professor of Hebraic Studies, Hebrew, and Yiddish, and she edits and translates works from those languages, as well as from English into Spanish. She is currently completing a translation into Spanish of Joshua Trachtenberg's *Jewish Magic and Superstition* and writing scripts for the radio program "La geografía del Yiddish" (radiosefarad.com), which she also hosts. Fiszbein is the author of children's fiction (for which she has won numerous prizes), literary reviews, critical studies, and adult nonfiction. Her work has appeared in *Jewish Fiction .net* and *Catamaran* magazine.

Eliya Rafael Karmona (Istanbul, 1869–1932) attended the French-speaking Alliance school. After four years he left, becoming tutor to the sons of the Grand Vizir. His family suffered grave financial losses, and Karmona lost his post, becoming a typesetting apprentice at the newspaper *El Tyempo.* He left, spending an adventurous youth in Salonika, Izmir, and Cairo, and returned to *El Tyempo,* where he stayed until 1908. From 1908, when the Young Turks' revolution removed the censorship on literature, until his death in 1932, Karmona edited and wrote most of his comic newspaper *El Djugeton,* as well as fifty novels.

Entela Kasi is a poet, essayist, novelist, and translator, born in Albania in 1975. Her poetry has been published in anthologies in English, French, Italian, German, Hebrew, Hungarian, Turkish, Spanish, Romanian, Slovenian, Serbian, Macedonian, Bulgarian, and Greek. She has been invited by different universities in Albania and abroad to serve as a Visiting Professor and writer, focusing on Albanian literature and freedom of expression and human rights in post-communist societies. She has received national and international literary prizes and is the president of PEN Albania.

Birte Kont is the former editor-in-chief of the Danish Jewish Community's magazine, a writer, and a woman of letters. Using her master's thesis on Franz Kafka as her point of departure, she wrote *Kafka's Guilt Identity,* published in 2002. She debuted as a fiction writer in 2011 with the novel *En by I Rusland (A Place Nowhere)*, and in 2012 received a grant from the Danish Arts Council for fiction writing. *No One is Speaking—A Loved One's Narrative* was published in 2021. She is the deputy chair of the board for Fiction Writers in the Danish Writers Guild.

Mario Levi was born in 1957 and studied French Language and Literature in Istanbul University. In addition to being a writer, Levi has worked as a French teacher, an importer, a journalist, a radio programmer, and a copywriter. His first articles were published in the newspaper *Şalom*. These were followed by other articles in literature magazines or newspapers like *Cumhuriyet, Milliyet Sanat, Argos,* and *Varlik.* His first book, *Jacques Brel: A Lonely Man* (1986), is a novelized version of his university graduation thesis. He currently gives lectures in Yeditepe University. He also teaches creative writing to people who have set their hearts on trying to express their thoughts. The past, minorities, and Istanbul are some of the most frequent themes in his books. Mario Levi's twelve books have been published in twenty-six different countries and a total of twenty-seven languages.

Norman Manea, born in Bukovina, Romania, was deported as a child to the concentration camp in Transnistria and was persecuted by the Communist dictatorship in Romania. He left Romania in 1986, lived for one year in West Berlin, and moved to the United States in 1988. He is the author of prose and essays translated into more than twenty languages, a Professor Emeritus of European Culture and writer in residence at Bard College, and the laureate of several international literary prizes, among them the McArthur and Guggenheim Fellowship Awards, the Italian international Nonino Prize for literature, the Prix Medicis Etrangere, and the German Nelly Sachs Prize. He is a member of the Berlin Academy of Art, an Honorary Fellow of the Royal Society of Literature in Great Britain, and was decorated as Commandeur dans l'Ordre des Arts et des Letters by the French government.

Maciej Płaza, PhD, born in 1976, is a Polish writer and translator. He is the author of the monograph *O poznaniu w twórczości Stanisława Lema* (On Cognition in the Work of Stanisław Lem) and three novels: *Skoruń* (Sluggy), *Robinson w Bolechowie* (Robinson in Bolechów) and *Golem,* which brought him several literary awards in Poland. He is renowned for his translations of H.P. Lovecraft, Arthur Machen, and Mary Shelley, and his scholarly works about Fredric Jameson, Marjorie Perloff, and others.

Augusto Segre was a well-known public figure in post-World War II Italy who worked as a journalist, educator, scholar, editor, activist, and rabbi. He wrote educational books on the Jewish festivals and commentaries on the Torah. He grew up in the northern Italian city of Casale Monferrato and fought as a partisan in the area during World War II. Segre retired to Jerusalem in 1978, publishing his memoir, *Memories of Jewish Life,* in 1979. "Purchase of Goods of Dubious Origin" appeared in his final work, *Stories of Jewish Life,* in 1986.

Peter Sichrovsky is an Austrian journalist, author, and former member of the European Parliament (1996–2004). In 1989, he co-founded Austria's newspaper *Der Standard,* where he served on the editorial board. He is the author of eighteen books, including many acclaimed books based on interviews, including *Strangers in Their Own Land: Young Jews in Germany and Austria Today; Born Guilty: Children of Nazi Families* (who themselves suggested the book's title); and *Abraham's Children: Israel's Young Generation.* Former foreign correspondent for publications including *Stern Magazine,* the *Sueddeutsche Zeitung,* and *Profil,* currently he is a widely read columnist for the Austrian weekly, *News.*

Gábor T. Szántó is a Hungarian novelist, essayist, and screenplay writer born in Budapest in 1966. Szántó is the editor-in-chief of the Hungarian Jewish monthly *Szombat.* His additional field of interest is researching and teaching Modern Jewish Literature. He has published several novels, collections of short stories, and a book of poetry. His works have been translated into many languages. One of his stories was turned into a feature film entitled *1945,* which won twenty international awards and has been seen in forty countries. His most recent novel is *Europa Symphony* (*Europa szimfonia*) (2019).

Luize Valente is a Portuguese-Brazilian journalist and writer, author of the historical novels *O segredo do oratório, Uma praça em Antuérpia, Sonata em Auschwitz,* and the young adult *A menina com estrela.* Her books—all about Jewish issues—have been published in Portugal, Holland, France, Italy, Albania, and Poland. Two of them had adaptation rights sold for cinema and television. She is the author, with Elaine Eiger, of the book *Israel Rotas e Raízes* and of the documentaries *Caminhos da Memória—A trajetória dos judeus em Portugal e A estrela oculta do Sertão,* about Jewish reminiscences in Brazil and Portugal. More information: www.luizevalente.com.

Elie Wiesel (1928–2016) was a Romanian-born American writer, political activist, and professor at Boston University. The author of more than fifty books, both fiction and nonfiction, he was a recipient of the United States Congressional Gold Medal, the Presidential Medal of Freedom, the French Legion of Honor's Grand-Croix, an honorary knighthood of the British Empire, and, in 1986, the Nobel Peace Prize.

The Translators

Michael Alpert is Emeritus Professor of the History of Spain at the University of Westminster in London. He has published *Secret Judaism and the Spanish Inquisition* in English (Nottingham: Five Leaves, 2008) and in Spanish. In relation to literature in Judeo-Spanish, he has transliterated and translated Eliya Rafael Karmona's *La muz'er onesta* (Nottingham: Five Leaves, 2009) and has published an article in *Ladinar* (Tel Aviv, IX, 2017, pp. xxxi–xli) on Viktor Levi's Ladino anticlerical novel *La Agua dela Sota* of 1889, as well as a survey of the Ladino Novel in *European Judaism* Vol. 43, 2 (Autumn 2010). He has published widely on the Spanish Civil War of 1936–1939.

Claudio Bethencourt is a Brazilian-Hungarian linguist and translator who grew up in Rio de Janeiro but graduated from the University of Florida. Being born in a close-knit family with Jewish values and devoted to show business, the theater played a pivotal role in his education. He is currently the curator of all the works of João Bethencourt (1924–2006), a dramatist and graduate from Yale University who wrote over fifty plays during his lifetime. He is the only Brazilian-Hungarian playwright who, to this day, is mainly performed internationally and is still relevant to the current show business scene.

Walter Burgess and Marietta Morry are Canadian. Six of their translations of stories of Gábor T. Szántó have been published. Other translations are short stories by Péter Moesko, five of which are in print, and a novel by Zsófia Czakó, two excerpts of which will soon come out. A more recent project is a book of stories by Anita Harag, four of which have been published or will be soon. Marietta Morry and Lynda Muir translate Holocaust memoirs for the Azrieli Foundation, and two of their book-length memoirs and many shorter works have been published.

Boris Dralyuk is the author of *My Hollywood and Other Poems* (2022), editor of *1917: Stories and Poems from the Russian Revolution* (2016), co-editor (with Robert Chandler and Irina Mashinski) of *The Penguin Book of Russian Poetry* (2015), and translator of volumes by Isaac Babel, Andrey Kurkov, Maxim Osipov, Leo Tolstoy, Mikhail Zoshchenko, and other authors. He is the former editor-in-chief of the *Los Angeles Review of Books*, and his poems, translations, and essays have appeared in *The New York Review of Books*, the *Times Literary Supplement*, *The New Yorker*, *Granta*, and elsewhere. The stories from *Red Cavalry* in this anthology are included in *Of Sunshine and Bedbugs: Essential Stories by Isaac Babel*, translated by Boris Dralyuk (Pushkin Press, 2022).

Jean Harris, PhD, is a novelist and translator who lives in Bucharest, Romania. She was the director of the critically acclaimed *The Observer Translation Project* (http://translations.observatorcultural.ro), and guest-edited an anthology of contemporary Romanian writing for *Absinthe 13: Spotlight on Romania*. Her translations have appeared in various periodicals including *The Guardian, Words Without Borders, The Review of Contemporary Fiction*, and *Exquisite Corpse*. Her translations include: "Beyond the Mountains" (Preliminary Ascent into Posterity: Celan-Fondane) for *The Fifth Impossibility*, a collection of Norman Manea's essays (Yale University Press), and Manea's "Words by Moonlight" for *Habitus: A Diaspora Journal*. She writes about literature and psychoanalysis.

John Howard, an American who lived in Berlin for more than two decades, has translated books from German to English and edited and translated many screenplays and treatments for film. He taught English language and literature in the U.S., Germany, and Beijing and has been engaged as a producer-director for German radio and television.

Ronnee Jaeger was a social worker in the Jewish Community until her retirement. She also taught at the Toronto Hillel Sunday School and is still fondly remembered by her students as a gifted teacher. Politically active in Israel for many years, she also served as the Jerusalem culture/political correspondent for *Outlook Magazine* (Vancouver) from 2005 to 2015. She has been involved in Yiddish poetry, literature, and translation since her arrival in Toronto in 1970. She has participated in translations to *Found Treasures* (1994, edited by Frieda Forman), and recently translated several works by Lili Berger, as a member of the Toronto Group of Translators of Yiddish Women Writers.

Mina Karavanta, PhD, is Associate Professor of Literary Theory, Cultural Studies and Comparative Literature in the Faculty of English Studies of the School of Philosophy of the National and Kapodistrian University of Athens. She has published articles in international academic journals such as *boundary 2, Feminist Review, Modern Fiction Studies, Mosaic, Symplokē, Journal Of Contemporary Theory*, and book chapters in international volumes. She has co-edited *Interculturality and Gender* with Joan Anim-Addo and Giovanna Covi (London: Mango Press, 2009) and *Edward Said and Jacques Derrida: Reconstellating Humanism and the Global Hybrid*, with Nina Morgan (London: Cambridge Scholars Press, 2008). She has translated George Steiner's *Heidegger* into Greek (Athens: Patakis, 2009), and Haris Vlavianos's poetry into English, *Affirmation:*

Selected Poems 1986–2006 (Dublin: Dedalus: 2007). She is the co-editor of *Synthesis: An Anglophone Journal of Comparative Literary Studies* (https://ejournals.epublishing.ekt.gr/index.php/synthesis/).

Entela Kasi (the translator of her own excerpt in this book, with assistance from Sarah Lawson) is a poet, essayist, novelist, and translator, born in Albania in 1975. Her poetry has been published in anthologies in English, French, Italian, German, Hebrew, Hungarian, Turkish, Spanish, Romanian, Slovenian, Serbian, Macedonian, Bulgarian, and Greek. She has been invited by different universities in Albania and abroad to serve as a Visiting Professor and writer, focusing on Albanian literature and freedom of expression and human rights in post-communist societies. She has received national and international literary prizes and is the president of PEN Albania.

Michael P. Kramer is Professor Emeritus of English Literature at Bar-Ilan University, Israel. He is the author of *Imagining Language in America* (Princeton) and editor or co-editor of numerous books, including *The Cambridge Companion to Jewish American Literature, Modern Jewish Literatures: Intersections and Boundaries* (Pennsylvania), and *The Turn Around Religion in America* (Ashgate). He is the founding editor of *MAGGID: A Journal of Jewish Literature* (Toby Press) and was co-organizer of Kisufim: The Jerusalem Conference of Jewish Writers. The above excerpt is from his annotated translation of S.Y. Agnon's *And the Crooked Shall Be Made Straight* (Toby Press).

Andrea G. Labinger translates contemporary Latin American fiction. *Gesell Dome,* her translation of Guillermo Saccomanno's novel *Cámara Gesell,* won a PEN/Heim Translation Award. Recent publications include *Proceed with Caution: Stories and a Novella* by Patricia Ratto, and *The Clerk* by Guillermo Saccomanno. *The Sanctuary,* Labinger's translation of Gustavo Abrevaya's *noir* thriller, *El Criadero,* is forthcoming from Schaffner Press.

David Livingstone is an American citizen living and working in the Czech Republic for the last thirty years. He teaches Shakespeare, Modernism, children's literature, and American folk music at Palacký University, Olomouc. His most recent book, *In Our Own Image: Fictional Representations of William Shakespeare,* looks at novels, plays, short stories, films, television series, and comics focused on Shakespeare as a character. His most recent project consists of a series of articles concerning American folk music. He also translates both fiction and nonfiction from Czech to English.

Antonia Lloyd-Jones has translated works by many of Poland's leading contemporary novelists and reportage authors, as well as crime fiction, poetry, and children's books. Her translation of *Drive Your Plow Over the Bones of the Dead* by 2018 Nobel Prize laureate Olga Tokarczuk was shortlisted for the 2019 Man Booker International prize. For ten years she was a mentor for the Emerging Translators' Mentorship Programme and is a former co-chair of the UK Translators Association.

Iskra Pavlović (1935–2022), born at Podgora, was a translator who translated a series of technical texts and literary works. She spent many years teaching English at the Center for Foreign languages in Zagreb, and as a supervisor for young teachers and students at Zagreb University. As a translator and interpreter, she worked for many state offices.

Steve Siporin is professor emeritus of folklore at Utah State University with a special interest in the culture of the Jews of Italy. He has published translations of Augusto Segre's memoir—*Memories of Jewish Life: From Italy to Jerusalem, 1918–1960* (Lincoln: University of Nebraska Press, 2008)—and a collection of Segre's short stories, *Stories of Jewish Life: Casale Monferrato-Rome-Jerusalem, 1876–1985* (Detroit: Wayne State University Press, 2020). His most recent book is *The Befana is Returning: The Story of a Tuscan Festival* (Madison: University of Wisconsin Press, 2022).

Nina Sokol is a poet and translator in the midst of translating plays, poems, and novels by Danish writers. She was a grant poet-in-residence at The Vermont Studio Center in 2011. She has received several grants from the Danish Arts Council to translate plays, including a play written by the fairy tale writer H.C. Andersen, which was published by the journal *InTranslation*. She has also translated numerous novels by writers such as Robert Zola Christensen, Thomas Lagermand Lundme, Anna Grue, and Kristian Himmelstrup, whose novel, *Pio*, has just been nominated for next year's DR Roman Prisen (literary prize in Denmark).

Catherine Temerson (1944–2015) was brought up bilingually in French and English and had advanced degrees from Harvard and New York University. She translated over twenty works of fiction and nonfiction, including works by Amin Maalouf and Elie Wiesel, and biographies of Francois Truffaut, Isaac Bashevis Singer, Marie-Antoinette, and Casanova, among others. She translated books for children, authored books in French on Hollywood and music, and while the Literary Manager of UBU Repertory Theater, did a number of translations of plays for the theater.

Leyla Tonguç Basmacı was born in Istanbul. After completing her studies at the Italian High School, she graduated from the English Language and Literature Department at Bogazici University in Istanbul, and then received her MA in Comparative Literature from Pennsylvania State University. She taught Italian at the Italian Cultural Centre in Istanbul, worked as copywriter and translator, and then became Arts Manager at the British Council, Istanbul. She currently works as a translator in Turkish, English, and Italian.

Printed in the USA
CPSIA information can be obtained
at www.ICGtesting.com
LVHW040753300923
759303LV00009B/5

9 798887 192062